BEYOND THE WALL

Books by the same author

For older readers
Hell and High Water
Buffalo Soldier
The Goldsmith's Daughter
Apache

For younger readers
Poppy Fields Murder Mysteries series
Sam Swann's Movie Mysteries: Zombie Dawn!!!
Sam Swann's Movie Mysteries: Tomb of Doom!!!
Flotsam and Jetsam
Flotsam and Jetsam and the Stormy Surprise
Flotsam and Jetsam and the Grooof
Waking Merlin
Merlin's Apprentice
The World's Bellybutton
The Kraken's Snore
Mary's Penny

BEYOND THE WALL

TANYA LANDMAN

WALKER BOOKS

First published in Great Britain 2017 by Walker Books Ltd
87 Vauxhall Walk, London SE11 5HJ

2 4 6 8 10 9 7 5 3 1

This book has been typeset in Bembo Educational

Printed and bound in Great Britain by Clays Ltd, St Ives plc

British Library Cataloguing in Publication Data:
a catalogue record for this book is available from the British Library

ISBN 978-1-4063-6627-3

www.walker.co.uk

To Caroline Royds. With love and gratitude.

"They have plundered the world, stripping naked the land in their hunger... They ravage, they slaughter, they seize ... and all of this they hail as the construction of empire. And when in their wake nothing remains but a desert, they call that peace."

Tacitus

"If I had to choose between betraying my country and betraying my friend, I hope I should have the guts to betray my country."

E.M. Forster

PART I: WOLF

I

Snow lies deep. Bitter cold days. Dark nights, when the veil between this world and the next grows thin. A time to shelter. To sit close around the fire. To rest. To remember.

I am a dreamer of visions. A shaman. A singer of songs, a weaver of words, a spinner of sights and sounds. Of stories.

Hear me now. Listen.

The tale begins with a birth.

Does it not always?

A birth. Or a death.

Sometimes both.

There was rain that year: so much of it. For a full six months it fell without pause from a leaden sky. The preceding summer had been unusually dry and so Mother Earth drank deep, sucking the water into her belly.

But at the turning of the year – in the very dead of winter – she could stomach no more. Instead, she spewed water out of the ground, which mingled with the rain until the whole country seemed awash.

This was Britannia. A land defeated; occupied by enemy forces these last three hundred years.

The estate of Titus Cornelius Festus – landowner, merchant, purveyor of stone to the city of Londinium and esteemed citizen of the Empire – was built along classic Roman lines. A great rectangle had been hacked out of the undulating land: order imposed on chaos. Now there stood a villa with straight walls, square rooms, regular columns. Around it, gardens with paths that neither bent nor swerved but crossed each other at crisp right angles. Vegetables stood in lines like soldiers ready for inspection. Fruit trees were staked to walls – every shrub was clipped into perfect symmetry.

At the heart of the estate was a spring where water gushed from the earth, cool and sweet, even in the height of summer. During the villa's construction a pool – tiled and paved and perfectly square – had been dug to contain it. A statue of Neptune stood in the centre for, though the current emperor was a Christian, who knew if his successor would follow the modern fad? Here, in the furthest, darkest, dampest corner of the Empire the old ways lingered on. Titus Cornelius Festus would not ignore the gods who'd bestowed good fortune on his family for generations.

But that year neither Roman gods nor Roman discipline could withstand the ancient, elemental power of water. The land was so sodden that the spring shifted and began to gush forth from a point five hundred paces away – high up the hill, behind the house. One night it cut a new stream through the soft chalk, winding in curves around the beds of harder flint before cascading into the gardens. Running unimpeded along those straight paths, it toppled Neptune's statue and carried the god away across the gardens. It poured into the villa, through the room where the master's wife sweated to push out her first child. The noise of the flood could not drown out her screams.

She was not the only woman who laboured that night. A short distance away, in the slave huts, another was silently enduring the pangs of childbirth.

A deer makes no sound when she drops her fawn in case her cries alert a predator. So it was with Cassia's mother. Shortly before dawn a girl-child slipped into the smoke-filled darkness of a roundhouse, and so quiet was her coming that the rest of its inhabitants neither woke nor stirred.

The hut in which Cassia took her first breath was built in the native style from stone and mud, wood and thatch. Its doorway faced the rising sun, its back pressed firm against the hill. Small though it was, it curled around its occupants like a parent's arms and steered the flood waters away from the newborn infant.

By the fire's glowing embers Cassia's mother took a bone needle and a pot of pigment, and pricked her daughter's wrists and ankles, marking her with the same pattern of whirls and dots with which her own mother had once marked her. And then she held her baby to her breast for the hours of darkness, weeping all the while for she expected that later, when the infant was examined by the steward, it would be killed as her other daughters had been. Why would Titus Cornelius Festus go to the expense of rearing a girl-child when full-grown women could be got so cheaply at market? None of Cassia's sisters had lasted the length of their first day. Their tiny bodies lay in the burial plot at the edge of the estate.

When the sun rose over the wreckage of the villa's gardens, the months of rain finally ceased. The flood water stilled, lying over lawns in sheets that reflected the sky so the whole world was turned crimson and gold. At its centre, the statue of Neptune was face down like a drowned man.

Titus Cornelius Festus looked out across his estate. The destruction of the shrine, the gardens, the water washing through the room in which his wife had given birth, seemed to portend something. But what? Were the gods angry? If that was so, he must pay for sacrifices to be offered at the Temple.

Yet there lay Neptune, overturned. Fallen. How was he to interpret that?

Perhaps he should also consider offering a few prayers

up to the Christian god? It could surely do no harm to appease both?

He shifted uncomfortably. His bladder was full to bursting, but he was reluctant to relieve himself. For months he'd been troubled by an agonized burning sensation every time he passed water.

A personal matter, some might say: hardly a fitting subject for a storyteller!

I agree. And I would not speak of such a thing were it not for the fact that his condition and Cassia's fate were intimately entwined.

Titus Cornelius Festus was grateful that the healer had at last effected a remedy, but the pain he'd suffered was seared into his memory. As was the cause of his infection. The local brothel. A new whore, lately brought from Gallia. Gods! She was so young, so fresh. She'd almost been worth the discomfort that had followed. He was recalling her in lurid detail when the steward came to report that a girl had been born in the slave huts.

Just then, his newborn son wailed aloud. An idea took root which grew and blossomed within a few heartbeats.

To the steward's surprise, the master did not at once give the command for the infant's death. Instead Titus Cornelius Festus went himself to the slave quarters to inspect this new child. Seeing that she was sturdy and straight in limb, hearing that her lungs were hearty and sound, he declared she was worth preserving.

For was it not significant, he thought, that this girl should have been born the selfsame night as Lucius – his son, his heir, a lad who would carry the family name like a legion's eagle into the future? Yes ... this is what the gods had been telling him! They had washed the world clean the very moment the children's lives began. Their fates were surely linked: this slave girl would be his son's playmate. She could keep Lucius amused while they grew and then – when he reached maturity... Every man has appetites that must be satisfied. But – as Titus knew only too well – brothels were insanitary places, and the women so often harboured some dreadful disease! It was the same at the market: one could not tell, no matter how carefully one looked, whether a woman carried contagion or not. Well then, when his son was grown, Cassia would be his. The gods surely intended her as a gift for Lucius: a gift who could be watched over and kept pure, clean and free from infection.

And so it was that on the very first morning of her life Cassia was marked by her master as a concubine. A mistress. A whore.

II

Things did not work out the way Titus Cornelius Festus had intended. His son Lucius was a thin, sickly baby who became a fretful, ill-formed child. He learned to walk unusually late and when he did finally get to his feet, he moved slowly, painfully, like an old man.

He and Cassia did not become playmates. The boy was too weak to take pleasure in the ordinary amusements of a child and the mistress, taking Cassia's good health as a personal affront, banished the girl from her sight. While Lucius remained confined within the villa's painted walls, Cassia was sent to work alongside the men wherever the steward saw fit. As soon as she could walk she was fetching and carrying – messages from the fields to the woods or the quarry, food and water for the animals, logs to the villa, vegetables to the kitchen. She grew strong and sturdy, warmed by the sun, cooled by the wind. The work was hard: grindingly so, from sunup to sundown. And yet her life was not entirely without its pleasures.

Cassia was five years old, or thereabouts. It was the Saturnalia – the midwinter feast – the one day of the year when slaves were allowed to drink and make merry. They had certainly made the most of the opportunity. After an hour or two of riotous delight the majority were lying insensible in the weak winter sunshine.

She was watching the adults' inexplicable behaviour with bemusement when a hand clamped over her mouth. Cassia felt a moment's fear before she registered that the fingers were too small and slender to be the steward's. A voice in her ear whispered, "We're for the woods. Coming?"

Silvio. Two years her senior. A fellow slave. A friend.

After nodding – with some difficulty given his tight grip – Cassia was released. She followed in his footsteps as Silvio darted between the roundhouses and into the woods beyond. There, the smells of fox and badger caught the back of her throat. Silvio ran for perhaps half a mile in silence with Cassia struggling to keep up. He stopped only when they reached a small clearing.

The sun stabbed beams through the canopy, hitting a stream that curled through the glade. Fractured by the water, splinters of light darted from trunk to trunk and from stone to mossy stone. She had thought spring was a long way off, but there in the woods bright shoots of green were already puncturing the earth. A week or two more and the snowdrops might be in bloom. The birdsong seemed louder here, more joyful, and the ground beneath her feet felt different.

Cassia was lost to sensation. Nothing grew between the roundhouses and along the roads that she daily walked. The rutted earth baked hard in summer and was a slop of mud and puddles in winter. But here it was covered in a carpet of leaf litter. There were things creeping and crawling all around her, the whole place pulsed with life.

Cassia's mother had often whispered about spirits and now – suddenly – the girl saw they were there in the trees. That flowing stream was as alive as she was. Mother Earth's heart was beating beneath her feet, her breath ruffled her hair, kissed her cheek. She would have been happy to stand looking, wondering. But Silvio had plans.

Suddenly he knelt before her. "My queen."

Baffled, Cassia said nothing.

He looked at her. Hissed, "You're Boudica. You know who she was, don't you?"

Boudica, defeated queen of the Iceni. Dead for near three hundred years, yet her name still burned like a flame.

"I'm your warrior," explained Silvio. "Ready to fight the Red Crests?"

The gang of boys divided into two. The strongest, the most daring of them, opted to be Cassia's men. The weaker,

19

the less popular, were forced to be Romans. Brutus, a lad so desperate to be liked by Silvio that he would do anything, was given the part of the Emperor. And then they went to war.

Brutus stood in the middle of the clearing, his army surrounding him while the Britons melted into the woods. Silvio strode into the trees dragging Cassia behind him. When they had gone maybe fifteen paces he hit the ground so suddenly she thought he'd tripped. But then his hand shot up and he was tugging her down. His face was in hers, his breath hot, his voice fevered with excitement.

"See him there?"

"Brutus?"

"That's not Brutus. It's Claudius. We're going to get him. Him and all his men. We've got to creep, Cassia. Wriggle on your belly, like a worm. Like this."

Obediently, Cassia copied him.

"We've got to surround them, understand? You come at him from behind those rocks. Don't let him see you. If he sees you, you'll be captured. Crucified."

For a moment she looked unsure, so Silvio hissed. "You're our queen. You're not going to let a stinking Roman beat us, are you?"

"No. Never!"

"Good."

Brutus was reclining on a flat rock, resting on one elbow, as if he was at a feast.

Cassia had been told to approach him from behind, which meant crawling through the stream and then through a patch of brambles that clawed at her knees and tore her clothes. She was scarcely aware of it. Only the attack mattered, only the victory. She edged forward, little by little, creeping then freezing, taking care not to break a twig, not to rustle the dry leaves.

But the other boys didn't have her patience. There was only so much creeping and freezing any of them could endure. Cassia wasn't even within striking distance when, without warning, a group of her warriors burst noisily from the cover of the trees. She was on her feet at once, wielding a stick in her hand like a sword, ready to fight.

In the clearing, two lads went down rolling, wrestling. Brutus was one. The other was Silvio. The rest stood in a circle to cheer them on.

To Cassia, they were no longer Brutus and Silvio. The Roman Emperor was battling her finest warrior. And the queen of the Iceni couldn't stand and watch. Brutus was astride Silvio, pretending to cut his throat. Cassia leaped onto her enemy's back, her arms tight around his neck, squeezing with all her strength. He was twice her weight. Twice her size. But her ferocity was enough to pull him backwards. He fell on top of her, punching the breath from her lungs before rolling sideways and landing on his back. She gasped for air. But then she was on her feet. Stepping onto his chest. Standing over him. Triumphant.

It was over as suddenly as it had begun.

The boys were laughing then. Playing. Tussling like puppies. It was all a game to them.

But Cassia had been in deadly earnest and the taste of that brief fight stayed fresh and strong on her tongue. In that moment she had *been* Boudica: a warrior queen not vanquished by the Romans, but one who'd driven the invaders from her land.

III

A birth or a death. Sometimes both.

For a storyteller, there is little of interest to relate in the life of a slave. Day follows day, hard, tedious and brutal. In all those years of captivity there were only three things worth remarking on.

The first? When Cassia was around seven years old a brother was born: Rufus.

Their mother was a slave, subject to the unwelcome attentions of any man who chanced to look at her. If she knew who had sired her children, she never said. Rufus was permitted to live, for a boy-child had a monetary value that his sisters had not, but when he grew up he had no more idea of who his father was than Cassia had of hers.

The second thing of note? Sad to say, their mother died when the boy was not yet a year old.

He was too young to understand. Rufus watched Cassia's grief in terrified confusion, staring wide-eyed and silent as she wept herself dry on that first bleak, motherless night. When she had no more strength to sob he crawled across the hut to his sister, whimpering, tugging at her blanket until she lifted it. Worming his way into her bed, he rested his head on her shoulder and pressed his face into her neck. Wrapping her arms around him, at last they slept, entwined, clinging to each other like the survivors of a shipwreck.

Thereafter, Cassia took his mother's place in Rufus's heart and for him life went on much as before. But Cassia was older. She felt the full weight of their loss and for many months she thought that sorrow might kill her too.

It did not. She lived. And eventually, a semblance of normality returned. By the time Rufus could run and wrestle and join Silvio and the other slave boys in the Boudica game, Cassia had mended enough for her to play once more at being their queen.

She grew. And the fact that she was marked for the master's son gave her a degree of protection that her mother had never enjoyed. Men might look at her. In fact, they did. Often. Eyes lingered on her breasts. Her buttocks. Her thighs. Yet no one dared touch her.

The third thing to happen was the most momentous. The third thing was what changed the course of the girl's life completely.

In her fifteenth year, Lucius's soul — that had always seemed reluctant to linger within that hunched, ill-formed body — finally departed. He was duly cremated, his ashes placed in a jar and interred in the family mausoleum. While the master stood watching, each of his slaves, one by one, had to kneel and press their heads to the stone edifice. Each had to weep and wail and make a show of abject misery.

Sometimes a name burns for longer than the life of the person who carries it. A name can rouse a population to rebellion; become a war cry. But sometimes a person goes to their grave and is forgotten in an instant. And so it was with Lucius.

His ashes had barely cooled when his father's eye fell on Cassia.

Titus Cornelius Festus watched the girl kneel. Watched her squeeze tears from her eyes.

He'd paid for her rearing, her upkeep. Why shouldn't he now reap the benefits his son was unable to enjoy?

Three days after the funeral, Cassia made ready the ox-cart, preparing to drive its stone cargo from the quarry to the river where a ship was waiting to carry the load to Londinium. The captain would already be there, watching the tide, waiting for her arrival.

But before she could leave, the steward sought her out. He declared that her day's work was done. Silvio would drive the cart in her place. She must go at once to the villa where a body slave was waiting to assist her. She was to be bathed. Oiled. Scented. Her hair must be brushed and braided in a fashion pleasing to the master. Fresh clothing had no doubt already been laid out for her, although – he added with a laugh – there was little point in that! She wouldn't be keeping it on for long. Once she was made presentable, then – at sunset – the steward said that he himself would come and get her and lead her to the room in which the master would be waiting. In case she'd somehow failed to grasp his meaning he slid a hand under the folds of her skirt.

"He's been waiting too long for a taste of this. Mind you treat him well, girl. For all our sakes."

Cassia knew what was intended. There was nothing to be said. Nothing to be done.

Had Cassia's mother been alive the girl could, perhaps, have better managed to perform the acts that the master expected. Her mother's spirit had been broken. She would have whispered into her daughter's ear as she plaited her hair in preparation for the night ahead, telling her to be meek, to submit, to endure whatever was done without a cry of protest. To fix a smile on her lips as though the master's attentions did not revolt her. Such words might have carried Cassia through her first encounter with Titus Cornelius Festus. But her mother had joined her murdered sisters in the ground and there was no one to tell her how a

26

slave girl should behave.

After stroking the oxen's necks Cassia handed their lead rope to Silvio. He cupped her hands in his for a moment.

"Courage, my queen," he said softly.

It was an attempt to comfort, but his voice cracked as he spoke. Silvio was looking at her with a furious pity, but she would not meet her friend's eyes or bid him farewell. Any more kindness from him would shatter her.

Instead she turned and walked slowly towards the villa, thanking the gods that her brother was working in the fields that day. She would not have to face Rufus until it was over.

It was as though she had been cast adrift on a stormy sea. The ground seemed to heave under her feet, the air was thick and foul-tasting. The cart track, the woods, the stream, the far-distant river — all the familiar scenes she had seen every day of her life, in all weathers and through every changing season — had become as flat and garish as a badly painted fresco.

The villa ahead was famed for its opulence, for the brilliance of its mosaics, the elegance of its furnishings, the artistry of its painted walls, the wondrous size and splendour of its rooms. Titus Cornelius Festus's proud boast was that there was no dwelling its equal this side of Londinium.

Yet Cassia did not see grace or elegance. She saw the violence done to the land in the villa's creation. Smelled the sweat of the slaves who had suffered during its construction.

Her skin seemed chilled by the ghostly breath of those who had gone before.

The bath-house was on the villa's westernmost side. Whenever Titus Cornelius Festus, his family or his guests wished to bathe they entered through the house. But they were Romans. Gods forbid that Cassia should walk on the villa's precious mosaic floors in her unclean state! There was an additional, external entrance at the rear where wood was delivered to fuel the fires and it was there she had been ordered to go.

The girl was numb by the time she gave herself over to Flavia, the aged body slave who had been sent to help her.

Flavia had been born among the wild tribes of Germania. But she had been captured by slavers and carried to Londinium for sale in the market there. A flaxen-haired girl with eyes as blue as cornflowers, she'd been purchased by the present master's father when she was scarcely old enough to be counted a woman. She'd borne his child but her body had been too young to make the birth an easy one.

She survived. The baby did not. And she was torn so badly by her labours that her body then repelled the master's father. It was a blessing of sorts. She was demoted from concubine to house slave before her fourteenth summer was out.

There was nothing Flavia had not seen. Nothing could surprise or shock her.

Except this.

This girl.

Cassia.

Flavia knew of her. How could she not? It had been the talk of the household when the mistress banished the girl from villa and gardens. From a distance, she'd watched her grow.

Cassia stood before Flavia, tall, sturdy, naked. Her muscled arms and legs were tanned from the sun but beneath the tunic the skin was so white it had a tinge of blue. Her hair copper-coloured, her eyes green, her wrists and ankles marked by her mother. She was so silent. Seemed so strong. So proud.

But she would be broken.

The thought burned through Flavia's head like a hot coal on ice.

Cassia must get on with it. Endure as best she could. She was young. She would recover. In time.

And if she was torn, hurt, bruised, beaten… If she bore a child? Well, then. It was the will of the gods, was it not? What could any woman do against them?

Flavia worked deftly, with the reverent care of a priest preparing an animal for sacrifice. She washed the girl. Rubbed her with scented oils. Dressed her hair. Fastened on a silken robe.

The very moment Flavia had finished, the steward was by the door, waiting.

Cassia had neither looked at Flavia nor uttered a single sound. Her mind had gone. Fled far away into the dark. She would be safe there. Nothing could reach her.

But Flavia was seized by a sudden impulse. She took the girl's face in her hands and pressed a kiss to her forehead. In her native tongue she uttered a blessing, a prayer, an invocation for Mother Earth to protect this daughter.

It was the kiss that pulled Cassia out of the cold, distant place she had retreated to.

One kiss made all the difference.

IV

Meekly, head bowed, Cassia walked towards the master's chamber. The steward led the way, his eyes bright, lips wet, his skin tingling with the thought of what Titus Cornelius Festus would do.

And tomorrow ... afterwards ... oh yes! When the master had finished with her she'd be ripe for picking by any man who chose to have her just like her mother had been. And he'd be first in line. Before long he'd find a way. Against a tree, in a doorway.

Wasn't he owed that much? A lifetime's bowing and scraping to Titus Cornelius Festus, a lifetime cowering and cringing? Whatever he could swipe from under the master's nose he'd take. A jug of wine, a loaf of bread, a slice of beef.

A girl.

As he left her, a broad smile spread across his face.

* * *

Cassia was resigned to her fate, or so she thought. Titus Cornelius Festus was already reclining on a couch. He rose and padded across the floor, wasting no time in talk, but letting his eyes roam every inch of her flesh. He walked around her once. Stood behind her. Then his arms snaked about her waist, pulling her against his thighs, her back against his belly.

While her eyes were tight shut, his fingers pressed and squeezed. The scent of his oil was thick in her nostrils: the essence of juniper, the stench of Rome.

He turned her around, face to face, his lips trying to latch on to hers. But he had just eaten and his fish-stinking breath was too much. She turned her head, and that small act of resistance, that small display of revulsion, incensed him.

A glancing blow. The back of his hand across her face. Then his palm under her chin, fingers and thumb against her throat, holding her still, his lips once again seeking hers. He expected no more trouble.

But Flavia's kiss had awoken Cassia. And the master's blow sent a wild wolfish rage coursing through her veins. It bunched her hands into fists, made claws of her nails. Raking. Digging. Piercing flesh.

His scream was high-pitched, girlish, comic, coming from so large a man. She laughed. As he turned to escape her nails the side of his head smashed into her mouth. In reflex, her teeth closed about his ear.

She'd seen dogs fight: one clamping its jaws around

the throat of another, and though it was shaken – though its back broke with the violence of the struggle – it did not release its grip. So it was with Cassia. There was no battle fury in her now, but simply a blinding terror that made her jaw seize. He threw her against the wall, the weight of his body crushing the breath from her, but her teeth stayed clenched. He writhed and twisted, howled in pain and still her teeth were locked. He stumbled. Both fell. Her head cracked on the floor. She lay, too stunned to stir. And now, only now was he free from her. Not because she had released him, but because the lower half of his ear was severed from his head. She had bitten clean through it. It was in her mouth, on her tongue. She spat it to the floor. Heaved, ready to vomit.

There was a sliver of stillness. She saw his blood, hers, on the mosaic, pooling in the cracks between tiles ... mingled.

He was panting. Shocked. As was she. For one breath, two, he made no move. Then he lunged. She rolled sideways. Before he could lay another hand on her she was on her feet running, fleeing from the chamber, from the villa, past the astonished Flavia, through the garden, into the night. Into the woods. The untamed forest. Where – though her breath was torn and ragged, and fear seemed to ring loudly in her ears – she could still hear the distant sound of wolves howling at the moon.

V

Running.

Terrified.

Weeping.

Blood on her lips.

Blood on her tongue.

Oiled skin and braided hair. An unfamiliar garment catching around her ankles.

There was a moon, although in the dense forest it gave little light to see by. But Cassia had played in this place with the slave boys. She knew every part of it, every tree, every glade, every rock. Her feet found their way with no conscious thought of hers guiding them. She ducked under branches, skirted hollows, picked a path between the badger setts that dotted the ground with holes deep enough to break an ankle.

She did not fear to die. But the thought of punishment – of

the pain that would be inflicted before she passed from one world to the next – suddenly filled her with such bowel-loosening terror that she had to stop and squat.

She had seen slaves burned with firebrands, their skin bubbling like a roasted boar. She'd heard of men staked to the ground and whipped, cut into pieces, chests opened up, their beating hearts fed to the dogs while they looked on. Men nailed to a wooden cross by their hands and feet, crucified, left to die by the sides of roads. And this for no more than spilling wine or dropping a platter of food.

And she had maimed her master! He would carry the mark of her rebellion for ever.

The taste of his skin, of his blood, was in her mouth. She spat and spat again, but could not rid herself of it. Neither could she wipe away the feel of his hands on her flesh, his fingers probing, pinching, taking possession. The smell of that oil in her nostrils. She wept. Vomited, the retching so violent it left her dizzied and weak.

When at last she went on she stumbled and had to lean a moment against the tree. Under her fingers was rough bark. Soft moss. The feel of it brought a recollection from childhood.

The steward had sent her with a message for the woodcutter. She'd been told to run, to hurry, but it was a bright spring morning, the bluebells thick on the ground. She'd ambled along slowly, breathing in their sweet smell.

A mist had been rising from the river and, while she

walked towards the sound of the woodcutter's axe, it had begun to wind through the trees, slowly, quietly, with the stealth of a hunting cat. Suddenly there was nothing but dull greyness. She could hear the chopping still, but the mist distorted sound. She couldn't tell which direction it was coming from. Frightened, she'd started screaming.

The woodcutter had come at once, striding through the trees. He'd plucked her from the ground, holding her in his arms until she'd calmed herself. When she'd recovered from her fear he'd pressed her hand to the bark of a tree. He'd pushed it across the rough surface until her fingers met something cool and soft and damp, like fur, or hair. Cold, dead hair! She'd recoiled but the woodcutter had hushed her and said, "You can't always take your direction from the sun or the stars, child. Feel here. It's only moss. It hates the sunshine. If a tree is out in the open, moss will grow only on the northern side. Even here, where the woods are dense, it grows thickest there. The river lies north of the villa. Remember that, and you'll always be able to find your way, even in the dark."

North.

There was something in the sound of the word that stirred another memory. She reached for it, but it melted like the mist. And then she heard barks. Yelps. The faint sound of baying hounds.

The master had called for his steward, and the steward had called for the dogs.

Cassia panicked. Four legs could move so much faster than two! She could not outrun them. If there had been a stream close by, she would walk along it, hoping they might lose her scent. But she knew the lie of the land. There was no water for a mile or more. They would catch her long before then.

As she had when she was small, she spoke her mother's name aloud. She begged for help. To be drawn into the clouds or to melt into the earth. Could some goddess not transform her into an animal? A bird? A tree? Into something, someone else? Where was she to go, what was she to do?

She prayed to mighty Jupiter.

Yet it was not mighty Jupiter who answered.

There are not words strange or subtle enough to describe the sensation Cassia had there in the forest.

She could not hear the voices but rather felt them. She could not see the speakers and yet knew them to be women. They surrounded her, and yet had no form. They were not flesh, not of this world, and yet neither were they divine. Not living. Not dead. She did not understand their words. She had never heard their voices before. And yet they were familiar.

"Help me!" she cried. "Help me!"

The women were gone as suddenly as they had come. Cassia was alone again. They had given her no answer. And yet she knew what she must do.

At her back, the baying of hounds, distant, but growing ever louder. Ahead — her skin prickled with awareness. The whisper of wolves. Fur against bark. Paws on leaf mould. Near, and coming nearer. A pack. Hunting. Scenting prey.

If she crossed their path, if she yielded to them, if she did not struggle or fight, they would kill quickly and cleanly. One bite to the throat would be all she would know. Oh, she would be torn apart. She would be consumed. But she would know nothing of it. Better to die now than live and endure torture at the hands of Titus Cornelius Festus.

Cassia started running towards the wolves.

VI

Do wolves mourn for their dead?

Does grief make them howl to the moon?

Who can say? A shaman, perhaps. But shamans keep their secrets to themselves.

I will say only this: the year before Cassia fled, Titus Cornelius Festus had entertained two merchants of great wealth and power. After days of feasting and whoring, the Romans began to crave a different sport. They went hunting in the forest with Titus Cornelius Festus's men and hounds. Hunting for wolves.

But a wolf is no easy thing to track and kill, no matter how many hounds run with you. A wolf is indifferent to the weight of your purse or the size of your ego. And the merchants were not the fine young warriors they imagined themselves to be.

They found only one animal – a she-wolf who had

recently whelped and was nursing her cubs. Full of wine-fuelled bravado, they dug her out from her den. She fought, killing two of the master's dogs before succumbing to their teeth. Her cubs were slain – all but one, who was brought back to the villa for the further entertainment of the master and his friends. Teased and tormented by them, the cub had not survived the day.

Do wolves know when one of their own is slain?

Given a chance of revenge, would they take it?

Cassia ran towards the pack fully intending to die, finding her way by instinct. With each step the hounds at her back drew nearer. They had her scent. And this time they were not running with corpulent, middle-aged merchants but only with the dog keeper and his boy, who were as fleet of foot as their animals.

They did not want this chase. To hunt a fellow slave? A woman? Their hearts recoiled. But they had their orders. They knew the price of disobedience. And so on they ran.

They were some fifty paces away when the girl reached a clearing. There was a small break in the canopy where the moonlight had broken through and lit the forest floor in a near-perfect circle.

Eyes glinting. A dozen pairs. Fixed on Cassia.

The deer the wolves had been hunting was forgotten. She walked to the centre of the circle. Knelt down. A human sacrifice. She turned her face to the sky. Waited for the bite.

The constellation of Callisto, the Great Bear, was directly above her. Callisto. Raped by Jupiter. Turned into a bear. Swept into the stars. Callisto looking down on Cassia.

She will give me strength, thought the girl. She lay back on the ground, leaving belly and throat exposed.

The pack leader, padding towards her. Stopping two paces short. The animal's breath billowing, clouds rolling over her skin.

And then the others. The air shimmering with their heat. They were close, fur brushing her flesh. She would feel their teeth. Soon. One heartbeat more. Another. Soon, soon, it would come.

But no.

A nose was pressed into her face. Another sniffed her hair. They were licking her neck, her face, her throat. Licking, not biting. As if she was one of their number.

When one snarled she opened her eyes. Its teeth were bared, yet its gaze was not fixed on her but on something beyond.

It seemed to Cassia that the wolf smiled.

When it leaped, it was not to pin her to the ground, but to soar over her head. For a moment it blotted out the sky. Moon, stars, Great Bear – all were gone.

When the wolf landed, the dogs were thirty paces away. Twenty. Ten. They entered the clearing.

Four hounds. One man. One boy.

A dozen wolves.

The keeper of dogs and his lad had come in pursuit of a runaway girl. They were not armed for battle.

The fight was as brief as it was unequal.

At its end, man, boy and four of the best hounds in the kennels lay dead.

Cassia was unharmed.

Her heart raced. Was she dreaming? It was fantastical. Impossible.

She, a girl. A slave. A nothing. She was of less importance than a strap on her master's shoe. Why, in all that carnage, had she alone been saved?

For a moment she wondered if the gods had preserved her for some purpose? But the idea was absurd – she dismissed it at once.

VII

Time had fractured. Broken apart. The two halves of Cassia's life – Before and After – were separated by a chasm. She could never go back. But there seemed no path forward. Nowhere to go *to*.

She sat at the edge of the clearing leaning against the trunk of a tree, her back pressed so hard into the bark it pierced her skin. Looking up at the stars, she prayed and prayed again. She called her mother's name. She listened for the strange women's voices.

There was nothing.

The fear and panic that had driven her suddenly evaporated. She was exhausted. Drained of emotion and of energy. She tried to force herself to stand. To move. But she could not. Sleep overtook her like a rising tide. Cassia fell into a doze, waking with a start shortly before sunrise.

Some strange compulsion then drew her north, towards

the river. The forest thinned, the pitch sky faded to pewter then smoke grey. She crested the hill as the sun edged over the horizon, streaking the sky with flames of red and amber. The river was below her, gleaming gold in the morning light. A vast mass of water flowing east.

And there! At the jetty was the ship bound for Londinium, heavily laden but still moored. Silvio had driven the ox-cart in her place the day before and he had obviously been slower to make the journey. The ship had missed last night's high tide but was even now making ready to leave.

Londinium. By all accounts a splendid city, teeming with people. If she could only reach it – could she not lose herself in the crowds?

She had come to the rutted track but it did not run directly down to the river. The hill was so steep that the weight of a loaded cart would have pushed the oxen off their feet. Instead it ran first one way and then the other, gradually descending the slope in a series of wide, sweeping bends.

But she was on foot. She took the most direct route, slithering down through bracken and brambles, scratching and scraping arms and legs, snagging the rich silk dress that was meant to please the master's eye.

She reached the jetty just as the last rope was about to be slipped, so out of breath she couldn't speak for a moment.

The captain regarded her with some surprise. Though a native Briton, he was a free man in name at least. But Titus Cornelius Festus had him so tightly bound in chains of debt that he was really no more his own man than the steward or the keeper of hounds.

Yesterday, when Cassia had not come with the cart, he'd asked after her. Silvio had flushed scarlet. Mumbled a reply that the captain couldn't hear. But he'd deduced where she'd been sent and why.

Her appearance could mean only one thing: she'd run away. Curse her! She must be returned to the villa. Now. At once. For his own sake, for that of his crew. He must give the order. *Come on, man. Speak.*

What was stopping him?

One, two, three heartbeats.

Her eyes.

He could read the outrage in them. The horror. The desperation.

He'd seen a look like that before.

A stab of sorrow slid under his ribs and pierced his heart. He recalled his daughter, violated by a Roman soldier and nothing he could do about it.

His crew were watching him. They were rough, unvarnished men, given to drinking and whoring come pay day. This girl had removed herself from any protection the master had once given her. She was alone. At their mercy.

But each and every one of them had mothers. Aunts, sisters, wives. Some had daughters. Women that not a man of them could protect if they happened to catch the eye of a passing Roman.

The captain felt the stirrings of rebellion in his chest.

"I expected you with the cart yesterday," he said. "Sent to the villa, were you?"

"Yes."

"Filthy old bugger!" He spat on the deck. "What are you doing here? Run away?"

She held her chin up. "Yes."

A smile passed like a shadow across his face. She was a fighter, this girl. Did she not deserve a better fate? He asked, "Did you kill him, girl?"

"No."

"More's the pity. Would have saved me a lot of money if you had."

"He's maimed. Missing half his ear."

The captain raised an eyebrow. "You cut him?"

"Bit him."

He laughed so loudly that the waterbirds nearby took flight. And then, in one smooth movement, he leaped from ship to jetty, took off his cloak and threw it about her shoulders. "Come aboard. Let's get you away before they catch up with you."

He could do nothing for his daughter now, but by all the gods in heaven he would assist this girl. As he helped her onto the deck, he said to his men, "Listen, and listen well. We have none of us seen her. Not hide nor hair. Understood?"

He was not a man to be argued with. There were nods, grunts of assent. He gave the command, the last rope was slipped and the ship was underway.

Cassia tried to find the words to thank him but he silenced her with a look. "Keep out of sight," he said.

She tucked herself into a corner where she would not be underfoot and where no one on the far banks could see her.

She had never been on a ship. Had never seen the country that lay beyond the jetty. All was strange and startling. Weary though she was, she drank in this new, wide world.

It was only many hours later – when they had journeyed the length of the river, skirted the coast and entered the mouth of the Tamesis which would carry the vessel to the city of Londinium – that Cassia's heart missed a beat. Her stomach heaved. She had to ball her hand into a fist and press it to her mouth to stop herself crying out.

In the heated rush of her flight, she had quite forgotten Rufus!

Rufus. Her brother. Her only family.

Eight years old now, a redhead like his sister, pale of skin, blue of eye: a small, slight boy, something of a dreamer. Since their mother's death he'd slept each night with his face pressed against his sister's neck, his head on her shoulder.

How could she have run without him? She'd given him no thought. Not once!

It didn't matter that Rufus knew nothing of where she was going or what she would do. It wouldn't stop the master giving orders to the steward. It wouldn't stop the steward trying to extract information that her brother simply didn't possess.

There on the deck of the ship Cassia felt as though she had been punched in the belly. She couldn't draw breath. Couldn't inhale, let alone gather her wits.

She would run back to him. Would offer herself up to the master – would do anything, endure anything, just so long as she could be with her brother.

But the vessel was midstream on a broad river and she couldn't swim. She leapt to her feet, she cried out, wept, wailed and keened until the captain took her by the shoulders and shook her. He begged her to calm down, to come to her senses.

"There's nothing to be done," he said. "Nothing. You can't go back. You do that and I'm in danger. Me, and all my crew. He'd have us killed if he knew we'd helped you. Is this any way to thank us?"

"Sorry. Sorry." Cassia slumped back to the deck and huddled tight down into a miserable heap. The weight of

awful knowledge settled so heavily on her shoulders that
she thought her bones would break: she was alone now.

As was Rufus.

VIII

The captain wouldn't take her into the city itself. Londinium heaved with people, he said. A vast population and from all the corners of the Empire. With luck, and if she kept her wits about her, she could remain hidden from her former master. But at the dockside there were too many eyes and ears, too many desperate souls who might seek to buy favour with Titus Cornelius Festus by telling him of the human cargo that had been transported to the city along with a load of stone.

The walls of Londinium were barely within sight when they lowered Cassia over the side of the ship. She was knee-deep, waist-deep, chest-deep in freezing water, the silk dress billowing around her, the ship dangerously close to running aground, before her feet found the river's silt bed.

She had returned the captain's cloak to him but he had bundled it up and now pressed it into her upraised hands.

"Take it, girl. And good luck to you."

A brief nod. That was all. They sailed on. She struggled towards the shore.

It took her some time to reach it, and when she did she found she was on an island, riddled with channels. She had to splash through mud, wade through streams and inlets, cross from one piece of marsh grass to the other. When at last she came to terrain that could claim to be called dry land she was sodden and chilled, her teeth were chattering, her skin was blue with cold. Wringing what water she could from her dress and hair, she wrapped the woollen cloak around her shoulders, pulling the hood up to conceal her face before starting the long trudge to Londinium.

What had she done?

As she walked towards the city she felt as though she'd swallowed lead. It made her heavy and dull-witted.

Until this moment, she'd never set foot on land that didn't belong to the master. And, until last night, she'd always known precisely where she was going and what was expected of her. Now she was heading towards an unknown destination and an unknown future, with a past that was a rope around her neck, tightening with each step.

The ship's captain had put Cassia down on the southern side of the river. Before long she came to a stone road that ran straight towards the city. If she turned to the left, she could have gone back to Rufus.

But there could be no returning.

Much though it pained her, she turned to the right.

It was late afternoon and there were plenty of people moving to and from the city. Ox-carts trundled slowly in both directions and were overtaken by horses, mules, even pedestrians. So many of them! Such an array of faces! In her fifteen years she'd never encountered anyone who didn't know she belonged to Titus Cornelius Festus. But now she was one among a crowd. Merchants and farmers, nobles and peasants: no one knew her, but they all stared. She moved so slowly – as if she was sick or simple or drunk. What was wrong with her?

The protective charm of being marked for the master's son had vanished. She was elbowed. Pushed. Yelled at. She felt herself slipping through her own fingers. She was nothing. No one.

Her courage almost failed her. Take heart, she muttered to herself. Keep calm. No one knows what you've done. No one will guess you've run away. No one will imagine you abandoned your brother to save your skin.

The thought doubled her over with pain. Rufus! He'd know she'd gone by now. Was he crying? Was he afraid? Was the steward even now taking his stick to her brother's back?

A pair of bare feet stopped in front of Cassia. Rough hands pulled her upright. A peasant woman, her face lined with concern, asked, "What's wrong, girl?"

Cassia didn't want to talk. She pulled the cloak tighter around herself to conceal her sodden dress.

"Bad meat," she said. "Stomach-cramps, that's all. It will pass."

Bidding her good afternoon, the peasant woman went on her way. Cassia tried to gather her wits but it was no easy task. Her guts churned with misery and regret, her head ached with thoughts of Rufus.

She'd gone half a mile or so more when she passed a graveyard that stood outside the city's walls. A funeral procession was coming towards it from out of the city and she stepped aside to let it pass. A small corpse wrapped in a winding sheet was laid out in a cart. A child. A string of mourners followed behind. A woman who Cassia took to be the child's mother could barely walk. Two slaves were half carrying her in the cart's wake. Her grief was so overwhelming she made no sound, but the wailing cries of the others seemed to echo Cassia's own sorrow.

She shivered, chilled, watching the procession enter the graveyard. Other passers-by hurried on their way, eyes to the ground, faces turned aside, not looking at the mourners. Sorrow, ill fortune: it could be caught as easily as a disease. Cassia turned her back on them and went on her way.

She neared the timber bridge that spanned the Tamesis. On the northern shore the city walls loomed high, taller than three men, wider than an ox. Titus Cornelius Festus's forebears had made their fortune supplying the stone to build them. But now perhaps, maybe, if the gods were with her, that fortified city might give her shelter.

The water was ebbing as she stepped onto the bridge, tugging at the posts. Through the slats beneath her feet she could see churning movement. Each step felt unsteady, as though she was still on the deck of the ship.

An arched gatehouse was at the end of the bridge. Two sentries in helmets and shining armour stood, one either side.

Red Crests.

People were coming and going, a human tide flowing in and out of the city. She forced herself to take a deep breath. The soldiers wouldn't pay her any heed amidst this throng, would they?

But they were bored and looking for entertainment. Someone advancing slowly, unsteadily – as if afraid, as if they didn't know where they were going or what they were doing – instantly caught their attention.

And they were Roman soldiers. And she was a woman. In truth, they needed no more reason than that.

Cassia approached the archway. Keeping her head down, she felt the soldiers' eyes on her. Every muscle tensed, every sinew tightened.

One stepped forward. Blocked her way. She dodged sideways. Straight into the arms of the second man.

"What have we here? See, Probus? Women can't help throwing themselves at me."

The violence of her reaction terrified her. She wasn't Cassia, she was Boudica: warrior queen. If she'd had a knife she would have disembowelled him without a moment's hesitation. She wanted to cut, to wound, to inflict damage. His arms were around her, pinning hers to her sides. She struggled, turning her head to bite, but the woollen hood was over her face, in her mouth.

Holding her so tightly, he couldn't fail to notice that underneath the cloak her dress was wet. "She's soaked to the skin! What have you been up to, girl?"

"Nothing!"

"Let's see your face."

"No!"

The second soldier jerked her hood back and recoiled at the savagery of her glare. Her teeth were bared like a wolf's!

"Hair wet too."

"No honest woman would walk around in such a state."

"Where are you from, girl?"

"Where are you going?"

When Cassia didn't answer, one of the soldiers said, "We should take her in."

The two men exchanged a glance. This girl was unaccompanied. Unprotected. She had aroused their curiosity and more besides. Cassia saw the lust in their eyes and fear inflamed her fury.

They tried to tie her wrists, to take her captive, but she fought like a wildcat, scratching, hissing. Yet there were two of them and she was alone. It wasn't long before they'd succeeded in pulling her arms behind her back.

It was then that a third man stepped forward.

Standing motionless in the shadows, he'd blended so perfectly into the background it was as though he'd emerged out of the stone wall. He might have been a painting, or a carved relief, come to life. The effect was so startling that Cassia stopped struggling.

They regarded each other. For a moment time itself seemed to pause and take a breath.

He was younger than the Red Crests, perhaps four or five years older than herself, she guessed. Tall, muscular, his features as perfect as a statue's. High cheekbones, black hair that curled at the nape of his neck, oiled skin the colour of a beech nut.

His eyes – that flicked from Cassia's wrists to her ankles, taking in the tattooed marks – were a brown so dark they were almost black. He had a pleasing mouth that was curled into a reassuring smile inviting her trust. Even so, there was something of the predator about him. *He's like a cat*, she thought. *Purring at me, but ready to bite if the mood takes him.*

His curiosity was self-evident. Brows contracted, he seemed to be making a decision. His expression changed. Mouth splitting into a wide grin, he said words that were so peculiar Cassia had no idea how to react.

"Where've you been, Tansy? Your uncle's been screaming for you since noon."

Tansy? What was this? Had he mistaken her for someone else?

"I…"

Before she could say more he interrupted.

"Clumsy girl! Did you fall in the river again?" He turned to the soldiers, jerking his thumb in her direction. "Pretty enough, wouldn't you say? But shit for brains." He looked at her once more. "Have you got the thyme?"

"What? I don't know…"

"Idiot! Thyme! The herb he sent you to pick? By all the gods on Olympus, you haven't kept the wits you were born with!"

One of the soldiers asked, "You know this girl, Aquila?"

"Oh yes. I've known her a long time. And surely you saw her pass this way earlier? Or are your powers of observation weakened by last night's ale? Tansy is the niece of Quintus Hortensius. I'm going there now. I'll see she gets home safe."

The lie was so smooth, so shamelessly told that Cassia herself was almost convinced by it. For a moment she thought her prayers in the forest had been answered; that her soul had been lifted from her own body and dropped into another form. Somehow she'd been transformed into a Roman.

The soldier clapped the man he'd called Aquila on the back. "Take her then. Get her away from here before she causes more trouble."

The stranger took her by the arm. Aquila. The name meant "eagle", did it not? The symbol of Rome. Of might. Of Empire. Of conquest. He was the living embodiment of it. His hand grasped her through the cloak's cloth so his palm was not in contact with her flesh and for that she was grateful. To feel his skin on hers would have been unbearable.

He didn't hurt her, but there was no escaping his grip. They'd gone perhaps twenty paces along the road before she found her voice.

"You're mistaken…"

He stopped, brought his face within a hand's breadth of hers and said softly, "I know a woman in trouble when I see one. I couldn't let you get arrested by those two. I know how they treat their prisoners. The female ones, at any rate."

She couldn't miss his meaning. "Thank you."

"How did you get so wet?"

"I don't want to say."

"Well, then… Where are you from?"

Did he take her for a fool? "I won't tell you."

"And I suppose you won't tell me why you're here either?"

"I am here … to live. To work."

"To work? At what?"

"At anything. That is ... anything honest."

"Ah, well, there I can help you."

"You? Why?"

He smiled at her again. "Why not? Let's just say it pleases me. Besides, I happen to know a man whose joints are failing him. He could use a younger pair of hands."

"For what?"

"He's a pharmacist. Cures. Remedies. Potions to heal the sick. He's a fine man. And he won't ask questions."

He seemed honest. There was something appealing about him: a charm that drew her. She was about to thank him again when a breeze from the river carried the scent of his skin to her nostrils. Juniper. The same oil favoured by Titus Cornelius Festus. Her eyes narrowed. She could not forget he was a Roman. An enemy. "And what would you want in return?"

"What do you think I might want from you?" He looked at her. She didn't answer. And so he said, "Ah ... you think I'm in search of a mistress?" His tone was a little mocking. "No... You're a delight to look at, but I've never needed to force a woman into my bed. I'll help you for the same reason that I'd save a bird from a cat. I have a soft heart."

"I can't accept."

"You'd refuse my introduction to Gaius Quintus Hortensius?"

"I would. I do."

"And where will you go? You're alone, aren't you? No food, no money, no place to sleep. Night's coming on. There's nowhere you can go. No honest employer would take you looking like that. There are inns and taverns by the docks but you don't look like the kind of woman who'd want to end up in a whorehouse. But if you don't accept my help, believe me, spreading your legs is the only way you'll get by."

The hopelessness of the situation overwhelmed her. Was that her only choice now? Had she run from Titus Cornelius Festus only to become a whore to any passing sailor?

She looked at the stranger in front of her. He didn't meet her eyes, but stood, staring down at the road, waiting for her to make up her mind.

Perhaps the gods who had preserved her from the wolves, who had steered her feet to the river and melted the captain's heart, had also sent this man?

In a voice that was softened by sincerity he said, "I really can't leave you alone here. Honour forbids it. Please, will you let me help?"

Cassia weakened and he seemed to sense it.

"I ask with all respect – will you let me help you?"

She yielded.

With a reluctant nod, Cassia put her fate entirely into the hands of an unknown Roman.

IX

Marcus Aurelius Aquila was the Roman's full name. He told Cassia to call him Marcus and – though it felt awkwardly intimate – she did as he asked. He had helped her. How could she refuse?

As Marcus led Cassia by the arm through the streets, he informed her that he was a trader. In the summer months he travelled the length of the country, all the way to the far north, selling salves and remedies for various illnesses. But with winter coming on, he planned to sit out the cold weather and sell what he could in Londinium.

A straight road appeared to lead into the heart of the city but he didn't take her along it. Instead he turned to the right and they walked along the dockside.

The ship that had carried her to safety was moored, its cargo of stone being unloaded onto the shore. They passed within a few paces of it, but the crew neither looked at her nor made any comment and she carefully avoided meeting their eyes.

But there were other vessels that drew her interest. There was one whose men were ebony-skinned, whose hair curled tight against their heads. Others who were the same beech-nut colour as Marcus, black hair slicked down on their skulls. They heaved great terracotta jars of oil and what she took to be fish sauce – from the smell of it – off the ship to a cart that waited on the land. The stink brought Titus Cornelius Festus to mind again and her stomach heaved. She missed a step and tripped. The sailors noticed and some whistled. Some called. Some offered her money. They'd taken her for a whore!

One who'd just set down his jar on the cart approached, swaggering, but before he could speak Marcus stepped in front of her.

"Don't you know an honest woman when you see one?" He batted the man away, and Cassia was grateful of his protection. She moved closer to him and he released his grip on her arm, instead placing his hand on her shoulder, pulling her against him. They moved away from the dockside and down a side street.

Here, things didn't improve. They'd entered a narrow lane where every second building seemed to be a brothel. The sounds – grunts, cries, curses – that came from doors and windows made the sweat bead and start running down her back. Had she wondered for a moment about the wisdom of escaping from the master, those noises wiped all doubt away.

Some women leaned through windows, looking for customers. One or two – the young, the pretty – called out to Marcus but he ignored them.

Aged whores sat in the doorways. Their eyes followed him but they were too tired, too soul-weary to speak or sell themselves.

Marcus and Cassia went on without a word and she – shocked by the squalid sights – offered up a silent prayer of thanks to whichever god had sent her this stranger. How could she ever have fared in this city alone?

She'd heard the story of the Minotaur whispered in the huts by firelight. A monster, hidden in a labyrinth so complex that no one could ever find their way out. Londinium seemed to be just such a place. It was as the rumours said: its scale and size was no exaggeration. But to hear a thing and then to see it are two vastly different things.

Marcus turned a corner. Then another. He walked fast and she had to almost run to keep up with him. They twisted and turned this way and that, finally emerging onto a broad thoroughfare. At one end lay the Forum, a building of such immense size and splendour that Cassia stared, open-mouthed.

He said gently, "Try not to look so astonished. Your eyes are on stalks."

"I can't help it. I didn't know there were so many people in the world! Or so many buildings."

"Don't let them take you for a newcomer."

"They'd harm me?"

"I haven't time to tell you the many ways you'd be taken advantage of. You need to act as though you've lived here all your life. As though that building there is utterly ordinary. From now on nothing must surprise or alarm you. Don't meet people's eyes. Don't invite conversation. Don't try to please anyone. It marks you as a country girl." He stopped for a moment. "Men here ... they're not respectful. They'll grab at anything female. Do you know how to protect yourself?"

Cassia smiled. The Boudica game had served her well. She'd wrestled and fought often enough to know exactly how to defend herself. "Yes."

"Good."

On they went. Sights and smells and sounds assailing her. Oil and steam thickened the air around the public baths, the amphitheatre reeked of sweat and blood. They passed countless villas that dwarfed that of Titus Cornelius Festus.

Eventually they came to a quiet street that was wider than most and lined with trees. The dwellings were elegant but did not scream of wealth and power and seemed more designed for comfort than for show. As they went on the houses got smaller and were spread further apart. Were it not for the city wall that hemmed them in, Cassia would almost have believed they were entering the countryside.

They had reached almost the very last building when Marcus stopped outside a modest villa. Square-built, of Roman style, walls enclosing a garden that was once neat and orderly but now overgrown and choked with weeds.

Marcus knocked on the door but did not wait for an answer.

"Wait here," he told her. Pushing the door open, he walked inside.

Cassia stood on the threshold.

She could run. The Empire was broad, wasn't it? She could go anywhere.

But she'd seen enough in the streets of Londinium to terrify her. She wanted to be let in. To shut the door against the world. To be safe.

The men's voices were low. She couldn't catch anything of what they were saying, but knew it must concern her. The conversation was brief. After a very short time, she was told to step inside.

X

⚜ ⚜

Gaius Quintus Hortensius, renowned pharmacist, was a most incurious man. Herbs and their healing properties were his consuming passion. Cassia had never encountered anyone who showed so little interest in his fellow creatures. A person was a body, that was all. A body that may – or may not – have a specific ailment that he may or may not be able to cure. He gave no thought whatsoever to the mind or soul of any particular patient. Or to that of his new assistant. For, the minute she stepped over the threshold, that was what Cassia became.

She'd entered a large room and it took her eyes a moment or two to adjust from the street to the dark interior. When they did, she saw a man hunched over a pestle and mortar, peering inside as though the bowl contained the secret of immortality.

He'd already lost interest in Marcus and didn't even

seem to notice that Cassia had come in: he was too busy reaching out a finger and thumb to sample the mixture he'd worked on.

"Too coarse," he muttered. He cursed and began to grind again, but his fingers were stiff, his knuckles swollen. Holding the pestle clearly pained him.

Marcus cleared his throat noisily. Reluctantly the pharmacist lifted his head.

"Didn't I say I'd find you help?" Marcus pulled Cassia forwards. "See. I've brought you a pair of strong and willing hands. She'll help you for as long as you need her."

Gaius Quintus Hortensius pointed a gnarled finger at her. "I'll not have my house filled with women's gossip."

"Oh, she knows how to hold her tongue."

The pharmacist asked Cassia only one question: "Are you healthy?"

"Yes."

He seemed disappointed. Without asking her name, he hobbled across the room, pressed the pestle into her hands and told her to grind the herbs he'd been struggling with. Where she'd come from, why she was alone, what her connection was to Marcus – he never asked. He didn't seem to wonder about her sudden appearance at all.

The job she'd been given wasn't a hard one, yet Cassia had never used a pestle and mortar in her life. She'd worked out of doors, alongside men, and was unfamiliar with women's more usual tasks. While she worked clumsily at the sage and thyme the two men talked.

"Your joints still trouble you, I see," said Marcus. "How goes the search for a remedy?"

The herbalist cursed again. "A physician should be able to heal himself, should he not? I wish it were that simple. I know many things. But how to ease these joints of mine? It eludes me still."

"I'm sorry to hear it."

"Not as sorry as I am to feel it."

The smell of crushed herbs drifted to him across the room. He hobbled back to Cassia, sampled the mixture and declared himself satisfied.

"I'll leave her with you then," said Marcus. "She'll need feeding, remember. And a warm place to sleep." He walked over to Cassia, took her hand in his, and bade her farewell.

Their palms touched.

His hand was warm, dry, unexpectedly rough. She'd thought it would be soft, smooth, oiled like the master's and found his callouses strangely reassuring.

She opened her mouth to thank him but before she could speak he dropped her hand as if he'd been scalded. A pained expression crossed his face and then he turned on his heel and walked out of the door without another word.

XI

For what remained of the day there was plenty to occupy Cassia's mind and body.

Following the pharmacist's command, she crushed the sage and thyme into a smooth, green paste.

"Now this," he said, pushing a pot of honey across the counter towards her. "Not too much, mind."

When that was done to his satisfaction he handed her an onion. "Chop."

She obliged, cutting the thing clumsily into chunks, her eyes beginning to stream as the juices were released.

"Add it to that. Crush it. It must be smooth. No lumps."

He watched the contents of the mortar like a hawk, oblivious to the fact that now Cassia's nose was streaming as freely as her eyes.

Last to be added was the juice of a lemon. She sliced it in two. Squeezed each half in her hands, the juice stinging the cuts she'd received during her flight through the forest.

When the task was done at last he commanded her to pour the mixture into a jar. He sealed it himself and gave no explanation as to what or who the remedy was for.

Snapping "Come along," he then led her into a garden that was badly in need of weeding. He couldn't bend to do the task himself, but neither could he bear the sound of slaves' chatter. "You must work silently," he said, "Or not at all."

Cassia simply nodded mutely and he rewarded her with a sniff.

He informed her in his querulous voice which were herbs and which were weeds and stood watching to make sure she did not tear up any of his valuable or beneficial plants.

But Cassia already knew which herbs were which. Titus Cornelius Festus never sent for a doctor to cure a slave. A physician's fees were so high, he reasoned, and able-bodied replacements could be bought so easily! It was cheaper to let sick slaves die. To have them smothered if they lingered too long in the process. Among the huts the slaves had developed their own cures. Cassia knew what would soothe an upset stomach, what would ease a headache or prevent a sore from festering, even if she had not brewed the remedies herself.

This was work she understood. Gaius leaned upon a stick and watched her pull away weeds, allowing his precious herbs room to breathe. When the sun sank below the horizon, he ordered her to light lamps and prepare his meal. Thankfully no cooking was involved, for this, again, was something she'd never learned to do. Bread. Cheese. Olives. Wine. When it was arranged to his satisfaction, she was permitted to sit in the corner like a dog and watch him eat.

She'd had no food since the day before but didn't wish to mention it. Yet her stomach betrayed her, rumbling loudly before he'd taken his first mouthful. He looked at her. Seemed to think for a while. Then he threw her a crust.

"There's more in the kitchen. Take what you need, but don't stuff yourself."

Ravenous though she was, she forced herself to take only a little and eat the food slowly, quietly. The hiding place Marcus had brought her to was perfect: she didn't wish to offend her new master.

When she'd finished her meagre meal Gaius told her she could make herself comfortable on the floor of the kitchen. He'd expect her to rise before first light and be ready to work. She curled up on bedding that was musty and damp but she was scarcely aware of any discomfort. Sleep overwhelmed her suddenly and completely; all thoughts of Rufus were rubbed out by exhaustion.

For most of the night, she didn't stir. But as the sky began to lighten a dream curled its way into her head, subtle and slight as a wisp of smoke.

71

She was standing in a strange landscape – on the lower slopes of a broad valley that seemed to have been scraped out of the hills with a gigantic spoon. It was edged on both sides by mountains so high that if she climbed them she'd only have to reach out a hand to brush the clouds. The plants that grew at her feet were unfamiliar. Wiry, purple-flowered, interspersed with peculiarly coarse grass. In the distance was a lake, still and silvered, a mirror to land and sky. A rushing stream close by flowed into it. There was a boulder in its middle and an ancient rowan clinging to a cleft in the rock. She had never seen these things in her waking life.

And yet she knew them.

In her dream she stood looking at the rowan, the red berries growing in such profusion that they weighed down the branches. She drank in the sight of it, breathing in the cool, clear air, thrilled with its familiarity. And then her heart began to pound faster. The women had come.

They had no form. Or rather, she could not see any. They were just out of sight. If she could only turn her head fast enough, she'd catch them. Yet she was frozen to the spot. She could neither move nor speak but only listen, and this appeared to be all they desired.

Their voices wreathed about her. Tender, gentle murmurings, not in Latin – in a forgotten tongue. A language Titus Cornelius Festus had forbidden any slave to speak.

She struggled to understand them. The words were like those that her mother had whispered in the darkness of the hut. She recalled the sounds but not their meaning. It was so long since Cassia had heard her mother's voice, so long since she'd died! She reached for understanding but it was beyond her. If she could stretch her mind, push her memory a little further... Yet the harder she tried to grasp it, the more the sense eluded her.

Moment by moment the women grew more irritated by her stupidity. They were frustrated. Angry. Their disappointment pierced Cassia but she could do nothing. They pleaded, as if by begging they could make her understand. There was something they wanted. Something she must do. But she had no notion of what. And so they began to vent their fury. At her back there were shrieks. Hissed curses. They rang in her ears and she woke wearied and confused, scarcely knowing where she was or how she had come there. For a moment she feared she was running mad, that pain and guilt over Rufus was turning her mind inside out. A desperate loneliness washed over her. There was no one who she could turn to for help. No one she could talk to.

No one but Marcus.

XII

The Roman did not show his face the first day, nor the second. The hours stretched long and thin on the third and still he didn't come.

Rootless and friendless, Cassia felt she'd become transparent. Insubstantial. She might be carried away by a strong wind.

Gaius kept her busy, and she was glad of it. Winter was approaching and the herbs the pharmacist needed for the dead months ahead had to be dried and powdered. She listened to his instructions, did as he asked, said nothing. But all the time she yearned for Rufus. Yearned too for the company of the men she'd worked alongside. Silvio, who'd been like an older brother; who she'd fought and played with as a child; who'd laughed and joked and called her "my lady Boudica" and "my queen". Who'd looked so stricken when she'd been sent to the master.

How painful it was to think that she'd never see him again!

The pharmacist's clients called on a daily basis and she made up salves and draughts according to his orders. In addition she was sent to fetch bread from the bakery and cheeses from the shop a hundred paces along the street. On top of that there was the huge, unfamiliar labour of working for a man who had no other slaves. She was clumsy with a broom, an inept cook and an inefficient housekeeper. But he seemed not to notice.

On the fourth day she was told to leave the house and deliver a remedy to a woman who lived on the other side of the city.

Her new master's directions were clear and precise: she was to head due west, and then south at the third crossroads. Directly opposite the barracks there would be a villa with a painted door and a mosaic on the step showing a picture of a dog. That was where she should deliver the salve. She must take payment, and on her return journey buy meat and vegetables from the market for their supper. The weather was growing colder and Gaius had a desire to eat something warming that evening. A stew, he said. And he expected her to make it.

She had no difficulty following his directions. She recalled Marcus's words and kept her head down, walking with purpose as though she knew her precise destination, meeting no one's eyes, looking too busy to stop or chatter.

It did not prevent unwelcome attention. An attractive young woman, out alone? There were comments. Catcalls. Lewd propositions. Offers of money. As the streets got more crowded she was jostled, and sometimes she felt a hand snake out to pinch her flesh. By the time she delivered the parcel, she was overheated, sweating, her heart thumping against her ribs. How was she ever to feel comfortable in a place like this?

She would have returned to the villa at once, but she'd been told to go to market. There the press of people was even closer. More pinching. More obscene suggestions.

To escape the thickest of the crowds she went to the quieter stalls, but there she discovered another problem. She didn't understand how to haggle for goods. She'd never had to handle money before, she didn't know the coins' value any more than she knew the cost of the things she'd been asked to buy. In the end she had to hold out a hand and allow the stallholder to pick the coins from her palm, not knowing whether he was an honest trader or not.

They were mostly not.

She ran out of money when she'd bought only half of what she'd been supposed to. The butcher had sold her gristly, half-rotten meat. The oil was rancid. The vegetables, mouldy. Looking at her meagre purchases, she felt like a child – so ignorant, so foolish! Once more she longed to see Marcus: there was too much to learn. She needed advice.

She wanted information. But could she trust him to give it to her?

Hot and distressed though she was, she'd noticed the streets of Londinium crossed each other at right angles. When she'd passed the Forum she'd seen that the road from it ran in a straight line all the way to the bridge. There had been no need for him to take her along the dockside or that street lined with brothels. So why had he? And why was he now keeping away from her?

Unhappy and confused, she walked towards the market's exit. But then she passed a throng of women who were gathered at one of the popular butchers' stalls and all thoughts of Marcus were forgotten.

"… the north."

It snagged in her ears although she didn't know why. She stopped.

"All along the frontier, I heard…"

"Coming down from the hills, across that wilderness…"

"Swarming like flies the other side of the wall."

"… harrying our men…"

"Our soldiers!"

"Barbarians!"

"Savages!"

"Boil their enemies alive, I heard."

"No!"

"Worse than that. My man was stationed up there before he retired."

"Mine too. They sacrifice their captives, he said. Eat their livers."

"Eat their hearts."

"Cut off their heads. Stick them on poles the birds to peck at."

"Eat their own children when they've a mind to, I don't doubt."

"They're animals."

"Worse than animals."

"It's about time our lads sorted them out once and for all. Torch the whole place. Burn it down to ashes."

"What's the Emperor thinking?"

"They need reinforcements. He wants to get a couple more legions up there. Crush them. Wipe them out."

"They should kill the lot of them. Everyone north of the wall. They want to clear them off the land. They're nothing but vermin."

There was a chorus of agreement, and then the women moved on to other topics. Their stories had sent fear prickling down Cassia's spine. But something else stirred in her heart too.

They had talked of a frontier. A wall. The land on the other side sounded like a wasteland, teeming with wild barbarians. Bloodthirsty savages. Vermin, they'd called them. As if they were a plague of rats.

Boudica was dead. Britannia had been defeated long before Cassia had been born.

But now – for the first time – she began to understand that the whole world was not ruled by Rome. The mighty Empire had a limit. And there were people beyond it that lived free.

The idea scared and thrilled her in equal measure.

XIII

That same evening Marcus called on Gaius with an order for different remedies for several of the soldiers in the army barracks. The pharmacist was in the garden, inspecting his herbs. Cassia was in the kitchen, struggling to make an edible meal from the foul ingredients she'd bought earlier that day. When Marcus came in, her heart soared.

He sniffed. Frowned. Lifted the lid and peered at the mess of stew in the pan.

Cassia was almost in tears. "He sent me to the market. He asked me to make him a meal."

"Ah…"

"I didn't know what to do!"

"How much did you pay for the meat?"

"I don't know. I held the coins out. I don't understand the money."

"You were robbed! Didn't you suggest a lower price?"

"No! Is that what I should have done?"

"Yes. Every time. Never accept the first amount you're told. Halve it at least. And this... Couldn't you tell the meat was rotten?"

"I didn't think to look."

"Throw it away. Quickly, before he smells it. I'll go now."

"What?"

"Don't worry. I'll be back. I'll bring something from the tavern. He'll never know the difference."

"I've spent everything."

"I have my own money."

Marcus was as good as his word. She'd emptied the stinking mess into the latrine and was busy washing out the cooking pot when he returned.

Pouring what he'd bought from the tavern's bowl into the pan, he asked, "Didn't your mother teach you how to cook?"

"No," Cassia snapped. Her mother was too raw a subject to talk about.

"And yet you don't look like a lady of leisure. You haven't been lying idle on a couch these last few years."

She didn't answer, but he persisted. "What were you before you came here?"

He'd been nothing but kind. And yet she couldn't bring herself to tell him the truth – the words died on her tongue before they could be uttered. The silence stretched out until at last he said, "Ah … don't trouble yourself. I don't intend to ferret out your secrets. Tell me them when you wish. *If* you wish. Meanwhile, I can see I've a lot to teach you if you're to survive in Londinium."

The next day he went with her to market. They stood at one of the four entrances, Marcus pointing out quietly which were the popular stalls. "The key is to watch. See over there. That trader flirts, that one teases. That's how they build the loyalty of their customers. But you're not a middle-aged matron that needs flattering, are you? Look – that's where the canny people buy their meat. No nonsense. No showmanship. Just fresh meat at a fair price."

They neared the stall and he made her listen for a while – observing other customers – until she felt sure what coins made a fair exchange for which goods. He didn't trade for her, but kept a watchful eye, only intervening if she made a mistake.

And then later – in his own lodgings – he taught her how to cook a basic stew. Or he tried to. When it came down to it, it seemed that he was as bad a cook as she was. He burned the meat and boiled the vegetables to within a hair's breadth of their lives. After an hour he conceded defeat, declared that the art of cooking was best left to those who knew how to do it and took her back to Gaius's house via the tavern, where she bought the meal she later reheated and served to her master.

After that, Marcus called on Cassia on an almost daily basis. Sometimes he brought her a gift: small things, chosen to please her and make her smile. A shell from the docks, a stone picked up in the street. Once he came with a bead of lapis lazuli that had dropped from a wealthy woman's necklace. It was the colour of bluebells; the colour of her brother's eyes. Soon after the turning of the year he brought her the first snowdrop of spring.

It was not the robust friendship she'd had with Silvio. It was more like a courtship, she thought, and yet he never touched her. He was always courteous. Warm, friendly, maybe a little flirtatious. Sometimes she'd catch him gazing at her, as if transfixed, but he made no demands and seemed to have no expectations.

Once, she asked him why he'd led her to Gaius by way of the dockside and the brothels. He'd smiled, a little red-faced. "I knew the danger you were in," he said. "But I didn't think you'd believe me if I tried to explain. I thought it best to show you where lone women sometimes end their days." It seemed reasonable enough and she pressed him no further.

He often asked her about her past but she told him nothing. It was too painful to speak of Rufus. And besides, there was some deep instinct of self-preservation that made her keep it to herself. She became adept at turning the conversation on to other matters: things she'd heard in the street, things she'd seen in the market. She demanded to hear his stories of gods and monsters. Of Perseus, slaying the Gorgon Medusa. Of Ulysses escaping from the Cyclops under the belly of a sheep.

Cassia looked forward to his visits. They were a welcome break from the dull routine imposed by Gaius. When she was sent out to deliver salves or remedies, she and Marcus walked the streets together and his talk was engaging. He spoke of his own childhood in Rome. He told her of his travels, too, of the rough country that lay on the Empire's side of the wall and the vast bleak expanses of hill and heather that lay beyond. Of the tribes in the far north he knew little, although she pressed him for information: he said only that he'd seen the occasional prisoner – men so wild they'd chew their own hands off rather than remain in chains, "the way a fox will bite through its own leg if it's snared". He was interesting. He made her laugh. She enjoyed his company. She would almost have craved for more than that but whenever he drew close, the scent of his oiled skin would catch in her throat. Juniper. Titus Cornelius Festus. The stink of Rome. Of decadence. Of debauchery.

As the weather warmed and the herbs began to emerge from their winter sleep, Cassia grew restless. She felt confined. Constrained. Her yearning to see Rufus, to have him with her, had not dulled and, as the days grew longer, the pain of his absence grew worse.

Marcus seemed as restless as she was. He was young. Energetic. He'd been too long in the same place. One morning he announced that his months in the city were over.

"I'll go north soon. The colder the weather, the more people suffer from it. There are people all along the wall prepared to pay well to cure the ills brought on by damp and cold."

Cassia listened with some irritation. He was a man and a Roman – he could go wherever he pleased. But she could not. She would have to remain in the city, labouring, keeping her head down. Avoiding attention.

And there would be no visits from Marcus to relieve the tedium. How would she manage?

XIV

The whole of that winter, Cassia's dreams troubled her. They were always the same. The women, calling to her in words she could not understand. Each morning she woke frustrated and angry.

But she was not the only one plagued by nightmares during the long dark months.

A storyteller may slip through time and across distance with a single word or phrase.

Back.

To the estate of Titus Cornelius Festus. Who had not been resting easy in his bed either.

He had been so sure the bitch would be caught.

The night she'd bitten him – after she'd run – he'd lain on the floor too shocked, too stunned to do anything but clutch the side of his head, feeling the stump, hot blood oozing between his fingers. His mind would not accept the

reality of what every sense was telling him: that he had
been maimed.

Maimed? Maimed, and by a slave! By a girl whose life
he'd spared! Who he'd fed and clothed for years. And at
what expense?! Is this what a man got for being merciful?

When he found his voice, he had screamed for his
steward, but his cries were so frantic, so alarming they
brought every house slave in the villa running. They did
not bring his wife. But no matter.

The girl would be hunted down. When they dragged
her back – by Jupiter and all the gods on Mount Olympus,
he would skin her himself!

Every slave on the estate had expected to see her
humbled within the hour. Sickened by the knowledge of
what would follow, a pall had hung over the huts.

But Cassia had not been dragged back.

As that night stretched on and still she did not appear,
there was a little whispering.

And when at first light the steward went in search
of the keeper of hounds he came back white-faced and
shaking, with a story that would have chilled the heart of
an emperor let alone Titus Cornelius Festus. After that, the
whispering became a murmuring.

She had injured the master! Bitten the bastard's ear off!
She had set a wolf pack on her pursuers! She had bent wild
animals to her will. And she herself had got clean away.
She had vanished. Become invisible.

There had always been something special about the girl, the other slaves muttered. The very fact she'd been allowed to live proved that. And on the night she was born – *do you remember?* – at the very moment she came into the world in a flood of blood and water wasn't the statue of Neptune overturned? What did it mean?

The slaves couldn't decide. But night after night they talked of it.

Titus Cornelius Festus, on the other hand, knew exactly what Cassia was.

A witch. A demon.

Proof, if any more were needed, came when his ragged wound festered. Foul-smelling pus oozed from the stump of his ear. She had cursed him!

He called for a soothsayer, he called for the healer but neither could help. For days he lay in a sweated fever. And he dreamed of Cassia. Kneeling. Meek and submissive, her mouth open, smiling, showing her teeth. Which suddenly clamped shut.

Each time he woke with a scream.

The master had lain in his bed for ten full days and nights. When the heated sweat and shaking abated, his ragged ear was a throbbing reminder of what had occurred.

The fever left him. The dreams did not. They continued all winter long. He didn't visit the brothel in town. He didn't send for any of the house-slaves. He didn't even look to his wife. The girl had unmanned him. He was wretched.

Angry. The healer had mended his body, but not his mind. That, he supposed, he must do himself.

After five months of torment, Titus Cornelius Festus remembered an accident he'd had as a boy. His father had bought him a new horse – a fine, black stallion, high-stepping and proud – a magnificent beast that had thrown him before he'd ridden ten paces.

How old had he been? Eleven? Twelve? He'd cried, he remembered – tears of shame more than hurt. And of fear. With its nostrils flared, snorting, pawing the ground – the horse had suddenly looked like a monster from the ancient tales.

How angry his father had been! He'd ordered Titus to get up off the ground, to get back on the horse, to show it who was master. "Conquer your terror, you screaming sissy. Or it will conquer you."

Perhaps the same principle could be applied to the girl? Titus began to think that there was only one way to recover his sanity.

He should buy a new slave. A redhead. An obedient virgin to take Cassia's place. He would select her himself.

And where was the best, the biggest slave market in Britannia?

Londinium.

A week later Titus Cornelius Festus set forth for the city. His temper had not improved these past months and the steward had been at the receiving end of it, day after day. He watched his master depart with a sense of glorious relief.

By road it was a journey of some forty miles from villa to the city – a ride that could have been managed in a single day had Titus Cornelius Festus the will to do so. He did not. He was soft and heavy of body and did not care to sit astride a horse. Instead he was propelled along in a carriage stuffed with silken cushions and pulled by a pair of well-groomed horses.

They had to proceed at a slow pace, for behind the carriage ran the master's body slaves. They were tied to the end of a rope in case they were tempted to run away like that bitch of a girl, Cassia.

Oh, he was aware of the effect she'd had on his slaves. Somehow she'd put a spring into their steps. They carried their heads higher these days. Often he felt their eyes straying to his ruined ear. They were not such fools as to let him catch them staring. But he could feel their suppressed smirks, their contained laughter. He'd had several of them whipped for it, his steward included, but the smiles were still there.

She'd given them a fable to cling to, given them hope.

Curse the woman! He'd never had any trouble managing his slaves before. Well … let them see how he treated the girl he'd bring home from Londinium. He'd break her, and break her well. She'd serve as an example to them all.

Titus Cornelius Festus stopped for the night at a wayside inn, where he demanded the best rooms to be given over for his use. He made straight for the bath-house, where his slaves scraped and oiled his skin. A jug of wine, the finest food the inn could offer. When he lay on his couch, clean and with a full belly, his mind turned to the satiation of his other appetites.

He called for the innkeeper to see what was on offer and the man returned with a woman. Her red hair was a wig and she was far older than he would have liked, but the creature was willing and able to please him and just then that was all he desired.

When he was done, he slept.

He'd planned to be on his way at dawn the next morning. But he woke late, his head aching from too much inferior wine. He groaned, rolled onto his back. Scratched himself.

And – oh, curse that whore! – his old problem had begun to flare. He recognized the telltale itch and that hideous burning when he urinated into the pisspot. Jupiter and all the gods on Mount Olympus! Were they playing some kind of joke on him?

Maybe it would pass off as they travelled.

It did not.

Moment by moment, mile by mile, the pain grew worse.

They reached Londinium at sundown and went straight

to the tavern where he was accustomed to stay. He spent the night in torment.

The following dawn was a ravishing one – clear and cool, with the welcome promise of warmth to come. But Titus Cornelius Festus missed all the beauty of the sunrise.

He needed help. A doctor. A healer. Someone. Urgently. He sent a slave to fetch the tavern owner and the man recommended a pharmacist at the edge of the city.

Before long the innkeeper's boy was running through the streets of Londinium towards the home of Gaius Quintus Hortensius.

XV

Dawn that day found Cassia in the garden, weeding between the rows of freshly sprung herbs. The smell of the earth, the feel of the sun on her back, the colour of the new growth – all conspired to make her miss Rufus more than ever. The bluebells would be out soon. He used to pick them for her, even though she always told him to leave them where they grew. He could never resist pressing bunches into her hands, bluer than the sky on a spring day. She'd like to breathe in that colour, to fill herself with it.

And here she was, trapped in Londinium, while Marcus, the only person in the entire city who was close to being a friend, was making preparations to leave. This week, or the next – any day now – he'd be back on the road, he said.

He'd offered to take her with him. She'd refused. She didn't know why. There was nothing to hold her here. But there was some nagging sense of a task undone. Something incomplete that kept her chained, unable to move.

Cassia had no inkling of what was to happen that day. She felt no prickling of the skin, no dark presentiment. She was so engrossed in her work and so far down the garden that she didn't even hear the innkeeper's boy arrive or the pharmacist questioning the details of the guest's condition.

The boy was sent back with word that the remedy would be delivered as soon as it was made. It would take an hour or two, no more.

It was only when Gaius called Cassia to come and grind dried berries into paste that she realized he had a new client. She walked into the house with no sense of foreboding and made the preparation as he instructed. Then she delivered the salve to the tavern.

And the fates of Titus Cornelius Festus and Cassia collided once more.

She smelled him before she saw him. She'd been directed to the large chamber at the top of the building and had climbed the stairs in all innocence. She was barely through the door when her nostrils were assaulted by the stink of wealth and over-indulgence. Of lechery.

For a moment she froze. Stood petrified.

He had his back to her. She could have escaped without him knowing. If only his slave's eyes hadn't widened; if only he'd not let out that astonished cry.

Titus looked at the boy. Turned his head to see what had alarmed him. Saw Cassia's red hair, bright in a shaft of sunlight.

And then it was as though he had unleashed the Furies.

He rose from the stool he was sitting on, leaping up so violently it crashed to the ground. "Get her, get her, get her," he shouted, the words melding together into one phrase.

He was a wealthy man, and he liked to display his affluence in the retinue that accompanied him. There were five slaves waiting on his every whim. Five men set on one girl. Though their hearts might not be in the chase, they'd seen what the consequences were when she escaped the first time. No one would willingly endure that kind of torment.

She was down the stairs, through the door and running. Her pursuers cast aside everything in their way – tables, stools, customers. Titus Cornelius himself discovered the use of his feet – running down the stairs, through the tavern and along the street in pursuit of Cassia for perhaps twenty paces before he exhausted himself.

As for Cassia – her work had been easier this last winter, much of it indoors. Her muscles weren't as hard as they had been: she couldn't run as far or as fast as she once had. Panic tightened her chest and her breath came in pained snatches.

The slaves were running to escape a certain beating. Cassia was running for her life, but so blinded by fear she couldn't think. She turned one corner, then another. Then a third. She thought she'd shaken them off, but had merely run around the outside of a tenement block and almost straight back into her pursuers.

Pushing her way through the crowds, splashing through mud and filth, she entered the market. It was the busiest time of day, with people pressed so tightly together she could not run. Indeed she could barely walk and had to go with the human tide as it flowed in and then moved from stall to stall. She had the presence of mind – just – to duck down a little, so her red hair did not act as a flaming beacon to her fellow slaves.

She saw them come in. Split up. They spread out, each heading to the separate exits. There they stood guard at each doorway knowing that the market would eventually end, that the place would clear: that she would not get through without having to pass them by.

And then they waited.

It was a long, weary morning. But by noon the crowds began to thin.

One by one, the traders began to close their stalls.

Cassia was in despair. She'd run herself right into a trap. The urge to weep, to scream, to tear her hair was overwhelming. She dropped to her knees. Crawled under the table of a stall where a sudden calmness descended.

She was seized with an odd kind of detachment, as though watching herself from above. A story slipped into her head. One Marcus had told her. Ulysses, escaping from the monstrous Cyclops under the belly of a gigantic sheep.

There were no creatures to hide under, but there were vehicles, being brought in now in ones and twos. The nearest was a four-wheeled donkey cart, low to the ground.

She tied her hair into a knot. Gathering her skirt through her legs she stuffed the hem into her belt and then crept underneath it. Ulysses had clung to the sheep's fleece. Could she not find something to cling to now?

Forcing her toes into the space between the rear axle and the floorboards, ramming her fingers into the hole at the front, she held on like a limpet, praying she would not be thrown down the moment the cart moved.

But first it had to be loaded and the stallholder was in no hurry to be off home. He chatted while he worked. Each thud of an empty amphora hitting the boards went through her, jarring her spine, setting every muscle on edge.

She was in an agony of impatience but soon discovered the folly of wanting to be underway. While the cart was stationary, clinging to its belly was bearable. As soon as the wheels began to turn, the axle moved with them, scraping against flesh and bone, bruising her, grinding her feet and hands. She would be crushed! Or she would be dislodged and flung to the ground.

They neared the exit. She could see the feet of one of her

pursuers. Saw him approach, walk around the cart, glance into it in case there was a stowaway crouched between the jars. But he did not think to bend down and look at what was underneath.

And then the cart was out of the market and into the street. Every stone, every pothole jolted the vehicle and gave her fresh pain. The blood was rushing to her head; her hands and arms had begun to shake. As the wheels turned, they cast manure into her face.

When they hit a particularly deep pothole, she could cling on no more. She fell, landing with a splash in a pool of urine.

The cart driver heard nothing over the grate of metalled wheels on stone.

For now Cassia was free.

But she could not go back to Gaius. She could not stay anywhere in the city now Titus Cornelius Festus knew she was here.

Once more she was on her own. Once more she must flee.

Where to?

She stood in the street, and at that moment a cart piled with hides trundled past. Bear. Beaver. Wolf. Dead, grey fur, stirred by a breath of wind.

The coolness that had overtaken her grew and spread. Her skin felt as though she had been stroked with ice.

The women's voices: the dreams she had been having

all winter came to her now in broad daylight. Still she could not understand the words. But the tone? They were desperate. But not angry. Pleading. Begging. Inviting. She could feel their invisible hands reaching out, pulling her towards them.

I will come, she thought. But where? Where?

The answer dropped into her head and she said aloud, "North."

Of course! For as long as she was within the Empire, Titus Cornelius Festus could pursue her, take her back, do as he wished with her. But the Empire had its limits. The thought of the wild tribes made her blood run cold. Savages, they were called. Vermin.

But was that not the same way the Romans talked of Boudica and the Iceni?

Romans. Who put men to death for their own amusement. Surely the savage tribes could not be more barbaric than the men who now ruled Britannia? Could she not take her chances with them?

Again she spoke aloud: "Yes."

And – as if in response – another thought came into her head.

Not without Rufus.

The fears and worries, the forgotten task that lay undone: the grief that had so clouded her head cleared. She knew precisely what she must do.

Even as her plan was taking solid form, her feet were

leading her to the place where Marcus had his lodgings.

She entered his chamber without knocking.

Before he could ask her what was wrong, the words were out of her mouth, cool and resolute.

"I need a Roman."

XVI

Cassia told Marcus that she would travel with him, as he'd asked. But first she had a job to do. There was someone she needed to find, someone of immense importance, who she must rescue from bondage and bring secretly away. Someone she needed to take north of the wall.

She expected him to refuse. He was a Roman, after all – why would he help her with something so clandestine? *At the very least*, she thought, *he'll want to know more about Rufus. To demand why he was so important to her.*

She'd expected to use every argument, every means of persuasion in her power. Gods! She'd even sleep with him, if necessary. There were times he'd seemed to burn with lust for her: she would use that, if need be, to gain his help. He was young. Handsome. How bad could it be? If she kept her eyes shut and tried not to breathe in, it would soon be over.

And yet she didn't need to offer herself.

He asked her nothing but agreed to help. No questions. No conditions. Indeed, he said it was probably for the best if she kept her secrets to herself. "What I don't know I can't tell."

It was astonishing! He seemed to be helping her for no other reason than that he was a good man. She struggled to believe it, then rebuked herself for being so surprised. Titus Cornelius Festus had surely twisted her mind out of shape. Not all men were like him, she reminded herself. This past winter Marcus had never given her cause to doubt him. It was foolish of her to not entirely trust him.

When she described to Marcus the place where Rufus was, he offered suggestions of how they could get there. He wondered aloud how best they might bring him away. But he never once asked for more information.

The land between Londinium and the villa was unfamiliar to Cassia but she knew the general direction they should take. Marcus assured her there was a road running east that would take them there.

He proposed riding – native ponies could be purchased at a small price and they were hardy and sure-footed, well used to travelling great distances at speed. Cassia had never ridden a horse in her life but was loath to admit it. *How hard could it be?* she thought. Surely, she'd only have to sit still and let herself be carried along? If children managed it, so would she.

And so her hair was cut. In the room where he'd spent the cold, dark months Marcus took his knife and Cassia's red tresses fell to the floor. What little remained on her head was dyed with a stinking concoction of dead leeches steeped in wine that he'd obtained from the barber along the street. Her arms and legs, her face and hands were darkened with walnut juice from the same source until the marks on ankles and wrists were almost obliterated and she looked like what she was pretending to be – the boy slave of a travelling trader.

They were agreed: they'd set forth at first light.

Leaving her alone in his room, Marcus went into the city. There was business he needed to complete before leaving, he said. Once it was done he went to Gaius, returning with jars of potions, pots of salves, pestles, mortars – a whole pharmacy of remedies that could be sold as they journeyed north. Cassia was concerned that Gaius, when he noticed her absence, would have reported her as a runaway – but Marcus assured her that she need have no fear. He had made things right with her one-time master, he said, and she didn't pursue the matter. For not only had he brought her the garments of a boy, he'd acquired a packhorse and a pair of panniers, one of which was stuffed with all manner of things that might prove useful. The other was empty, but – if the gods were willing – it would conceal a small boy for long enough to bring him to freedom.

They slept that night in the same room and in the same

bed, Marcus facing the wall, his back to Cassia.

He did not lay a finger on her. He'd complained of tiredness and shut his eyes, yet he did not seem to sleep. Cassia dozed fitfully, but each time she woke she felt his spine at her back. His breathing was slow and steady, but she'd slept in the slave huts all her life: she knew the difference between real and faked slumber. She wondered at it, but soon her puzzlement turned to gratitude.

He'd helped her so much already, and asked for nothing in return. Now, together, they would free Rufus. As she lay in the dark, feeling his warmth against her, for the first time she thought his touch would not be at all unwelcome.

XVII

Cassia was used to handling oxen. She knew and understood their temperament. A pony, she soon discovered, was entirely different. Alert, wary, sensitive to her every movement and reacting, so it seemed, to her anxious thoughts. She looked at the creature, wondering how to get astride. The task seemed impossible and, perplexed, she let out a sudden hiss of breath. The animal threw its head up and pulled away, wheeling in a circle at the end of its rope. It took her some time to calm it. When it was finally standing still she scrambled in an ungainly manner onto its back.

Marcus, to all intents and purposes now her master, sat on a much finer mount. As slave, it was Cassia's job to lead the packhorse, but – thank the gods! – the animal was old and steady and knew his job so well that the rope remained slack in her hand as he followed along, his chin almost resting on her thigh.

Cassia's balance was good, but riding required more concentration than she'd expected. As they passed through the streets of Londinium it occupied all her thoughts and for that, she was grateful. How they would get onto the estate; how she would spirit Rufus away from under her old master's nose — well, those were matters they hadn't decided. They were problems that could be solved as they travelled, Marcus said. Opportunities would present themselves. They'd seize what Fortune offered.

They neared the bridge. The river was unusually high, almost lapping at the planks and completely covering the marshes on the far side. The water had reached the moment of stillness before the tide turned. It lay glassy and unmoving and, when the sun began to crest the horizon, the whole river was turned blood red. Cassia shivered.

But if it was an ill omen the soldiers on the bridge were blind to it. They greeted Marcus by name.

"Are you off on your travels so soon?"

It was inevitable that he would stop a moment to talk to them. Cassia kept her head down, her hood pulled forward, shading her face.

She felt him glance in her direction before replying, "I've big plans this year. I'll take advantage of the good weather."

"Get rich quick, huh?" said the first soldier.

"He'll drink it away, same as ever," joked the second.

Marcus protested, "You're wrong. I'll be a man of substance some day, you'll see."

There was a moment's pause, then one of the soldiers said, "If you're after easy money you'd do better to stay in the city."

"Oh?" asked Marcus. "Why?"

"Haven't you heard? It was the talk of every tavern."

"I was busy last night."

"I'll bet you were. Was she blonde or brunette?"

"Rosa from the waterfront? Or Paulina near the Forum?"

For what felt like a very long time the soldiers compared the talents of the various whores of their acquaintance. Marcus laughed along with them before finally protesting his innocence. "You do me wrong. I was simply preparing for my journey."

"More fool you." The soldier lowered his voice, but it was loud enough for Cassia to hear and his words chilled the blood in her veins. "There was a slave girl escaped from her master yesterday. She's running loose in the streets. A real looker, by all accounts. He wants her back. He's prepared to pay a pretty reward for her, too."

"How much?" asked Marcus. Cassia tensed.

"Five thousand denarii," the soldier replied.

Marcus whistled. But he didn't seize her. Didn't turn her over to the soldiers. Didn't appear to make a connection between the girl who'd escaped yesterday with one who'd been in the city all winter. Instead, he said, "She must be the best whore in Britannia to be worth that much."

Cassia wished she could block her ears. She must give no sign that their talk was of any concern. She was a boy now. Only the reddening of her skin under the walnut juice gave any indication of her discomfort.

"Wouldn't mind a taste, eh?"

"Virgin, I heard. Or she was when she ran away."

Marcus laughed. "She'll not be one by now. And he'll not pay for soiled goods. No, I'll put my faith in selling cures to lonely wives and rich widows. That's the way I plan to make my fortune."

"Good luck to you."

After bidding the soldiers farewell, Marcus gave the command and Cassia urged her pony on. Her stomach was churning but she had to ride at a steady pace, the packhorse plodding along beside her, its drool running down her thigh.

It was only when they'd crossed the Tamesis and were well out of the soldiers' sight that Marcus spoke to her. They were on a stretch of empty road when he reined in his horse and waited for her to draw level. Softly, he said, "I apologize."

She didn't reply. He was helping her. He'd asked her no questions. She could scarcely complain about his behaviour. And yet he seemed to feel the need to explain himself.

"I was only saying what they expected to hear," he murmured. "I'm a tradesman. I have to rub along with other people no matter how vulgar they are. It's an act, nothing more."

"I understand that."

"Good. Well ... be warned. There'll be plenty more of that kind of thing in the coming days. You're a man now. Better get used to the way we talk when we're alone."

There was no chance for more conversation. A flock of geese was being herded along the road towards them. At their back the loud wheels of a cart heralded the approach of more traffic. Marcus turned his horse and went on. Cassia rode behind, eyes fixed on his back.

She was puzzled. He had been so careful with her, so tender and courteous all winter long! To hear him talking to the soldiers – to hear him sounding so coarse – was a revelation.

She'd thought she knew him. But the man she'd seen on the bridge had worn an entirely different face. An act, he said, but how could she be sure? Which was the real Marcus?

XVIII

They travelled slowly that day. The road was busy; a steady stream of traffic going to Londinium. Besides the geese, they met a flock of sheep and later a herd of scraggy-looking cattle. Each time they had to wait by the side of the road for the animals to pass. By the time stragglers and strays had run off and been rounded up, they seemed to spend more time stationary than on the move.

There was still an hour or more of daylight when the sky turned leaden and rain-sodden clouds bloomed like bruises overhead. It had started to spot with rain when a roadside inn came into view. They had covered only half the distance to the villa, but stopping for the night seemed preferable to riding on beneath a gathering storm.

They were on public view and so Marcus treated Cassia as any passing stranger would expect: with the cool indifference of master to slave.

The remedies that had been loaded so carefully into the panniers were too precious to leave unguarded. After Cassia had rubbed down the horses to Marcus's satisfaction, he took himself inside to eat and then to sleep. Cassia was left in the stables to mind both beasts and cargo. While the animals had a generous quantity of hay she had only a little rye bread and goat's cheese from the supplies Marcus had purchased in Londinium the day before.

The storm had broken by the time she settled down to eat, and soon she found herself joined by a pair of stable lads, slaves to the innkeeper. They were friendly enough. Eager to share food and gossip with a stranger.

It turned out that the inn where Cassia and Marcus had stopped was the selfsame one in which Titus Cornelius Festus had stayed on his way to purchase Cassia's replacement. It was inevitable that there would be talk of him. What Cassia found more surprising was that there was also talk of herself.

"You should have seen him!"

"Great fat bugger, wanting to get his end away!"

"Imagine being poked by that."

"No wonder his last one ran."

"She never got caught, that one. Vanished into thin air, they say."

"I heard she set a pack of wolves on the man sent to fetch her. Got ripped to pieces, he did. Him and his boy."

"There were signs when she was born. A great storm,

just like this one. Flooded the whole place. Knocked Neptune's statue right over."

"There were dragons in the sky."

"Never!"

"My old mother saw it. Honest."

The tales went on, growing more and more fantastical. Cassia listened, apparently agog, and the boys' stories continued to tumble out until their yawns came more often than their words. They crawled off to sleep in the loft. Cassia settled herself in the stall with her pony but it was a long time before she could sleep. She had a strange sense of disembodiment, as though she was seeing herself across a great distance. The stories she'd heard that evening were entirely removed from the reality of herself. It was odd. Unnerving. Somehow she was becoming a creature of legend.

She was sleeping, curled on the straw in the corner, when Marcus crept in and shook her awake. She jerked upright, back pressed to the wall, her hands claws – ready to rake his face.

"It's mc. You're safe," he said. His speech was slurred, but she relaxed.

As soon as he saw her hands go down, he squatted, meaning to rest on his haunches, but the quantity of wine he'd imbibed threw him off balance and he landed hard on his buttocks.

He grunted, then sighed, before saying, "While you've been sleeping, I've been working hard on your behalf."

"You've been drinking."

"Sometimes it's the same thing." He lowered his voice to a whisper. "I've been finding out how things lie on the estate where your Rufus is kept. It's the villa of Titus Cornelius Festus, isn't it?"

"You know it is."

"By strange coincidence he stayed here two nights ago. According to the landlord, he has a … *personal* problem … that's known to flare up on occasion."

"What of it?"

"They say he's gone to Londinium. Some business transaction or other. He'll stay there a week or two, no doubt. But I gather his wife remains at home."

He looked at her. Smiled knowingly. "If he suffers a personal affliction, she will too."

"So?"

"Fortune is smiling on us. We have a remedy in that pannier that will help. We won't have to creep onto the estate like thieves. We'll go openly, in broad daylight. While I'm selling a salve to his wife, you can do what you need to. Will that give you enough time?"

XIX

They travelled on the next day. By late afternoon, Cassia found herself riding back onto the estate she had fled from a few months before.

On either side of the road that led to the villa, there were slaves working in the fields.

Her heart leaped to see that Rufus was there – she could see his red hair in the distance near the line of trees that marked the beginning of the forest.

But there was the steward, supervising. She could not ride up to her brother without him noticing and demanding an explanation. And there was no reason that one boy slave would approach another at his work. Her disguise was good, she thought, but the steward had known her all her life. The risk that he would see through it was too great. She would not escape a second time.

To be so near her brother, yet so unable to do anything,

strained every nerve. She'd have to come back at night – to creep into the roundhouse. But did he still sleep in the same place now she'd gone? Had he found another shoulder to rest his head on? How could she find and wake him without disturbing every slave in the huts?

Marcus gave the command and Cassia was sent riding ahead to announce that a renowned healer was passing by and was the household in need of remedies?

As Marcus had predicted, he was invited inside for a consultation with Livia Tertia, the master's wife.

Cassia's head was full of her brother, and yet she couldn't help but see how very skilled an actor Marcus was. Last night, with the men in the tavern, he'd been so loud, so noisy, so full of friendship and good cheer. She'd heard him while she'd been in the stables trying to sleep. But now, with Livia Tertia, he was courteous, respectful, polite. The way he should be.

Cassia had never seen the wife of Titus Cornelius Festus as anything other than a smudged blur on the far-distant horizon. The woman had banished her from sight when Cassia was just a child and – as a result – had grown into a mythical monster in her mind. Livia Tertia was a screeching harridan. A thing of wild tempers and furious sulks. A slattern who shared her bed with the master.

But now, here they were in the same room. Breathing the same air. The creature of Cassia's imagination melted into mist.

Livia Tertia was small. Sick. Her hands shook and her voice trembled. She was riddled with pain, and only a small part of it physical.

Alone in Londinium, Cassia had sometimes felt herself dissolving. She recognized in Livia Tertia a woman clutching at threads. Trying to hold them around herself to maintain some semblance of what she'd once been.

The master's wife talked with Marcus not of ailments or cures, but of the terrible weather in Britannia. The damp. The cold. The grey skies. Of how she missed the heat of her homeland. The olive groves. Lemon blossom. The azure sea.

And he listened. His head inclined to the left, nodding, sighing in sympathy as she carried herself back to different times. She'd been married at twelve to a man she'd never met. Taken away. Never seen her mother or her sisters again.

Marcus spoke little, and when he did, he only asked questions that prompted her to reveal more.

After she'd been talking and he'd been listening an hour or more, the old slave Flavia came in with a tray of victuals. She set it down. Left the room. The conversation flowed on.

Another hour passed and then — with Marcus's prodding — Livia Tertia started to speak of the only good thing that had come of her marriage. Her son. Lucius. Of the illness that had killed him. How she feared the gods had mistakenly taken him instead of her...

At that, Marcus coughed. Said – very gently – "The Jews would say that the sins of the fathers are visited on the sons."

Livia Tertia flinched. Turned away. Turned back. Stared at Marcus with panicked eyes.

Gently, so gently, he ventured, "And perhaps also on their wives?"

Blanching, she whispered that *yes, yes indeed*. She suffered.

"I can help you."

At that, Livia Tertia dismissed her slaves from the room. After a nod from Marcus, Cassia also scurried away.

Cassia had always moved in a different world to Livia Tertia's house slaves. She was faintly amused to notice that they took themselves off only a short distance. They were discreet, they were stealthy, but they remained within earshot so they could hear every last word. Details of the mistress's private consultation would reach the roundhouses long before nightfall.

Cassia had never thought to feel sympathy for Livia Tertia. But she was surprised now to feel a pang of pity.

Gah! She couldn't afford that. Crush it, crush it!

There was a job to do.

She went in search of Flavia and found her in the kitchen, alone.

She didn't know the woman. And yet there had been that one kiss. There was a bond there that was deeper than reason.

The old woman's spirit had been crushed many years before. She was hopeless, helpless, devoid of joy, devoid of any expectation but death.

And yet something extraordinary happened when Cassia laid her hand on Flavia's arm and said, "Don't you know me? I'm Cassia. I've come back."

Cassia feared Flavia would faint, or scream, or both. The old woman clasped a hand to her mouth. She paled. But her eyes! Some ancient fire was reawakened in them. There was wonder. Excitement, as well as shock.

"Why are you here?" she asked.

"For my brother. For Rufus. I'll take him with me. To freedom."

"Where? How?"

"I have no time to explain."

"The danger…"

"Sshh!" Cassia put her fingers to the old woman's lips. "Please. Can you get word to him?"

"Yes."

"Tell him I'll meet him where we played Boudica. The Emperor's clearing. He'll know. Can you do that without anyone else hearing?"

"I'll do my best."

"I'll wait there as soon as it's dark. Tell him to slip away only when it's safe. He can't be followed. We can't be found."

XX

Cassia burned to see her brother, to have him once more under her protection. But things could not be hurried. Once Marcus's consultation was completed, they left the estate, proceeding south towards a town where Marcus had told Livia Tertia he would find more customers.

The day was warm, the horses slow. They had gone only three miles or so before Marcus said it was time to stop for the night.

They found a tavern and as soon as the horses were settled, as soon as Marcus took his place among the drinkers and started loudly regaling them with stories, Cassia slipped away.

A slave lad out alone: she dared not go along the road in case she was taken for a runaway. Instead, she cut through the fields of the estate that neighboured that of Titus Cornelius Festus.

It was dark when she reached the woods, but her feet knew the tracks and the trees and carried her straight to the clearing. Here she'd stood, playing the mighty Boudica. And now what was she? A woman disguised as a boy. A woman in the debt of a Roman. A stranger fate than she could ever have imagined.

The moon came and went as clouds scudded across it. There was the far-distant howl of wolves.

She waited. And waited. And Rufus did not come.

Where was he? Why was he taking so long? Surely the slaves must all be sleeping by now?

Was that it? Had he been unable to keep himself awake?

Poor Rufus! Some days he'd fallen into a doze on his feet as they'd walked back from the fields.

Suppose he didn't come?

Could she creep into the huts herself? But where would she find him?

In an agony of indecision Cassia paced, grinding leaf mould to dust beneath her feet.

It was not until the sky started to lighten that she finally heard the heavy tread of feet on dead leaves.

Rufus came into the clearing.

But he was not alone.

Her brother was held between them, a dark trickle of blood leaking from the corner of his mouth. Eyes shut, insensible, his head lolled to one side. He breathed, though. He breathed.

Flavia had her hand about his waist, his arm around her neck, but it was Silvio who shouldered most of the boy's weight.

Silvio. Her friend. She'd grieved for him in Londinium, thinking never to see him again. Yet now here he was and there was no pleasure in the reunion. All her attention was on her brother.

"What happened?"

"Nothing." Silvio let Rufus slide to the ground. He turned to her. Threw her an apologetic smile. "I had to hit him."

"You did what?"

She was almost ready to strike. Silvio's hands came up in his defence. "It was nothing. He'll recover soon enough."

"You hit him? Why?"

"He wouldn't come."

"What…?"

Flavia interrupted. "He's angry with you."

"Me?"

"You left him."

"I had no choice!"

"He's a child. He doesn't see it. He'll come to his senses. In time."

Cassia looked at her brother. His tunic was torn and in the moonlight she could see his back, marked with lines where his flesh had been cut with a whip. So many of them! Healed now. On the surface. But beneath, the wounds still smarted.

And she was the cause.

She could have wept. But there was no time. She needed to be off the estate now, to be back at the tavern before sunrise, to have Rufus concealed in the pannier before anyone there stirred. But how could she carry him on her own? On her back, perhaps? He would be a heavy burden. But it must be done.

She looked at Silvio. At Flavia. "Go now. And thank you. I'll take him from here."

"You won't." Silvio bent down and in one easy movement hoisted the boy across his shoulders as though he were a sack of grain.

Cassia's mind was slow. It was not until Flavia spoke that she realized what they planned.

"You're going to freedom. And we're coming with you."

The plan had been so simple. One small boy – a willing fugitive – could be concealed with relative ease. If they went on their way slowly, circuitously, selling cures and remedies to whoever would buy them in plain and open view, no one would guess they carried a secret cargo.

Slowness would be their salvation she'd told Marcus that night in Londinium. That, and the sheer unlikelihood of a Roman assisting a runaway. No one would suspect him. If they were brazen, if they did not lose their nerve, they would succeed.

But now it was not only one small boy they had to conceal, but a full-grown man and a frail old woman. And her brother had resisted going! He was not a fugitive, but a captive. The plan, such as it had been, was in pieces.

All Cassia could think to do was get back to the tavern. The sky had already shifted from pitch to lead. It would not be long before the sun was up, the world awake, and then all would be lost.

So they followed where Cassia led, crashing through the woods. Speed was of more importance than caution now, she thought, in the last moments of fading darkness. But Silvio was labouring under the weight of her brother. And Flavia's age and infirmity made haste impossible.

They were free of the trees and onto the grass. It was wet and Cassia was painfully aware that their trail would be clear to anyone who came in pursuit. Yet she could not disguise their direction by doubling back – it would take too long. All she could do was pray that the sun dried the grass by the time the absence of the three slaves was noticed. Or that they would be searched for in the opposite direction first. And so she prayed, not to the gods of her Roman master, but to those strange women she had dreamed of, the whisperers who had told her to run towards the wolves. Who were even now calling her north.

They were watching. She could feel them. Eyes on her

flesh. Breath on her neck. Their hands tugging her forward, pulling her on, towards the road where there was no cover, nowhere to hide, but where their footprints would not be seen.

Fortune was with them. It was barely dark but the world slept on. They met no one and soon the inn was in sight.

But what was she to tell Marcus? He had agreed to help her find Rufus. But to help two others? How could she expect him to do that?

There were no signs yet that anyone was stirring. She urged her companions forward in whispers. She would get all three into the stables. If she could bury them beneath the hay stored in the barn, then she could go to Marcus. They could decide together how best to proceed.

He was waiting for her. She'd expected him to be sleeping in his chamber, but as they entered the stables he stepped from the shadows, scaring her almost out of her wits.

"I see the plan's changed," he said, looking from Flavia to Rufus and Silvio. He seemed more curious than alarmed and she felt a rush of gratitude.

"They must hide in the hay," Cassia answered.

"No. It's the first place anyone will look. Up to my room, now, before anyone sees. Come."

Distrust and suspicion showed in every line of Silvio's face, but – after a nod and a shove from Cassia – he followed where Marcus led, Rufus dangling over his shoulder. Flavia went next. Cassia, last. Up the stairs, through a door whose hinges had been oiled, to a room whose bed had not been slept in, and whose occupant had lined his few possessions up with military precision.

Rufus was stirring by the time Silvio lowered him onto the bed. He was dizzied, but his eyes – when they opened – flamed with fury at the sight of his sister. He tensed. But before the yelp of rage could escape from his throat, Marcus was there, his knife in his hand, the point at the boy's neck. His voice was soft. Deadly.

"I don't know what goes on here. But if you speak now, if you make another noise, I'll cut the tongue from your throat. Believe me, I will kill you, boy, before I let you betray us."

There was no doubting the sincerity of the threat. Rufus clamped his jaw tight shut.

"You'll be hidden in that chest. It will be uncomfortable. But you'll not move a muscle unless I give you permission. Do we understand each other?"

A brief nod was the boy's only answer.

"As for you two," Marcus said to Flavia and Silvio under the bed. "Press tight against the wall. Do not move, do not stir until I tell you it's safe to do so."

They did as he instructed while Marcus went to work on the room.

In a few deft moves the chamber was transformed into

one apparently occupied by a lone man who had drunk far too much the night before. A flagon of wine was spilled, a half-finished bowl of stew overturned, its congealed contents spattered across the floor. His pack was opened, his clothes strewn across bed and stool and chest. When the entire room was in disarray he turned to Cassia.

He stood close, so close she could feel his warmth. "Go to the stable. You must seem as though you have slept there all night, yes? I'll call you soon."

She expected him to show anger. Fear. This was not, after all, what had been planned and now four slaves' lives were in peril. But his eyes were gleaming with excitement despite the danger – or perhaps because of it.

Briefly he took her hand. "I play a part today. You must play yours. Let's make it convincing, or the entire game is lost."

XXI

Cassia had barely settled herself in the stall when the stable lads began to rise, stretching, yawning, pulling the straw from their hair. Then they were up, fetching water, feeding the animals, mucking out their stalls. Cassia – who had not slept at all that night – did the same, knowing full well that the slaves on the estate of Titus Cornelius Festus would also be stirring. The three fugitives would be missed at once, of course. But she guessed that no one would remark on their absence until the steward himself observed them gone. How long that would be was anyone's guess. If Livia Tertia called for him, if she sent him on an errand of her own – they might be lucky. He might not notice for several hours. Each moment that passed would help. But when he did know they were gone – what then?

Men on horses. Dogs. A hunting party on their trail. And all of them staying here at an inn not three miles away, beside the road, not making any attempt to run.

What had she done, putting herself so entirely into the hands of a Roman? Marcus could turn them over the very moment a search party appeared. Claim a reward. Hadn't he heard on the bridge how much was offered for her return?

Be calm, she told herself. *Be reasonable.* He hadn't betrayed her in Londinium – why would he do so now? All winter long he'd been nothing but a kind and true friend: so why did she continue to doubt him? The smell of juniper. Was that it? Was that all?

Fear and faith wrestled in her mind for the length of that morning.

Marcus did not stir, but slept and slept and slept. The other stable lads remarked on it.

"He must have had a skinful, right enough."

"Of the landlord's wine? He'll pay for it. His head must be splitting."

"If he sleeps past noon, he'll get charged an extra night whether he stays or not."

"Do this often, does he?"

"Often enough," replied Cassia. Recalling the way Marcus had behaved on the bridge, she fell into conversation with them. Aping the soldiers' tone and manner, she started grumbling about her master's drunkenness and lazy habits. She seemed perfectly at ease, but with each moment that passed her apprehension grew. Each footstep, each hoofbeat might be the steward approaching. She had to go about her tasks as though she had no concern other than the horses she tended. When she mucked out their stall, she had the presence of mind to accidentally spill the trug of manure before she reached the muck heap, dropping it by the door to the inn, masking the scent, she hoped, of those who had taken refuge inside.

She fed the animals, and groomed them until their hides gleamed. It would perhaps have been more convincing had she taken advantage of her master's state by sitting in the sunshine, enjoying a little unexpected leisure, but she could not keep still.

It was almost halfway to noon when the yelping of dogs heralded the steward's arrival.

He was mounted on the master's fastest horse, three hounds preceding him, panting and barking as they came along the road. He had two other men with him.

They didn't ask permission to search but went straight into the barn, seizing pitchforks from the rack on the wall and ramming the spikes into the store of hay and the animals' straw bedding.

Hearing the commotion, the landlord came out to see what the matter was. When he was told about the runaway slave, he shrugged and told them to look wherever they pleased.

They began with the outbuildings, poking into every nook and cranny that might conceal a fugitive. And when no one was discovered they moved into the tavern itself.

It was then that Marcus – apparently disturbed by the noise – woke and opened the shutter of his window. He blinked at the light, then yelled into the yard, "Boy! Get up here. Shift your lazy arse!"

His voice was slow and thick, his tone petulant, pained, as though wine had dulled his tongue and his head ached from the excesses of the night before. He seemed a man in thrall to a hangover and when Cassia did not cross the yard at a run, he cursed loudly until she arrived outside the door to his room.

The first and the second man were searching the tavern on the ground floor, but the steward was close behind her. As she crossed the threshold, his hounds barged past. For a moment she thought they'd caught the fugitives' scent but no, they were attracted by the stew that Marcus had spilled across the floor and at once began to squabble over it.

He was standing unsteadily, pissing into the pot beside the bed. The blanket hung half off it, concealing those who lay beneath.

He looked appalling, Cassia noticed with shock. His skin was sallow, his eyes reddened, dark shadows beneath. He appeared to be shaking. What had happened in the hours since she'd last seen him that had made him so unwell?

He didn't speak to her but jerked his head, silently commanding her to empty the pot. Then he squinted at the steward and asked, "What goes on? Have you lost something?"

"Three slaves."

"Runaways, eh?" His face brightened at the thought of a chase. "Can't have that."

The dogs were licking the last of the stew from between the floorboards. One had already begun to nose at the corners of the room.

Heart in her mouth, Cassia had picked up the brimming pot and was heading for the door when Marcus walked towards the steward as if eager to help in the search. All three were close together when his legs buckled and he stumbled.

Marcus saved himself from a headlong fall by clutching the steward about the shoulders, but in doing so he knocked into Cassia, who upset the pot's contents. Hot piss splashed over the steward's feet.

"Clumsy oaf!" Marcus's hand caught Cassia under the chin. It was not a hard blow, but her teeth snapped shut on the end of her tongue.

For the briefest of moments her temper flared. She would have brought the pot crashing down on his head, but a glance from him reminded her she was a slave boy. Defeated. Her spirit crushed.

And so she cowered, cringing away from him, mumbling an abject apology, edging out of range in case he hit her again.

Her eyes were on the dogs. One was sniffing the air, its tail up, the hair on the back of its neck standing to attention.

She glanced at Marcus in panic. But he had other things on his mind. His colour had suddenly worsened. His skin was ghastly pale and his eyes looked as though they might at any moment burst out of his head. His arm was still about the steward's neck and the man was looking at him with some alarm when Marcus began to retch. He clapped a hand over his mouth, but the noise in belly and throat announced the impending eruption.

Revolted, the steward moved swiftly, freeing himself from Marcus's clutches, stepping through the doorway and whistling to his hounds. He had not yet shut the door when Marcus brought up a copious quantity of vomit.

The stench was foul to human senses, but to the hounds it was ambrosial. The one who had caught Rufus's scent was the first to start lapping at the fresh-formed pool.

The sight made the steward blanch. Seizing the animal by the scruff of its neck, he hauled it from the room, kicking the other two hounds ahead of him.

The door was slammed shut. They were alone.

Her relief was so strong Cassia had to lean against the wall. She took a breath to steady herself, but the stink of vomit only made her head reel. With a glance at Marcus she left and went in search of a rag and bucket. She forced herself to behave as though cleaning up after a drunken master was an occurrence so common it was scarcely worth mentioning.

It was only when the task was done, and sufficient fresh air had passed through from window to door to carry away the unpleasant reek, only when the steward and his men and dogs had finally gone from the tavern to continue their search further along the road, that she asked what had caused his sudden illness.

She was expecting him to reply "rotten meat" or "bad wine". Instead he smiled weakly and took a vial from the chest beside his bed, which he placed into her hand.

"A little trick I learned from Gaius," he whispered. "A powerful emetic. It's served me well many times before. But gods, the effect is vile. Let me lie here awhile."

The door was closed and barred but the window was left open. For the benefit of the innkeeper and the lads outside in the yard, Marcus lay in his bed groaning and occasionally berating his idle slave, ordering Cassia to do this and that, loudly cursing when she was too slow. But under his breath his instructions were different. The runaways could not talk or move about freely, but they could breathe more easily for a while. They could stretch their limbs and eat what little remained of the food in Marcus's pack, even if the very thought of eating made the Roman gag once more.

That he would have willingly made himself so ill moved Cassia beyond words. That he would have gone so far to help Flavia – a woman he had never even met, one who was old and frail and would be nothing but a burden to them as they travelled – showed such generosity of spirit! Cassia had had no choice but to attempt to free her brother but Marcus was under no compulsion to do the things he did. She was overwhelmed by it. By him.

When Rufus was allowed to emerge from the chest he glared at her. She longed to talk to him, but could utter not a word. How were they to make the long journey north with a lad who would fight them every step of the way?

As for Silvio...

Silvio.

Enforced silence and stillness these last hours had stretched his patience tight as a drum skin. She remembered seeing him this way in childhood, creeping through the undergrowth, pretending to be the mightiest of Boudica's warriors, freezing, keeping still until his nerves could stand it no longer. Then he'd erupt into action at the wrong moment, spoiling the game. She hoped he was a better master of himself now than he had been.

There was nothing to be done until Marcus was recovered. No plans could be made, nothing could be decided.

The day passed agonizingly slowly.

Late in the afternoon, Marcus sent her running to the kitchen, ostensibly in search of food and drink to settle his stomach. When she returned, he told her to distribute it among the others, for he could still hold nothing down.

Flavia accepted hers gratefully, her hands closing around Cassia's for a moment, a gesture that the girl found immensely comforting.

Rufus snatched his food without meeting her eyes.

But when she offered Silvio his portion, he bowed from the waist and said softly, "I thank you, my gracious queen."

He remembered the game, then. His thoughts had been running in the same direction as hers. She felt a pang of affection for him.

"My faithful warrior. I will not make you kneel before me," she said, smiling. "Not here, not now."

Cassia was between Silvio and Marcus, so the Roman did not see Silvio's answering smile or the wink that followed her words. When she turned she caught a flash of something on Marcus's face that alarmed her. It was that same look she'd seen when she first met him. The look of a cat hunting a mouse: watchful, alert. But it was gone the moment their eyes met and she was left thinking she'd imagined it. Anticipation of the journey ahead was making her see things that were not there.

It was not until the evening that Marcus was recovered enough to stand. He took himself down to the tavern to eat and make merry. It was part of his performance, he'd told her: he must seem to be a wastrel of a man, intent on pleasure, letting all the money he'd made from Livia Tertia run through his fingers like water. Only then would it be plausible for them to move on in order to earn more.

Cassia was banished to the stables with the horses. If she could only be doing something, it would have been more bearable. Enforced idleness was painful in the extreme.

Word of what had happened spread, of course. The stable lads were on fire with the story that Cassia's brother had now vanished, and two other slaves along with him. She had to listen to tales of them being drawn into the clouds, or melting into the river. Something wild and supernatural had occurred. It must have done. How else could three people – one of them an old crone – not have been hunted down by those dogs?

When the lads finally slept, Cassia lay awake. She could barely keep still. Her mind ran in circles, trying to fathom how they were going to get safely beyond the reach of the steward and his men. She could find no solution, and the more she worried at the problem, the more tangled her thoughts became.

Once more Marcus came to her at night, when the tavern slept. He stank of wine, but he must have poured away more than he drank because his voice was sober and steady.

They talked, foreheads so close they were almost pressed together, breath mingling as they whispered.

"How do we get them away?" she asked.

"I have no idea. The boy can be concealed in the pannier as we planned. But the others? Your warrior friend is too tall to be hidden. As for Flavia? She might fit in the second pannier if we abandon everything stored inside. But I think she's too fragile to endure such rough treatment. Bent double, crushed like that? Her bones would break." He paused. "Perhaps we should keep to our plan with the boy? They could go on alone."

"No. We cannot let them loose. They will be caught."

"They must take their chances."

"They will talk. They would be forced to." He gave a nod of understanding. "We need to get all three away together, but I don't know how." Pressing the palms of her hands to her eyes, she said, "We will all end up dead!"

Dead.

Dead.

In her mind's eye she saw the funeral procession she'd passed on her way to Londinium.

Her skin prickled into goosebumps. The small corpse in the back of a cart. The grief-stricken family walking behind. The mother's face.

People had stood aside to let them pass. They had turned their heads away, avoiding looking at the mourners for fear they might catch their misery like a disease.

A funeral procession.

Who would question such a thing? Who would look for the living among the dead?

Her palms prickled. A sudden wild excitement gripped her.

"My friend," she said, her eyes glinting, a slight smile playing at the corners of her mouth, "we need a corpse."

XXII

The idea was a daring one: a concept so outrageous that Marcus declared it had to succeed. Yet the practicalities of its execution took all their combined ingenuity.

Cassia – knowing this small part of the country well, knowing its inhabitants by reputation if not in person – had the advantage over Marcus. It was she who drew the fine detail, she who would have the responsibility for carrying out the greater part of the plan.

The next morning – as they had agreed – Cassia rode the distance to the nearest town. Tied to her waist she carried a bulging purse of coins. It banged against her hip as she rode, a thudding reminder that Marcus was still a mystery to her. The longer she spent in his company, the more she liked him. And yet the more perplexed she became.

He was a working man, so he'd always told her. He had

to earn his own way, pay his own keep. She'd been under the impression that he'd left Londinium with nothing, and she knew precisely how much Livia Tertia had paid for the remedy he'd sold her. So where had the bulging purse he'd produced that morning come from?

He'd put his finger to her lips as he'd pressed it into her hands and told her to ask no questions. She was hardly in a position to do so. She supposed she should be grateful that he had coins that he was willing to use for her benefit. But she was now uncomfortably in his debt and it weighed heavily on her.

She had left the inn apparently on an errand for her master who, once again, lay in bed with a sore and aching head. The three fugitives remained concealed in the room with him, their nerves strained almost to breaking.

But when the town was barely in sight, she left the road, giving the place a wide berth, skirting its perimeter through woodland and field, until she had reached its far side. There she rejoined the road, finally approaching from the opposite direction at a steady trot, as though she had ridden from the coast.

Cassia had spent years of her life listening to slaves' gossip. The rumour ran that there was a farm on the outskirts: a grubby, run-down establishment whose owner was known to be a drunkard and a lecher who would have sold his own children for a jug of wine. He was, by reputation, a man of both great laziness and great greed: a combination she could now make use of.

Her months in Londinium had served her well. She adopted the accent of someone who'd come from overseas. Slowly, as though unaccustomed to Britannia and its modes of speech, she hailed the landowner, and asked for his help.

His curiosity was aroused by seeing a stranger before him. He listened while Cassia spun a tale of a tragedy: the death of a young boy, mortally wounded by an accident in Gallia, a lad whose dying wish was to be laid in the family plot beside his mother.

His corpse, she said, had been brought across the sea. She'd been sent by her master to find a means of transport that could carry the lad to his final resting place.

"Why didn't you hire a cart at the port?"

"I tried, believe me. But the place was too busy. No one can spare a vehicle for the length of time we need it. The lad's home is in the far north."

"Well, you can't have mine either."

"Are you sure? My master's family are wealthy. I pay a good price and I'll buy it outright. I'm desperate, sir."

The unmistakeable gleam of greed was in the man's eyes although he feigned indifference. When she produced the pouch of coins, his hand was out before he could stop himself.

It took more than half the purse's contents to persuade him to part with two ill-fed oxen and a rough-looking hooped cart covered with a sheet of moth-eaten canvas. Even then he sold it with noisy protests, saying that he was being robbed, he was a fool to be so generous, he was too kind-hearted for his own good.

Cassia knew the money would buy women. Women and wine. If there was any justice in the world, it would buy a barrel big enough for him to drown in.

She harnessed the oxen, tied her pony to the rear of the cart, and led them away, apparently heading towards the coast.

She wasn't even out of sight before the farmer had called a slave to bring his horse. In a few moments more he was off to the town brothel. All being well, he would not return for a day or two.

She planned to conceal the oxen and the wagon on the boundary of his own land. She'd noticed a byre, no doubt used to shelter cattle in winter but standing empty now.

When she reached the place, she discovered it filthy, no one having given the order to dig out the manure that had accumulated during the winter. A vile stench was emanating from one corner where some creature had died and lay rotting. She worried for the oxen's health: leaving them breathing in such bad air for the length of the day would do them no good. And yet there seemed no choice. With luck, no one would pass this way. She assumed that the farmer's slaves would make use of his absence and snatch a day of rest. There was, of course, the danger of the steward and his men searching the byre but surely they'd already done so? Might they do it again? It was possible. They'd scour the countryside until the fugitives were found. What would he think if he found an unattended cart and pair of oxen standing in a filthy byre? He might find it odd. But it was more likely, wasn't it, that he'd put it down to the farmer's lazy incompetence? She could only pray that would be the case.

Besides the steward there was the fear that Titus Cornelius Festus would tire of searching for her in the city and return to his home. The prospect of encountering her former master on the road was enough to turn her bowels to water. It was some time before she could mount the pony once more and ride through the woods, skirting the town and coming at it now from the other direction.

This time she spoke in the accents of a travel-weary slave from Londinium, complaining of a master who was insensible at the tavern some few miles further along the road. A man who would spend all he had made and be empty-handed again before the week was out. A man of inordinate vanity who had sent her out to buy luxuries he could barely afford. Two lengths of fine cloth for tunics. Two thick woollen cloaks – when summer was coming on and he would hardly have use for them! And food – luxuries he had a sudden desire for, as though the tavern he stayed in could not supply all he needed!

She grumbled convincingly enough, but the slave who

served her soon tired of the subject and turned their talk towards the runaways.

"Four have gone from that place these last few months!"

"Four? I heard three."

"No … there was a girl back last autumn. Bit half her master's ear off, can you believe? Then she ran."

"And was she caught?"

"No. She disappeared. It was like she was drawn into the sky. I reckon she flew away. Maybe she's in the stars, eh? Drowned in the river, some said, but a body was never found."

"The river? Perhaps these others have gone that way. They must be halfway to Londinium by now."

"They'll be found, soon enough. I wouldn't want to be in their skins when they do. Not known for his forgiving nature is Titus Cornelius Festus."

They exchanged a look. One slave to another. Whatever was said aloud, in their hearts they both hoped that the fugitives would get clean away. The conversation came to an end. Packing her purchases onto the pony, Cassia returned to the inn.

She could hear Marcus yelling for her from half a mile away, or so it seemed, calling her a lazy good-for-nothing scoundrel. Threatening to whip her, or sell her in the market of Londinium. The hatred on her face when she glanced up at the window before dismounting required little of the actor's skill.

XXIII

Rufus would be the corpse.

A child's body would be the most pitiable: the mourners' grief raw, overwhelming and dreadful to behold. Anyone they passed on the road would be eager to avoid close contact with such a procession. People would turn their eyes away; they would not be questioned.

Rufus accepted his role in sullen silence. As Cassia outlined her plan, the boy would not meet his sister's eyes. "You'll be tightly bound. You'll see nothing. And you must keep perfectly still. It will be hard."

He wouldn't speak to her, but pursed his lips, resentment rising like a shimmering haze of heat.

Marcus asked him, "Are you up to this? All our lives depend on you. It's a man's job, truly."

Cassia was surprised to see her brother lift his chin and look directly at Marcus, eyes eager, shoulders squared. He nodded and was rewarded with, "Brave lad."

It stung her. Marcus had held a knife to her brother's throat and threatened him! Yet he shrank from her and sought the Roman's approval. She was a demon, but Marcus had become a god!

She opened her mouth to speak, but Flavia drew her aside.

"Swallow the pain," she whispered. "Push it from your thoughts. There will be time to heal the rift when we are living free. But there is much to be done between here and there. One thing at a time. One step, then the next."

It was sound advice. Soothing. Gratefully, Cassia embraced the frail old woman. She was glad to have Flavia with them. Perhaps she would not be a burden but a source of wisdom? Maybe the gods had meant it to be this way?

As for Silvio – what part did they intend him to play in this? He'd already carried Rufus to her. Without him, could she have got her brother away from the estate? Unlikely. That was enough reason to be grateful for his presence. Besides that, he'd continued to call her "my queen". Each time he said it, it made her smile. Silvio had always been part of her life. She trusted him. But the depth of that trust only served to highlight the reservations she still had about Marcus...

As the day wore on, the Roman continued in his role of libertine.

146

But the landlord had met men of his kind before. When Marcus called for more meat and wine, payment for board and lodging was demanded before anything else was brought to his room.

Marcus reached for his public purse – the one he'd given to Cassia having been concealed. When his coins were counted out, there was barely enough to pay one more night's keep.

"Time to move on," Marcus told the landlord. He said he'd do so in the morning. His slave must make ready to leave: he'd expect the horses to be packed and prepared so they could be off the moment the sun was up. Yes … at first light he'd be on his way. But until then, why, he'd drink the last of his money in the form of the landlord's wine.

He kept up the pretence of carousing as he'd done for the last two nights. Cassia emptied the room of Marcus's possessions and stacked them in the stable, ready to be loaded onto the packhorse. After that it was a matter of waiting for the night to come – that was all. But it was the hardest part.

While Cassia was hounded by worries, one by one the travellers at the inn retired to bed. Gradually their chatter and noise ceased. Even the beasts slept. Eventually all was quiet. All was still.

And then – as stealthily as she could – Cassia loaded the pack animal. She muffled its hooves with cloth and did the same to the ponies. She made ready to go.

Only then could the fugitives leave the room they had been trapped in. This was the time of greatest danger.

Cassia had taken the horses from their stalls. Marcus now lifted Flavia onto one and Rufus onto the other.

Cassia led the way, Silvio walking beside her. Marcus brought up the rear with the pack animal.

It was no easy journey in the dead of night with no flaming torch, no oil lamp to light their way. The moon was almost full, but there were stretches of road where the trees grew so thick either side that its light could hardly penetrate.

They did not dare go through the town, but skirted it and in the density of undergrowth they could not pass swiftly. Brambles snagged skin and clothing, nettles stung flesh. Their progress was slow, but not disastrously so. There was an hour left of the night when they finally reached the byre.

The oxen – who had been tied up but neither fed nor watered – lowed in greeting. To keep their noise from disturbing anyone Cassia untied them and led them out to drink from the stream and graze a little.

Marcus, meanwhile, began to dig deep in the panniers for all manner of things that he'd brought from Londinium.

In the moonlight he began to bind Rufus in a length of rough linen.

Her brother stood still and calm while it was done. Only when Marcus reached his face, did Rufus show some alarm. To have to go through a long journey and not see any of the dangers. To be bound so that he could not run – it was too much to ask of him!

Marcus said nothing, but clenched his fist and placed it under the boy's chin, bringing his face up so he could look into his eyes. Rufus seemed to draw strength from it. When the Roman wound the cloth about his head her brother made no sound or sign of protest. Something about Marcus poured courage into him. It was strange. She was so slow, so reluctant to absolutely trust the man. Was there something Rufus saw that she did not?

They laid him in the cart. The makeshift linen shroud was fresh and bright. Even in the moonlight Cassia could see it would look too clean to have made their supposed journey across the sea. When she said so, Marcus scraped up dirt from the floor, apologizing to Rufus as he rubbed it into the folds.

As he was doing that, the stench from the corner of the byre reached Cassia's nostrils – and gave her an idea.

"So many days since he died. Would he not now be ... decomposing?"

Marcus nodded, at once understanding her train of thought. He searched out the source of the odour. A small dog, or maybe a wolf cub? Hard to tell. It was long dead, and reeking of decay. With more apologies to Rufus, he tucked it into the shroud under the boy's legs. Nothing would convince a passing stranger of the genuineness of the

149

corpse more effectively than that smell of death.

Cassia harnessed the oxen to the cart. And now she and Marcus turned their attention to the mourners.

Flavia: supposedly grandmother to the dead boy.

Taking the knife, Flavia's hair was cut in token of mourning – long strands of grey and gold that were then buried in the byre.

But she was still too recognizable. If the steward saw her, he would know her.

Cassia thought the only solution was for her to keep the hood of her cloak pulled down, over her face, but Marcus surprised her.

Among the jars and vials he'd obtained from Gaius he had an array of women's cosmetics: thick white face cream, rouge. He plastered Flavia's wrinkled skin with it, outlined her lips with a brush, painted them scarlet. Dressed in the cloth Cassia had purchased from town and with the cloak around her shoulders she had the look of an elderly woman – a Roman – who, despite her grief, was making a huge effort to maintain a respectable appearance. Only her calloused palms gave her away, but who would inspect those?

Silvio – tall and well muscled from his days labouring in the fields – would be less easy to transform. True, he could pass as an athletic youth – the kind of wealthy noble's son used to spending his days hunting and wrestling and whoring. But his face: nothing could alter that jaw, that nose, those blue eyes. If they were to pass along the street in broad daylight as they intended, he would be seen. The chance of him being identified was too great…

But Marcus, it seemed, had been working on Silvio during the hours of their confinement. The Roman's silver tongue was very persuasive.

Silvio's yellow hair was also cut to show deep mourning. His face was painted white and red. And then he donned the garb of a woman. The second length of cloth was fashioned into a robe. The second cloak was thrown around his shoulders.

Silvio was transformed into the boy's older sister.

He looked at Cassia with a rueful smile. "Our places are reversed. Now you are the warrior. And I am the queen."

She stifled her laughter. Said only, "Marcus – he is too tall to pass for a woman."

"If he stays crouched in the far corner of the cart beside the corpse, he'll get away with it. He'll be hidden by the canvas. In shadow. Silvio, you must seem to be bent double in grief. Can you do that?"

"I can."

"Well then, take your place."

Marcus was to pass as uncle to the dead boy. Brother to his mother: the man charged with returning the corpse to its final resting place.

His hair was cut almost to the scalp. He too applied a little cream – not the thick caking mask of the women, just sufficient to give his skin the pallor of grief. Charcoal was smudged under his eyes to form deep, weary shadows. Such efforts would not be enough, Cassia thought – he was still recognizable as the man who had spent three days and nights drinking in the tavern. Someone was sure to know him.

He looked at her, reading the doubt in her eyes. In response he moved his shoulders, bringing one a little higher than the other, hunching his back so he was lopsided, uneven. When he walked towards her, he took on a gait that lurched slightly, one leg dragging awkwardly behind him. He seemed to have aged twenty years, and when he addressed her, it was in the irritable, impatient tone of a man who had spent too long on a journey and was sick to the heart of travelling.

"Get on with you, boy. We've a lot of miles to cover before nightfall."

Only Cassia now remained to be transformed. She, he informed her, was already playing her part. She would be the family's slave. Taking his knife, he hacked her hair yet shorter, and then pulled a different coloured tunic from a pannier. It would be sufficient. What Roman ever stared at a slave for long enough to remember their looks? The innkeeper wouldn't give her a second glance. As long as the stable lads didn't notice her – and they would surely be too busy to even observe their passing – a change of clothing was all that was required.

As for the animals – the smaller pony and the packhorse were turned loose. There were enough people in the region who'd snatch up a stray and take it along home, no questions asked. The panniers were stowed in the cart.

Only the finer horse was kept – a mount suitable for a Roman. It too received Marcus's attention. A star was painted on its forehead. A sock on its right foreleg. When it was done, he vaulted onto its back. But he did not sit upright, as he had done before. Instead he hunched and twisted a little at his waist. His shoulders were rounded, giving him an aged and weary air.

They were ready to start the journey.

The party's transformation exceeded Cassia's wildest expectations. It was all so ingeniously contrived by Marcus. So practised. So easily and swiftly done that they were on the road before sunup.

Cassia felt exhilarated. Optimistic.

But as she looked sideways at Marcus, questions pricked at the corners of her mind. When had he done such things before? Where? And why?

XXIV

They were on their way, cart wheels creaking, hooves thudding on the hard road and the stench of death thick in their nostrils. Marcus had said they would no doubt get used to it but that hope seemed forlorn. As the sun rose higher and the day warmed, the decayed animal stink only grew stronger.

Cassia, walking at the oxen's heads, was at least some distance removed. For Silvio and Flavia sitting in the covered cart it must be unbearable. For Rufus – lying inside – gods! How was he to survive?

They passed the inn without incident an hour or so after sunrise. Any curious looks were averted as soon as the watchers realized a party of mourners was on the road. Death was a disease that no one wished to catch.

They reached the fork where the road divided, one branch heading towards Londinium, the other to the villa of Titus Cornelius Festus. This too they passed without anything untoward happening.

They were two or more miles west of the estate and Cassia had almost begun to relax when she saw ahead a number of dogs in the middle of the road. Amidst them was a man on horseback yelling orders to half a dozen harried slaves.

Cassia knew that voice. Had she been blindfolded, she would still have recognized the steward. Their way was blocked.

She missed a step. Her hand tightened on the oxen's lead rope. Softly – so softly that she could barely catch his words – Marcus murmured, "Courage, my love. Hold firm. We get past this and we are home and dry."

The dogs came running towards them, drawn no doubt by the reek of rotting flesh. The cart was suddenly surrounded by hounds, slobbering, sniffing, yelping. All was noisy confusion as the steward attempted to get them under his control. When they were leashed and held by the slaves he'd brought with him, the steward raised a hand and greeted Marcus, his tone respectful and courteous as he addressed the man he took to be a wealthy Roman noble.

"My apologies, sir! May I speak with you?"

"If you must."

"Where did you come by the cart? It looks familiar."

Marcus shrugged, an expression of extreme indifference on his face. "I don't know. My boy obtained it."

"Have you travelled far?"

"From Gallia."

"Your destination?"

"The north."

"I doubt the cart will last that long."

"Then we will buy another." Marcus sighed irritably. "We must be on our way. We have many days' travel ahead."

"I won't detain you long. Sir, we're looking for three runaways."

"We have troubles of our own."

The steward had been so intent on his manhunt he'd paid little attention to the inside of the wagon. It was only then that he noticed the shrouded corpse. When the stench reached his nostrils, he paled a little. "You've seen no one?"

"We have seen many people. Seen and not seen. In truth the living are like ghosts to me."

"Sir, I'm a desperate man. May I speak with your slave?"

"Why?"

"They sometimes see things their masters do not."

"If you must."

Marcus gave a wave of the hand, urging Cassia to walk forward towards the steward. She did so, feeling as though her feet were carved from wood.

But he didn't immediately ask her about the runaways.

"Who lies dead?"

"My master's nephew. He fell from his horse a month since."

"You've carried him all the way from Gallia?"

"Indeed."

"Why didn't they bury him there?"

"They're Christians, sir."

"So?"

"The boy's dying wish was to be laid beside his mother. When the Good Lord calls for their resurrection, they'll ascend to heaven hand in hand."

The steward spat onto the road in response. "Crackpots."

"I couldn't say, sir."

The steward turned his attention to more pressing matters.

"Have you seen anyone, boy?"

Cassia avoided his eyes. "No." Her voice had faltered. Even to her own ears, it sounded like a lie.

As, indeed, it was meant to.

The steward turned his back to the wagon so that Marcus couldn't see his next move. Reaching into his pouch, he produced a coin. "I'll give you this. Slip it into your hand and your master won't even see."

She accepted it. And then whispered, "There was a fire. Smoke, in the woods, some five miles from the coast. It could be your fugitives are there."

He would have questioned her more, but in the wagon

Flavia had begun a soft, keening cry. As if in response Silvio gave a whimpering groan. It spoke of distress, of unbearable grief. The steward winced.

In a flat, dead voice Marcus announced, "We must be on our way."

No further command was necessary. Cassia took her place by the oxen. She clicked her tongue. They moved on. She forced herself to set one foot in front of the other, made her shoulders relax, ordered her legs to move naturally. The steward's eyes seemed to bore into her back, she felt the heat of his gaze on her flesh. It seared into her and when she could bear it no longer, she turned. But it had been Marcus's eyes on her. When she looked back, the steward was already mounted on his horse, urging the slaves to hurry, to run, to head towards the coast.

Marcus wore his mask of misery. But for a brief moment he grinned at her. She could not return it – what slave would ever grin at their master? – but inwardly she felt a thrill of triumph.

The many years she'd worked under the steward's command his eyes had been on her so often! And yet he'd looked her full in the face without a glimmer of recognition. It seemed little short of a miracle. She sent prayers of gratitude to the gods before she realized with bitter amusement that in truth it had never been her face that had held the steward's attention. She dismissed him from her mind and began to consider a different matter entirely.

Marcus had called her "my love". She had to pull the hood of her cloak right down over her face, for no matter how hard she tried, she couldn't entirely erase her smile.

XXV

Oxen are strong and steady, but their pace is woefully slow. They didn't make as much as fifteen miles that day and there was no town or tavern in sight when the dark began to gather. Only a house, whose owner couldn't be persuaded to give them lodgings for the night – not even in the barn – when she realized they were transporting a supposedly month-dead corpse. She feared contagion and Cassia could hardly blame her. But she did at least sell them bread and cheese, and they made camp, such as it was, by the side of the road.

In the dark, Rufus's shroud was unwound: an ungainly grub released momentarily from his cocoon.

Cassia tried to embrace him, but he pushed her away and in the moonlight would neither look at nor speak to his sister.

Yet to Marcus he displayed a dog-like devotion. When

the Roman gave him bread, Rufus took it eagerly. Then he sat at Marcus's feet, watching his face.

Cassia had seen beaten hounds, cringingly grateful for the smallest kindness shown by the owner who'd whipped them. Dogs who'd whimper and wag their tails in a desperate attempt to please. She'd known slaves behave in much the same fashion, yet she'd never thought her brother would be among their number. She was exasperated by it. Furious with Rufus. Enraged by his lack of dignity and irritated beyond belief that Marcus encouraged her brother's abject loyalty. The Roman was feeding him scraps. Any moment now he'd be ruffling his hair, scratching his ears, petting him. And Rufus would roll over and beg like the most brainless puppy.

She turned away from them towards Flavia. She longed for the old woman's reassuring wisdom. Flavia pressed her hand, told her, "All will be well, in time," but was too tired to talk any further. Too tired to do anything but eat a little and then fall into an exhausted doze. She looked smaller asleep. Weaker. Cassia felt suddenly unsure about whether she would survive their journey at all.

Silvio. Where was he? He, surely, could be relied on? He'd treat her as he always had – with a smile and with mocking, gentle humour.

"Your cry of sorrow," she said, sitting beside him in the grass at the side of the road. "It was most convincing."

She'd thought he would retort with a joke. But no.

161

He'd eaten his food in silence and now she saw his face was tight, drawn, as though that day had been one long agony. He seemed ashamed and made no reply.

She realized then that if she'd been scared during the encounter with the steward, he'd been almost unmanned by it. The whimper that escaped him – that she'd taken to be part of their communal act – was the real and genuine sound of terror.

"Some warrior I have turned out to be," he said bitterly. "I am sorry, my queen."

She would have comforted him, but he turned his back on her, not wishing to show any more weakness. She could feel him withdrawing into himself like a snail into its shell. Gods! He was near to breaking already. And they were so far from safety. There was Londinium to pass through, the city where Titus Cornelius Festus was – as far as she knew – still searching for her. Word may even have reached him by now that he had lost three more slaves! There would be a price on all their heads.

Could Marcus resist so much money? And if he could – why? Why had he so thrown his lot in with her? Why did he take such risks with his own safety for people that were not his kind?

He had said "my love". Was that it? Was he truly doing all this for her sake? And if he was … why did he refrain from touching her? She was beginning to think she'd be only too willing to respond. Instead he kept her brother by him – as if Rufus was a human shield.

It was too strange to comprehend. Instead, she turned her mind to more practical problems.

There was no way to avoid or go around Londinium. All roads led to the city and there was but one bridge across the river. How they were to get through the place kept Cassia awake.

There were several burial grounds outside the city walls. But, as she'd observed that long winter, bodies went from deathbed to cemetery in one direction, and one direction only – from the inside to the outside. They did not travel from the outside in. The house owner they'd bought bread from had been terrified of contagion. In the confined streets of Londinium that fear would be so much worse. They would have to go over the bridge, in one gate, cross through the very heart of the city and out through another. They were sure to draw attention to themselves. Was carrying a rotting body through the streets even permissible?

She had no answer to that question. And there was another thing that troubled her. The city was teeming, populous. She should have been safe there. But Fate had made her run headlong into her former master once before. If it happened a second time – if they all came face to face with Titus Cornelius Festus – could Silvio be trusted to hold his nerve?

As for Marcus – she'd seen herself that he was well

known by many of the soldiers who guarded the gates. Would his disguise bear the weight of their scrutiny? Suppose it didn't?

She thought of the marks on her brother's back.

Whipping would be the very least of it.

XXVI

Cassia slept badly, and was troubled by restless dreams in which the women's calls sounded more threat than invitation. She was awake long before first light.

As was Marcus.

It seemed the matter of their getting through the city had been giving him as much cause for thought as her.

By mutual consent they strolled down the road a little, out of the hearing of the others.

"This disguise is good," Marcus began. "It will get us to the outskirts of Londinium unchallenged, I think. But a corpse can't be carried through the city without permission. I can arrange matters, but it will look strange if I undertake the task myself. When we near the city, I should send my slave ahead, alone. Are you up to that?"

"Of course."

"Good. I'll write a message, and you'll deliver it. And

then all our fates are in the hands of the gods."

The oxen, at their stately pace, took two and a half more days to reach the city. Two and a half more days that stretched everyone's nerves until they were ready to snap. The mourners could at least cling to each other. Flavia and Silvio sat with heads pressed together and hands clasped. Cassia and Rufus had to manage on their own.

When the walls of Londinium were within sight, Marcus took a wax tablet from the pack and made marks on it – marks that Cassia could not begin to understand. And then he described the place she must go to, and the person to whom it should be delivered.

"There is a man called Constantius Scipio. You will find him in the Forum."

"You know him?"

"Only by reputation. I've heard he's the kind of man who gets things done. You must appear to be a stranger – say you were given his name in a tavern, or something. Ask directions to the Forum at the gate. We're foreigners, remember. We don't know the city or its streets. We don't know their ways. Take the purse, be prepared to bribe the man. He'll expect it."

Cassia manoeuvred the cart onto a stretch of grass by the side of the road. She unhitched the oxen and hobbled them so they could graze awhile. Then, purse banging against her leg, she walked swiftly towards the city.

Alone, without Marcus riding at her back, she felt exposed. Vulnerable. But she did as she was told. Asking for directions at the gatehouse, going to the Forum. Pushing her way between slaves and supplicants. Asking for the man, Constantius Scipio.

She found him eventually in a small room at the rear of the building.

He was old. Grey-haired, balding. But he was lean and fit, and had a stillness to him that she found unnerving. There was something alarming about his eyes, though he barely gave her more than a passing glance. She felt, rather than saw, the close attention he paid her, and tensed, wondering if she was going to have to run.

She handed him the tablet as she had been told. Holding the purse in her hand, she jiggled it up and down so the coins clinked together. From the corner of her eye she studied his expression while he read.

She expected curiosity. Surprise. A little distaste, perhaps. She braced herself for a comment about the folly of carrying a decomposing body with them all the way to the north. Some mention of likely disease.

And yet Constantius Scipio said nothing. His face remained perfectly immobile. Not even an eyebrow was raised. He asked no questions. Not one. And this in itself made her wonder what was written on the tablet.

She had no reason to doubt Marcus and yet, and yet ...

something didn't feel right. What? What was it? Perhaps that it was too easy? Too straightforward?

A few coins in his palm was all it took.

He wrote a reply, accepted the bribe, said everything would be arranged and that was that. He instructed her to wait on the far bank of the river until after dark. Then they could pass without arousing undue attention. Sentries would turn a blind eye to the corpse being carried through the streets. He would see to it all. They would travel unhindered, he assured her.

She was turning to leave when her eye fell on a sculpture – a marble relief in the shadows hanging on the wall. It showed a woman being forced to the ground, dress torn, breast uncovered, face frozen in a silent scream. A soldier was standing over her – a Red Crest, in armour, holding her by her hair. His intention was plain.

"What's that?" she asked.

Constantius Scipio glanced at it. "My predecessor's taste. It's a copy, I believe. The original was carved to commemorate the conquest. It's the Emperor Claudius, vanquishing Britannia. Do you like it?"

She ought to say she did. Or perhaps shrug. Feign lack of interest. But she could not. The marble made her so angry her head was reeling.

"No. I don't."

The Roman smiled glibly and waved a hand, dismissing her. "Ah well. Each to his own."

Cassia left Londinium unchallenged, unremarked, unnoticed. Pausing only to buy food and drink at market, she walked back to join the funeral party.

It was as Constantius Scipio had promised. They travelled through Londinium entirely without incident. Long before the sun rose, they'd passed through the Moorgate on the northern side and the city lay behind them. By the time the sky lightened, they were well clear of it and Cassia felt the grip of Titus Cornelius Festus loosening with every step.

Her face was to the north and to freedom.

XXVII

Thereafter the days fell into a pattern. Though they itched to travel as fast and as far as they could during the hours of daylight, nothing could be more suspicious than a party of grieving people moving rapidly. And so the oxen plodded slowly, and they maintained their masks of sorrow.

They were not the only travellers on the road, and, as Cassia soon discovered, travellers liked to talk. Many of them were on horseback, or in light two-wheeled carts, and so word of the runaways' escape travelled north far faster than the runaways themselves. There was mention of them in each wayside tavern, each village or town they came to. As the days passed and they were still not found, the accounts of the escape and of the generous reward that would be paid for their capture grew wilder and more fantastic.

The strain told on all of them. Had they been able to

converse freely, they might have been better able to support each other. As it was, they were each trapped in their own silent hell. Silvio: ashamed of his fear. Flavia: terrified that she would be the burden that broke them all. Rufus: lying in the dark, day after day, his mind coming loose from its mooring, drifting he knew not where.

As for Cassia: she knew that Titus Cornelius Festus would not forget or forgive the fact that so many of his slaves had escaped him. The hope that they would be free was harder to bear than the dread that they would not. Freedom was a concept that filled her with a dizzying lightness of head. She bore the journey better by letting her mind run along dark lines. She imagined capture. Punishment. Not liberty.

Some nights they stayed at taverns, Cassia sleeping with the animals, freeing Rufus from his winding sheet for the hours of darkness so that he could relieve himself and take food and nourishment. Total silence and absolute stealth were all that stood between them and capture. They could not speak. And each night he shrank from her touch and looked only at the ground. The boy who'd slept with his head on her shoulder was dead to her. She had to trust what Flavia said: that he would come around, given time. She hoped it was true. She feared it was not. Her greatest dread was that she'd left him abandoned for too long, and that now her brother's heart and soul were irretrievably lost to her.

★ ★ ★

As they journeyed northwards, the land became flatter, the weight of sky oppressive and heavy. Another week more and hills began to rise. The countryside grew wilder, expanses of moor alternating with vast swathes of thick, untamed forest.

Gone was the gentle heat of early summer in the south. Here the land seemed to be only just shaking off the grip of winter. Though buds were bursting into life, the trees were crusted with frost every morning. Settlements were more sparsely populated. Small hamlets of roundhouses containing Britons who clung stubbornly to the old ways were half-hidden in folds of the land. The people would come out to stare as the grieving Romans passed by, their faces impassive, but their hostility making the air feel thick and clammy, as though a storm was about to break.

Cassia knew Britannia was at peace. There had been no fighting in her lifetime, nor, as far as she knew, in her mother's. Living on the estate of Titus Cornelius Festus, she had swallowed the belief that the entire country was settled and at ease under Roman rule.

But as she walked beside the oxen, she began to feel that the appearance of calm was nothing more than a thin skin drawn over a seething pit of discontent. She could not help but notice that the further they went, the more heavily guarded the forts were and the soldiers more ruthlessly drilled. There was something brewing. An edge of menace that Cassia – even though preoccupied with her own concerns – was increasingly aware of.

They were five days short of the wall by Marcus's reckoning. Though they had planned to reach the next town by nightfall, the oxen were tired. One was starting to go lame and could not be pushed. Hour by hour the prospect of hot food and a dry place to sleep receded as the weary beasts' pace slowed to almost nothing.

As the sky darkened, so did the mood of the company. Trudging in silence – the wind gusting, the clouds hurling handfuls of hailstones at them – they were passing through a stretch of woodland, trees crowding either side, when the oxen stopped dead and snorted in alarm.

Marcus was riding close behind, hunched over his horse's withers to keep out the worst of the cold, when the animal threw up its head so sharply it almost cracked into his face. It too snorted, hot panicked breath billowing from its nostrils. Quarters bunched tight, it was poised for flight. Only Marcus reining it in tight, turning in circles, crooning softly between his teeth, stopped it bolting headlong back down the road.

The oxen stood twitching nervously, eyes rolling, lowing in distress. What had alarmed them Cassia could not at first tell.

There was no cry of wolves. Yet – there on the breeze –

was the faint scent of something. An animal smell. Large. Carnivorous. Getting stronger.

And then there was the sound of something heavy padding over dry leaves.

It seemed that the stench of rotten flesh that had protected them for so long was now attracting unwelcome attention.

In the gloom Cassia caught a glimpse of an animal. Large as an ox. Thick fur. Teeth. A bear. Awake now, after its long winter's doze. Desperately hungry, and looking for an easy meal.

There were no other travellers in sight. No soldiers marching from one fort to the other, no well-armed merchants. No one at all within hailing distance. And they had no weapons, save the knife at Marcus's waist.

To Cassia it seemed suddenly vital to unwrap Rufus. To discard the rotting creature that had been his companion these last weeks. If she could throw it into the trees it might distract the bear for long enough to get them clear.

She had no time to explain. Indeed she had no time to consciously think what she was doing. Instinct alone made her abandon her place at the oxen's heads and run towards the back of the cart to free her brother.

But she had gone no more than two paces when the bear was on them. With no Cassia to calm them, the oxen panicked, roaring in distress, one trying to flee, the other trying to turn to face its attacker, both pulling in different directions, swinging the cart around, sending the wheels sliding down the road's camber and into the ditch. The oxen were screaming now, their harness twisting, the axle groaning. The shaft that held them splintered, cracking along its length, and the sharp end pierced the first ox between the ribs as the whole cart toppled onto its side. Silvio, clinging to the struts, lost his grip and was thrown bodily onto Flavia. Rufus — who could not even put out a hand to save himself — was flung to the very end of the cart, within easy reach of the bear.

It seized the conveniently wrapped parcel of human flesh in its great jaws and dragged Rufus from the cart, across the road and into the forest.

Cassia felt its heated breath, its force and, even in its weakened, hungry state, its overwhelming power. The stink of carrion, of blood and death filled the evening air.

She could not hope to defeat the creature. And yet without a thought she followed, shouting in fury, not words that any human could understand, but a noise from the throat, a primal howl of rage that it should dare to take her brother.

Her cloak impeded her as she ran so she tore it off, wrapping it around her hand.

A bear could easily outrun her, but this one did not intend to lose its meal. It lumbered steadily but slowly, the shroud snagging on roots, catching on branches. What it had thought would be easy pickings was not a simple thing to drag through thick undergrowth. And so Cassia gained on it. It had reached a small clearing when it stopped, released Rufus from its mouth and turned its attention on her.

There were no bears in the south where Cassia had been born and raised, but enough tales of them had been told around the fire to make an impression.

"Don't let them go thinking you're a meal. But don't go making them angry either. Respect each other. Pass each other by. That's the only way to deal with a bear."

And yet here she was, facing it. Standing within striking distance, ordering it to be off, to leave her brother alone, to go find itself something else to fill its belly.

It stood on its hind legs. It would strike her, she knew it. But better she should die than let Rufus be eaten. She stood her ground. Faced it. Shouting, bellowing, roaring at the thing, whirling the cloak above her head to make herself look bigger.

It was incensed. But it was also confused. What was this strange animal that looked human but sounded wolf? It had not quite made up its mind to attack when there was a crashing from somewhere behind her. A horse, trying to find its way through bramble and bracken at speed, being urged on. Struggling to obey its rider.

And then there was Marcus, his knife held out. Riding at the bear, yelling at Cassia to stand aside, to move. She did. But only to move closer to the beast, walking towards it to drive it back, to drive it away from her brother.

It swiped at her. But in its confusion it misjudged and when she ducked, its claws did not even graze the top of her head.

And then – instead of tackling these two roaring, screaming creatures – it chose to flee, lumbering through the undergrowth and into the night.

Marcus was off his horse.

It happened so swiftly that afterwards she wondered if she'd dreamed it. His arms were around her, he was holding her tight to his chest. His cheek was pressed to hers and then his lips found her mouth.

And there was no scent of oil to repel her. The stench of Rome had vanished with each mile they'd spent on the road. She was kissing him back.

But he thrust her away, pushed her so violently from him she tripped and fell over Rufus, who was lying inert and helpless in the leaf mould. Marcus's arms were folded across his chest, he was almost bent double, as though in pain.

Cassia was hot with confusion, appalled and angry with herself. She'd been so wrapped up in responding to Marcus that she'd momentarily forgotten Rufus. Bending over her brother, she pulled the torn shroud from him.

He was pale as death. Eyes tight shut. Frozen with the shock. His mind almost lost with the horror of being dragged, arms pinned to his side, legs tied together, unable to see or move.

She held his rigid body to her, uttering soothing, meaningless phrases over and over again, smoothing his hair, pleading with him to speak, to say something, to tell her he was all right.

For a very long time he did not respond. But then a cry came from somewhere deep within. He buried his face against his sister's neck. Holding him tight, Cassia wept as she had done long ago, when their mother died.

XXVIII

The bear had not given up the prospect of a meal. It had fled only as far as the road.

Silvio had been desperately trying to release the surviving ox from the cart's broken shaft. The first had died, punctured through the chest by a great wooden splinter. As soon as the second was unbound, it swung its head, scraping Silvio with its horns before it fled, footsore and maimed. Bent double, Silvio watched helpless as it lumbered a distance of perhaps fifty paces. And then the bear reappeared.

The predator's choice was simple. One ox already dead, but too close to humankind to be appealing. The other lamed. Dazed. Stupid.

The bear attacked.

It had eaten its fill by the time Cassia, Marcus and Rufus found their way back to the road.

★ ★ ★

Nothing, it seemed, could have been bleaker.

Flavia – though she uttered not one word of complaint – was badly bruised, her ribs aching, possibly cracked by the fall. Silvio was lacerated across the belly from where he had freed the ox. Cassia and Marcus were cut and torn from their wild pursuit of the bear. Astoundingly, Rufus was the only one not physically harmed but his mind was in tatters. He would not speak, but made only strange, animal noises in his throat when he saw what had happened to the oxen. When Cassia put an arm around him, he clung to his sister so tightly she feared he would choke her.

They had lost their mode of transport. The disguise that had taken them safely this far was gone. Even were they to find another cart and pair of oxen, Cassia knew – as did Marcus – that they could not ask Rufus to go shrouded again. He would lose his mind completely if he were to be confined in the dark once more.

Cassia tried to comfort her brother, to soothe his pain away. But he whimpered so pitifully and she felt so helpless that soon she found herself crying alongside him.

It was Marcus who took the boy's face in his hands and said, "You are back from the dead. You have escaped the Underworld and returned to the living. No more of that winding sheet. You walk with us now. In the open air. Can you do that, Rufus?"

Still, the boy didn't speak. But he gave Marcus a small nod.

They had now one horse, and some fifty miles to go before they reached the border. Four or five days by ox-cart. Two on foot if the walkers were healthy and strong and they could travel in daylight. Who knew how long it would take with Flavia so weary, Silvio injured and Rufus almost out of his mind?

Cassia was riddled with anxiety, but Marcus seemed relatively untroubled by their change of circumstances.

"It was time to lose this disguise in any case," he told her. "We could not have carried it off for more than another few days. People in these parts know each other's business. Any day now the questions would have started. People would want to know where exactly we were going, and where the corpse was to be buried. Who was his mother? His father? Where was his home? We couldn't have answered without someone knowing we lied. Yet now that strange family of foreign mourners are gone. Killed by beasts, their packs looted by bandits. It solves a problem that's been troubling me for a while: of how and where we were to change our plan. We'll take the horse. Two can ride, but the rest of us will walk. You must trust me to choose the way. Will you do that?"

"Of course."

"Good. I know the land here. There's a river not five miles west. We can follow its path. If anyone should come looking for us, it will mask our trail. It flows beneath the wall. That's our way now."

They took only what they could carry with ease. What little food they had. The near-empty purse of money. Such salves as would serve to remedy their own injuries.

Marcus led. With Flavia and Rufus riding double, Silvio and Cassia walked behind in the path the horse cleared through the underbrush. Silvio had changed into his old slave clothes and was a man again. As he rubbed the white paint from his face, a little of his old self seemed to return. He gave her a pained smile, he called her "queen". There was some comfort in that.

No longer hiding in plain view, they trudged all the hours of darkness. When dawn broke, they found a hiding place on a small patch of shingle under an overhanging bank, where the river curved and the trees grew thick either side. After eating a little, they slept, Rufus with his head on his sister's shoulder. They took turns watching for danger as long as it was light. And at dusk they moved on once more.

On they went. Sodden, cold. Injured.

Four nights later, when dawn broke they were within sight of the wall.

XXIX

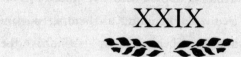

The frontier was as imposing as Cassia had imagined. A wall, taller than five men. Broader than an ox-cart. Manned by soldiers who were used to being harried by the savage tribes on the other side of it. Whose fingers twitched on the hilts of their swords even in their sleep.

It was a barrier that was impossible to scale. But here – where Marcus had led them – the wall became a bridge. The river was shallow, the arches wide enough to pass through. But how could they do so without being seen? It would be impossible to go unchallenged.

Yet here too Marcus had a plan. And once more, they were all entirely dependent on him.

He would ride back down the river then cut across country to the nearest town, he said. It was just over the next hill. At dusk he would come back to this spot in a loop, as though he had just then come from the west. He'd greet the soldiers, bringing them a jug of mulled wine on a cold night. In short, he'd distract them.

"It's a cheerless spot. They won't refuse my gift."

Cassia asked, "They'll have no suspicion?"

"I'm Roman. And I'm known here. I've traded this far north for the last two years. I can talk to them, keep them occupied for a while. Let Flavia go first – she'll take the longest time to get clear. Silvio, you'll help her, won't you? Then Rufus. Cassia last. Go from here straight under the bridge, as far as the first bend in the river. There's a copse that will give you some shelter. I'll meet you there."

It was a long day's wait, keeping themselves concealed in the scrubby vegetation that grew along the length of the river. But Marcus was as good as his word. At dusk they heard hoofbeats and there he was, calling the soldiers, engaging them in conversation.

Flavia – bruised in the bear's attack and now stiff from keeping motionless all day in the cold and damp – was awkward and slow to get going. Silvio almost carried her the distance to the bridge. It would take only one false step, one glance from the soldiers down at the water and all would be lost.

But Marcus had said he would distract them, and he did. Cassia couldn't catch his words, but knew he was telling a tale from the way he held their rapt attention. When Silvio and Flavia had passed beneath the stone arches, Cassia prodded Rufus forward. He was reluctant to leave her and flung his arms around her waist. Her hands were on his back. Her fingers could trace the scars.

"Go," she said. "On the other side you will be free. No master. No steward. No men with whips. I promise."

He went. Limbs weakened from spending so long lying motionless in the cart, Rufus's gait was awkward and shambling. But he too passed through without incident.

And then came Cassia's turn.

She stepped into the water, ice-cold, fast-flowing, feeling the crunch of stones beneath her bare feet. In the dark it was impossible to know where to tread. She kept low to the water, fearing that she'd slip and that her splashing would alert the soldiers to her presence. Their loud laughter as she drew closer made her flush. They were talking of women. Foul jokes. Crude remarks. Coarse and unpleasant.

Marcus was doing what he had to and doing it well. She had to hold firm to that. But there were times when he didn't make it easy to like him!

She was beneath the bridge now, feeling her way through, her hand on the mossy stones steadying herself.

Go to the first bend in the river, he'd told her. But she did not. As she'd worked her way towards the bridge, the wind had been veering around. By the time she reached the other side, it was against her, blowing a squall of rain into her face. She'd said she'd give him a signal: the call of an owl would let him know they were all through safe.

But with the wind and the rain she knew that if she went too far, he wouldn't hear her. So she stayed close, and was still in the shadow of the wall when she raised her cupped hands to her lips, blew between her thumbs and hooted like an owl.

By chance, or by fate, the wind dropped at that moment. And so she heard his remark fall from the bridge like a stone.

"Ah. So the bird flies free. Now I will see where it makes its nest."

XXX

At dawn the next day Marcus met them at the place he'd described. How he'd passed through the wall without being questioned or stopped Cassia didn't ask. She did wonder at it. And at the words he'd spoken.

But to question him – to look as though she didn't trust him – would seem too ungrateful. They were free. Free! Breathing air where no master could give orders.

When he joined them he looked at her expectantly, as though now she was leader of their expedition. "Where to?" he asked. "I have brought you here. Now we're all in your hands."

Cassia wanted to get as far away from the wall as she could. To hide herself in the hills where she could neither see nor hear nor smell the influence of Rome. She looked at the horizon. Fixing her eyes on the furthest peak, she nodded towards it. "There."

They set off. With each step Cassia filled her lungs with the sweet air. She looked at her feet – not those of a slave any more, but those of a free woman. They could carry her wherever she wished. There was no one to answer to but herself. With each step she felt a weight lifting from her shoulders and her euphoria was infectious: it spread throughout the party. Silvio picked Rufus up and swung him through the air.

"We have arrived! Gods be praised!" He threw back his head and laughed.

Flavia linked her arm through Cassia's. Frail though she was, there was a light in her eyes that Cassia had not seen before. "I thought to die a captive," the old woman said. Her mouth was open as if she wanted to add more but the words would not come. Her feelings seemed too large to be contained in language.

What they would do, how they would live, how they would eat: Cassia had not given such things any thought. For now they had food. But in the months, the years ahead?

Well … Silvio had always been skilled at setting traps. The slaves on the estate had been fed a meagre diet and Silvio's trapped hares and squirrels had supplemented many a supper. There was no reason to suppose they wouldn't find ample food in these hills.

The weather was warm now, but they would be needing shelter when the winter came. Oh, but there would be ways and means of building it. They were their own masters and not afraid of hard work. They could build themselves a roundhouse in time, and none of them need be driven by the whip.

And if they were to meet the barbarians?

They would deal with that problem if or when it came.

There would be time enough to worry about that then.

It was late morning, maybe an hour before noon, when the skin of Cassia's arms prickled into goosebumps.

She could not have said how she knew it – she had heard nothing, seen nothing – and yet she felt they were being watched.

She stopped. Turned full circle.

There was nothing. The hum of insects. The cry of a buzzard. The footfalls of her companions.

"What's wrong?" asked Marcus. "Are you tired? Should we rest awhile?"

"No. I thought… Someone's looking at us."

He cocked his head to one side, an eyebrow raised enquiringly. His hand went to the knife at his waist as he looked about him at the empty hills. "I see nothing."

"Neither do I. But I feel it."

They stood, scanning the horizon. But there was no movement. Nothing to see, nothing to hear.

But she could not rid herself of the sensation of eyes, pressing on her skin.

She exchanged a troubled glance with Marcus. He shrugged, but did not put the knife back in its sheath.

The others had seen them and now stopped walking. A look of panic passed across Rufus's face. She didn't wish to alarm him.

But when she took a step forward, the earth erupted at her feet.

A bird, startled from the heather, flew up into her face, squawking, flapping. She swung aside, her foot catching in undergrowth, so she fell sideways.

Marcus, throwing his knife, cut the creature from the air. It fell in a flurry of feathers, blood dropping like rain onto Cassia's face and arms.

"That was your watcher," Marcus assured her. "These hills are empty of any human life."

They shared the bird over a fire that evening.

Cassia was still preoccupied, and Marcus had no more to say on the matter. And yet she could not shake off the feeling that there was something out there other than birds and beasts. Something that was studying their every move.

For two more days they pressed on, one morning coming across the traces of a road that ran in a straight line from one horizon to the next. It was undoubtedly of Roman construction, but crazed with cracks, grass running between them, tree roots growing underneath, lifting stones, forcing them aside like an earthquake in slow motion.

"Romans were here?" Cassia asked Marcus.

"Once. Long ago. But no more, as you can see. There was a wall, I believe, some miles north of here. It was abandoned many years ago."

"Why?"

"It could not be held."

They said no more, but the conversation ignited something in Cassia's mind.

Rome held the rest of Britannia in a stranglehold. There seemed no escape from the Empire's rule. Her only chance of freedom had been to remove herself beyond its borders.

Yet here, in the land she now walked on, Romans had been driven back. That mighty army had been repelled. A road of Roman construction lay in ruins. Which must surely mean that Roman rule was not inevitable?

Things could change.

The same day they saw the Roman road Cassia began to feel something tugging at her.

It was faint to begin with. A sweet smell on the breeze. The call of a bird, the distant whisper of a mountain stream. The cry of a wolf, one calling to another.

But with each step it became stronger. She felt as though a cord was tied to her belly pulling her on.

She'd never set foot on this springy turf, never seen

that line of hills, those mountains, those crags, that vast expanse of silvered lake in the far distance. Yet there was something familiar in it.

They were moving along a river valley, the hills rising high on either side. It was Cassia's turn to ride awhile.

She had only just climbed astride the horse when she heard the voices.

"Can you hear that?"

"There is nothing," Marcus said. "Nothing but the wind. The bees."

She looked at Silvio. Flavia. Nothing.

Rufus.

Her brother had his head on one side. He seemed to be listening intently.

"Rufus, what do you hear?"

His eyes were glazed.

"Rufus?"

He did not reply. He heard them, though. She was sure of it. They were in his ears too. The women of her dreams. Not weeping or wailing now, not shouting or desperate. Singing softly, insistently. Calling.

Welcoming her.

She urged the horse forwards and then she was cantering, galloping ahead, ignoring Marcus's yells to stop, to wait. Ignoring his increasingly desperate pleas to know where she was going, what she thought she was doing.

She rounded a bend in the river.

A few paces more and she would see it. The rowan tree, rooted in a rock.

She pulled the horse to a halt. Slipped from its back. Went on foot.

There it was. A pool, seemingly still, but one in which deep currents stirred, one that brimmed and tipped over flat rocks into a waterfall.

How was it that she knew this place? How was it that she had seen it in her dreams?

The women's voices were at their loudest now, but still she could not make out the words. She was struggling so intently to catch their meaning that she did not hear the thud of approaching hooves, the slide of a man dismounting, walking steadily towards her.

She was gazing into the pool when a shadow appeared, gliding across the surface. Only then did she swing around.

A man. Club in hand, raised, blotting out the sun. Behind him, a line of warriors on shaggy ponies.

Bare-chested, bearded, wild-haired.

Spears, extended even as she watched, ten or more, pointing at her heart.

She saw it all in the instant before the club came down.

And for a long time after that, she saw nothing.

XXXI

It was dark when she woke. She was lying on a bed of bracken beside a fire. In a hut. A roundhouse. The smell of smoke and food was so familiar, and yet so strange.

For a moment she thought she'd been carried back to the estate of Titus Cornelius Festus. That these last months had been nothing more than an illusion. A dream.

She turned her head. It hurt.

Then she realized she was not alone. A woman was with her. Old. As old as Flavia. Watching her with an avid interest. There was a hunger in those eyes that struck fear into Cassia's heart.

She spoke, but Cassia could not understand her. The old woman gestured to Cassia's head, pointing to where she'd been struck. Cassia's fingers went to the wound. The skin had split, she could feel the soreness of it, but it had been carefully washed and dried. Her fingers came away sticky, but not with blood. Some sort of herbal paste had been put upon the wound. Whatever they had used was effective. Considering the violence of the blow that had knocked her out, it ached surprisingly little.

She was dazed, though. She could not seem to order her thoughts clearly.

The woman held something out to her. A bowl. Meat. A few vegetables. The smell was appetizing. Sitting up slowly, she took the stew, along with the hunk of bread the woman proffered. Dipping it into the gravy, Cassia began to eat.

"Am I a captive?" she asked between mouthfuls. "A slave?"

The woman looked puzzled. She frowned and spoke again, but the words made no sense to Cassia's ears. Both at a loss as to how to communicate they sat in silence until Cassia had eaten her fill.

And then the old woman stood, picked up a folded garment and shook it out for Cassia's inspection.

The cloth was fine: a tightly woven dress of wool. In the firelight the colour was hard to tell but seemed a deep blue, threaded with lines of green that criss-crossed over each other. The woman appeared to want Cassia to put it on and there was no point resisting.

She stood. Allowed herself to be draped in it. The woman tied it around her waist with a belt made of finely tooled leather. And then a cloak of the same rich hue was fastened at her shoulder with a brooch.

When she was dressed the woman braided her hair, carefully, gently, winding it around her head, pinning it to conceal the dressing that she placed over Cassia's wound.

And then a box was pulled out from a hole in the roundhouse wall. Inside was a twisted golden necklet, as thick as Cassia's thumb. At each end of it was fashioned the golden head of a snarling wolf. Then earrings of coral and shell. Armbands with the same wolf motif, then rings of silver and copper twisted together.

They were put on, one after the other, until Cassia was dripping with jewellery.

It seemed a strange act of kindness, but it brought memories of Flavia, preparing her for Titus Cornelius Festus.

Was she being readied for the same reason? Had she come so far to escape the master, only to be violated by a barbarian? Or worse. What had they said in Londinium? That the savages north of the wall sacrificed their captives. That they ate their enemies' hearts. Severed their heads and impaled them on poles. Was this some kind of ritual? Had she been cleaned and dressed simply to make a more attractive trophy?

Tears began to prick at the corners of her eyes.

Where was her brother? Where was Silvio? Flavia?

Marcus? Gods, what had happened to him?

Just then a man entered the hut, ducking low under the

door lintel then stopping, standing, fixing her with his eyes.

It was the warrior who'd struck her.

A moment of blind terror squeezed her heart. But she raised her head, thrust out her chin. She wouldn't show her fear. She wouldn't give him that satisfaction.

But dimly, in the flickering firelight, she began to see that the look on his face was not triumph. Instead there was a hint of apprehension in his eyes. Regret, perhaps? Maybe even fear.

He skirted the fire, surprisingly light on his feet for so powerful a man. Stopping before her, he stood for a moment before sinking to his knees, taking her hands in his and pressing his forehead against her knuckles.

He was muttering in his strange tongue and, while she could not understand the sentences, she recognized the tone as one of deep and profound apology.

She found herself making soothing noises in response. Uttering words of forgiveness.

It was only when he raised his head that she saw the marks pricked into the skin of his wrists. Whirls, patterns of dots that exactly matched her own.

XXXII

The night took on the quality of a dream.

The warrior got to his feet. He did not touch her again, but extended an arm, gesturing that she should follow him out through the door.

In the open air she realized they were high up, on top of a hill, she guessed. There was something in the clearness of the air that suggested it. A fence, a circle of stakes, enclosed a flat ring of turf. Huts – roundhouses – were grouped in clusters. But there at the heart of the settlement was one larger than the rest.

She walked towards it between two lines of people. Men on one side, women on the other. Dogs on both. Huge animals, with amber eyes, grey coats and wolf blood clearly running through their veins.

Children poked their heads between their parents' legs. She was surrounded by barbarians, who jostled and strained to see her face. They muttered to each other. Smiled if she caught their eye, before casting their gaze down in apparent respect.

She walked into the great house, where torches flamed and a fire danced in the centre, throwing shadows onto the roof beams.

There was Rufus – similarly dressed and bedecked in jewellery – his eyes round as an owl's. He stood to the left of a great chair. A throne, in which a man sat. A woman was at his right side, and Cassia was shocked to note that she seemed the more powerful of the two. All eyes were on her as Cassia entered. The men only sat down when the woman nodded her permission. Certainly it was she who gave the order for the mead cup to be passed from mouth to mouth, and for the harpist to step from the crowd.

Cassia could see Flavia and Silvio. The light was too dim for her to read the expressions on their faces but they were not bound or chained. Marcus was standing at the far edge of the crowd, and he too looked unharmed.

A sip of mead. An invitation to stand behind her brother. He leaned into her and she put her arms around his chest.

Then a harpist began to play. Long fingers, plucking the strings. A single note. Repeated. Once, twice more. Steady, insistent. Like the start of a storm. Single drops of notes. Then a flurry. A patter. Building steadily to a shower raining down on her. A tune, filling the great house, circling the fire, coming back on itself, dancing, whirling. A tune that made Cassia's heart contract, that brought rapture and longing and terrible sadness all at once. A tune Cassia had long forgotten. But now remembered.

A song. That rose and fell.

A song. A story.

Of a tribe that lived in the valley of the split rock.

A story sung in the barbarian tongue, which until that very moment she would have sworn she did not know.

When Rufus glanced up at her, his face was blank. He understood nothing.

But she did.

The words.

She knew their meaning.

A veil had been pulled aside in her mind.

She stared into the fire.

And in the rising smoke she saw shapes stirring, taking form. The face of her mother, close by hers. As it had been night after night before the fever came and carried her away.

A long-buried memory was prised from the depths and floated to the surface. Their mother's body had been burned. Cassia – eight years old – had stood and watched, holding Rufus in her arms, seeing the black smoke rise, feeling it writhe into her soul like a serpent that then coiled about her heart.

This singer, this song: the serpent loosened its grip. It slithered away. Left her. Joined the smoke that rose through the thatched roof.

The singer sang of the coming of the Red Crests, of the battles that followed, of the building of the wall.

And then the song departed from the words that were familiar and told a tale she did not know.

They drew a picture in her head so clearly it was as though she had been there.

She saw a boy, climbing a hill. A boy older than Rufus, but who looked like him: the same hair, the same skin, the same eyes.

She watched him from afar, as though she was an eagle soaring above. But then the picture changed and she was inside the boy's head, seeing through his eyes, feeling the wiry grass beneath his feet, breathing the chill morning air with his lungs, sharing the stream of thoughts that passed through his head.

Ten days he had been gone.

Ten days in which he had been tested to the limits of his endurance. He had neither eaten nor drunk, but sat in the mouth of a cave, praying to the gods of heaven and earth, waiting for the vision that would bring his spirit guide.

And last night it had come. He had left his human body and walked with wolves, tumbled with the cubs, hunted with the pack.

Ten days ago he had gone from the village – a stripling youth. He was returning a man. His heart, his mind, his soul were transformed. When the men were back from their long hunt, he would join his father and brothers at council. He would sit with them and eat.

As he crested the hill, the broad valley was spread out before him, the early morning mist lying in a thick blanket, obscuring the village below.

Smoke curled through the layer of fog in faint wisps.

But it was not the smoke of hearth fires, welcoming him home.

The smell of cooked meat drifted up to him in the cold air.

But not roasting hare, or deer.

Burned flesh. Burned hair.

The rank reek of blood and death.

His smile was gone. He was running, pelting through heather and bog. Falling, rolling, getting up again, running, running, running, breath ragged, coming in pained gulps, crying out the names of his father, his brothers, his sister, screaming each of them in turn. Getting no reply.

Reaching the village. The mist burning off in the sun. Rolling back, peeling away from the dead. The old men butchered. The women nowhere to be seen. Neither them, nor their children.

Scatha! Scatha, his twin. His sister. Scatha, one half his soul. Gone!

There was but one woman left alive. A woman too old to be desirable. A woman too old to be of use. A woman of no value as a slave.

Mortally wounded, but not yet dead.

He cradled her in his arms.

"Stay. Stay with me," he begged. "Do not go."

But he could see in her eyes her conviction that the tribe was destroyed. Broken beyond repair. Dead. Its daughters had been carried away. With no women, there could be no future. What reason was there for her to live?

"They are gone," she whispered. "Scattered. Like dust."

"Not dust," he said. He must find some shred of hope where there was none. "Not dust. Seeds. Scattered indeed. But will they not take root? Can something not yet grow from them? This is not the end."

She shook her head. Bubbles of blood frothed at the corners of her mouth.

As she died in his arms, the boy swore by all the gods of heaven and earth that this was not the end of it.

This was a beginning.

Cassia was scarcely aware that the singer had ceased. That she herself had taken up the tune.

That she was singing aloud the other half of the song. That of the boy's sister, taken south.

"Scatha. Sold at market.

Scatha. Slave to a Roman master."

A list of names began to pour from her mouth.

She was chanting them, as her mother had done. Night after night they had been whispered into her ear.

"My child, my daughter, you are daughter of
    Annys,
who was daughter of Brighid.
Brighid, who was daughter of Scatha.
Scatha, stolen by the Red Crests.
Scatha, of the valley of the split rock
With the rowan, growing from its heart.
The valley of the Wolf People."

Cassia's words dried in her throat. She could not utter what had come next. Instead it echoed in her mind. Her mother's voice, come from the world beyond to accuse her. "You are the only daughter of mine to live. Remember your slain sisters. Their future was stolen from them, from the children they would have borne, from the generations that would have followed. Remember them. Never forget who you are. If we lose our memories, we lose everything."

A great storm of sorrow broke Cassia's heart.

For she had not remembered!

She had wiped her mother from her mind. She had not held the story in her heart. She had never – not even once – told it to Rufus.

She had betrayed her mother. Forgotten the women – the ancestors – who had called her home.

Crushed under a great weight of guilt, Cassia sank to her knees and wept.

XXXIII

A very long time later Cassia found herself alone with Marcus.

She had been claimed: a lost daughter of the tribe. When she'd recovered from her weeping, the celebrations had gone on far into the night. She'd been too dazed, too overwhelmed to feel anything but confusion.

When the Wolf People had dispersed, she'd lain down to sleep in the place allotted to her, but had woken only a few short moments after falling into an uneasy slumber. Unable to lie still, fearful of disturbing the others who slept there, she'd risen and left the roundhouse.

She felt bruised. Battered by the waves of opposing emotions that had swept over her. She'd been welcomed. The chief himself had taken her by the hands and called her daughter. Bretha, the woman who'd sat at his right side – the one all had deferred to – had embraced her and wept salt tears into her hair.

In turn, each person had come to her, laying a hand on her arm, on her hair, calling her sister, cousin, friend. The joy was beyond anything Cassia had ever experienced. And yet there was an overwhelming sadness mixed with it – a terrible grief that while she understood their talk if they spoke slowly and clearly as if to a small child, Rufus could not decipher a word.

"He is young," Bretha had said. "He'll learn. Before the turning of the year he will have forgotten he ever spoke the Red Crests' tongue."

Cassia was not so sure. Rufus had been damaged these last few months in more than body. She was afraid her brother could never be the boy he was or the man he was meant to be. Quite what he'd now grow into she couldn't imagine. He'd looked strange that evening. His eyes focused, but not on her. It was as if he was looking beyond, seeing things that were not there.

She'd translated what words she could for him, explaining that they were welcomed, that they were home, but he seemed scarcely able to take it in. He'd accepted food and drink as if he was in another world. She wondered if he expected to wake to find himself back on the estate as she had, abandoned and alone once more.

She left the roundhouse, walking out into the cold night. The moon was full, lighting the clouds that drifted across the sky. Marcus was silhouetted against them, standing near the gate, looking down over the valley.

★ ★ ★

If he'd taken her in his arms then, she would have given herself to him without reservation. Indeed, she longed for nothing more than to stop thinking, to lose herself to a pleasure that was entirely physical.

He smiled at her approach, but kept his arms tightly folded across his chest. And there was something icily polite in his voice when he said, "A splendid feast, wasn't it? You must have looked forward to coming home these last months!"

"Home?" she echoed. "Oh Marcus! I didn't know it was here."

He frowned. Tilted his head to one side. "How could you not?"

"I was a slave. I was born in the south."

Disbelief showed in every line of his face. "And yet you know the tongue?"

"From my mother. But she died... I'd forgotten."

"You've never set foot on this land before? Truly?"

"Only in my dreams."

He seemed oddly unnerved, as though this happy outcome was profoundly disturbing to him. She moved closer, but he stepped back.

"I can hardly believe it..." he said, shaking his head. "You knew nothing of this?"

"No... Dreams. Memories. Fragments. Nothing that made sense."

"You were a slave?" he asked. "No! I can't believe it! The dress you were wearing when I first saw you – that wasn't one that belonged to a slave girl."

"No, it wasn't…"

"You couldn't sweep a floor! You couldn't cook a meal!"

"I worked in the fields. Among the men."

"Silvio… He called you queen."

"He was mocking me! You didn't think him serious? It was a game we played. When we were children, there were times we were able to slip away. We went to the woods. Played Britons against Red Crests, battling with sticks as swords. Silvio was the first of my warriors. I was the mighty Boudica."

"A child's game?" He looked utterly bewildered. A silence fell between them broken only by the distant howling of wolves. And then he asked, "You were truly a slave?"

"For the third time of telling! I was."

"Your master was who?"

"The same as Rufus's. That was where I was born."

"Why did you run away?"

"Titus Cornelius Festus wished to … use me."

"Use you?"

"Yes!"

"How?"

"How do you think? Do I have to describe every detail?"

"And you wouldn't submit?"

"No. I fought. Hurt him. There was nothing for it but to run."

"There was talk on the bridge – that day we left – a runaway girl. The offer of a reward. That was for you?"

"Yes."

He breathed out between his teeth. A harsh, sudden hiss. Slapped his hand against his forehead.

Cassia felt as though a cold fist squeezed her heart. The more she explained herself, the closer she tried to get to him, the further she seemed to be driving him away. It was as though they were having two quite different conversations. She had the strange sense they were divided by a screen that rendered communication impossible.

"Had you known who I was, would you have behaved differently?"

Silence.

She persisted. "Marcus ... you've protected me these past months. You've done more than I could ever have asked from you. I thought you did it from kindness. You said you helped me the same way you would have saved a bird from a cat."

"Those were my very words." There was a bitterness in his voice that made her flinch.

"Did you lie? Marcus, tell me. What goes on here?" She put a hand on his arm, her fingers pressing into his flesh. "Who did you think I was?"

He didn't answer. Instead, he looked at her, taking in every detail of her face, as if seeing her now for the first time. He dropped his eyes. "It doesn't matter. I was wrong."

He reached out his hand and traced the line of her chin with one finger. Leaned towards her as if he wanted – as if he yearned desperately – to kiss her.

But something in his nature fought him. Mind and body seemed at war with each other.

Suddenly he threw back his head and yelled, "Gods of Olympus, how you mock me!"

Pulling his cloak tight about him, he turned and strode away, out of the hill fort and into the night.

She waited and watched all the hours of darkness.

But Marcus did not come back.

PART II: EAGLE

I

There are two players in this tale: Cassia, and her Roman. I turn my attention now to him.

A storyteller can travel through time and across both land and sea in a heartbeat. I go back ten years. To the city of Rome, and to Primus Aurelius Aquila, the father of Marcus, who was returning home that morning having sold his daughter's mother at market.

The woman was a slave and he was perfectly entitled to dispose of her as he saw fit. Though Hera had been his whore these last fourteen years he had felt no guilt about her sale. She'd served him well. He'd enjoyed her while her looks had been intact. And he'd treated her kindly. She'd been fed. Clothed. Rarely beaten. She'd had better care from him than any slave had a right to expect. But his appetite for her had waned as her breasts sagged, her stomach slackened, her buttocks hollowed. These past few months, she'd begun to revolt him. Her time was done. He needed someone younger.

How very convenient then, that as Hera had faded, her daughter had bloomed.

Phoebe.

The mere thought of her made the blood race in his veins. Why would he buy a new girl when she was there, ripe for the picking?

Phoebe may have been daughter to Primus and half-sister to Marcus, but she was born a slave, like her mother. She was her father's property. Besides which, Primus had created her. He could do with her as he wished.

He'd not told mother or daughter what he planned, of course. The weeping and wailing of their separation would be more than he could bear. Women made such a fuss! Their noise would have been enough to curdle cheese. No... Instead he'd taken Hera with him to market the way he had so many times before.

But she'd known, he thought, long before he handed her over to the dealer. She'd said nothing, but there was accusation in her eyes. He was surprised to find that it pricked him a little. He needed a distraction to wipe the memory of her look from his mind. What could be better than to find Phoebe and enjoy her right away?

Marcus was then ten years old. He should have been at his lessons, but his tutor had been taken ill and, it being a bright spring day, he'd walked out into the gardens with his sister. He and Phoebe were lying on their backs in the dappled shade of a lemon tree. They didn't see their father return.

They stayed side by side in the shade until noon, she begging him for stories of gods and monsters, of death and destiny. Only when their stomachs began to growl with hunger did Phoebe – his sister, but still his slave – go in search of food and drink.

Marcus waited. And waited. She did not return. Puzzled by her disappearance, he went to the kitchen himself.

She was not there. And no one would say where she'd gone. So he went looking.

He searched all the usual places, but couldn't find her. And then he passed his father's room. From there he could hear strange, muffled noises. An animal grunting. A gasp of pain. A cry of distress.

Phoebe's!

Thinking robbers had somehow broken in and attacked her, Marcus burst through the doorway.

His father was kneeling on the bed.

Phoebe was crouched on all fours in front of him.

She was crying.

A boy should not attack his father.

He was permitted to beat the slaves. To kick a dog, whip a horse, strike a woman: all were necessary to maintain discipline.

But to raise a hand against the man who'd sired him?

That day, Marcus committed an unforgivable sin.

And he was duly punished for it.

It is possible to take a child's mind apart. To dismantle a personality. To fragment a soul. Marcus Aurelius Aquila had been systematically destroyed by his father.

Not with cruelty. He might have withstood that. Brutality would have bred hatred, and with it a fire that might have sustained him.

Instead it was done with kindness. With compassion. With love.

After the first beating, when Marcus was bloodied and bruised, afraid and alone, his father had approached him.

The boy had cowered, but Primus had opened his arms and said tenderly, "Come to me, my son."

Marcus had run to him. Begged forgiveness.

And afterwards?

Gently, with infinite care, he was made to see the error of his ways.

Phoebe was a bitch. A two-faced, treacherous, self-serving whore who'd knowingly tempted his father. Willingly turned her back on Marcus.

She'd made her decision. She must live with it. She was no sister of his.

He'd not spoken to her again. If he'd chanced to pass her, he'd looked through her as if she was invisible: like any other slave.

Piece by piece, stone by stone, the boy was remade. Rebuilt in his father's own image.

By the time he encountered Cassia on Londinium's bridge, Marcus Aurelius Aquila was a true and perfect son of Rome.

II

The night he left the Wolf People, turning his back on Cassia and striding into the night, Marcus had never felt so disturbed.

He could not keep still. He had to get away. To walk and keep walking. A plague of wasps was buzzing in his mind, ants were crawling through his blood vessels, some idiot demon was tightening every nerve.

How could he have so misjudged the situation?

By Jupiter and all the gods of Mount Olympus! How could he have got it so wrong?

How could he have so completely misunderstood *her*?

It was not possible. He could not have made a mistake so monstrous, so colossal...

He thought back to the first time he'd seen her.

There on the bridge: those marks on her wrists.

What more evidence had he needed?

He'd seen dots and whirls like that before. At the wall. Prisoners, captured by patrols. Warriors, brought in for interrogation by his superiors.

Not that they'd revealed anything. The bastards would rather die than talk. But he was well aware that there was a tribe somewhere in the wilderness beyond the Empire's furthest limit where mothers pierced their children's skin in just that way. Barbarian savages who hid in the hills and plotted against Rome. Whose lair was unknown, undiscovered.

Two years he'd been stuck on this wretched island. Damp. Cold. Forsaken by the gods. He should have stayed in Italia. Accepted the role his father had carved out for him. He could have been playing at politics in the city of Rome all this time but instead he'd wanted to forge his own future, to stand on his own feet. Two years he'd been away, hoping to make his father proud of him, desperate to show he was a worthy son and deserving of the family name. Perhaps, even, trying to prove himself an equal to the man who'd sired him.

And where had it got him?

Oh, he was a good salesman. He'd served Gaius well. But that was a mask that concealed his true purpose. Posing as an itinerant trader, he'd travelled the length of the wall, backwards and forwards, befriending barbarian drunkards who'd deserted their own people for an easier life in the taverns and whorehouses of the frontier towns. Not just posing as a trader, either. He'd adopted disguises. Taken pseudonyms, play-acted different parts. He'd worked so hard, extracting names, gleaning fragments of gossip, gathering information to pass to his employer.

But he hadn't told Constantius Scipio anything he didn't already know. Each time he made a report he could feel his superior's contempt growing. He felt more like a messenger boy than a spy!

The rumours had been running wild that year. In every tavern, in every flea-bitten inn he'd heard tales of native tribes forging alliances both among themselves and with Saxons from across the sea. Soon it was common gossip. He'd returned to Londinium to tell Constantius Scipio.

And there on the bridge, he'd seen Cassia.

She'd arrived in the city just when the rumours of barbarian conspiracy were at their height. He'd known she was an enemy agent the moment he'd laid eyes on her. The way she'd bared her teeth like a wolf at the guards on the bridge. She'd looked ready to bite their throats out! And she was so well muscled, so tanned. He'd had no doubt at all: she was a warrior. He could have arrested her right there, but self-interest had stayed his hand. She'd come south for some particular reason. If he could find out what it was, what a coup that would be!

Constantius Scipio had believed him when he said she was a spy. In fact Scipio had ordered him to dispose of her right away. A dark corner, a knife: he could have ended it the day she arrived in the city.

But by the time Marcus had reported to Scipio, he'd touched her. Standing there in Gaius's house: the feel of her palm against his had overwhelmed him. What was it? Lust? No… He'd felt desire before now. It was more than that. Something else. Something dangerous. And as a direct result of that he'd persuaded Scipio to let her live.

"Cut her down and others will spring up to take her place," he'd insisted. "We'll never know what they're planning. Better for me to befriend her. I'll see where she goes, what she does. That way we'll know what the enemy intends."

Scipio had been sceptical. And so, in desperation, Marcus had invoked his father's name. Used the power of his parent's reputation to add weight to his own argument. Even so, it was with reluctance that Scipio had agreed.

Nothing had happened all that winter. For months he'd played the part of a lovestruck fool. It hadn't been difficult. He'd burned to touch her. But he'd been so very respectful, not wanting to lay a finger on her skin without her consent. And it had never come.

Why not?

He knew how to charm a woman. It was the one thing he did know how to do better than his father. His looks alone often carried the day, and women were so generally overlooked, so thoroughly despised by the men they lived with, that they succumbed easily to his attentions. Women were so hungry, so desperate, that the smallest crumb of kindness was enough to satisfy them. He needed only to listen to what they had to say, to respond as though their words mattered to him, to murmur that their thoughts were intriguing and original, to look as if their company gave him great pleasure. He had plucked many men's secrets from their wives and daughters with a sympathetic smile and tender look.

Yet Cassia had been a challenge of a different order. She was polite. Courteous. Sometimes she'd seemed positively pleased to see him. Yet there had always been that distance.

And she had told him nothing. Nothing at all. He'd never known a woman so self-contained, so self-controlled. He'd put it down to her skill. He'd thought that she was a consummate professional.

But then there'd been her plan to rescue the slave boy. When she'd turned to him that day and asked for his help, triumph had overwhelmed him. All that watching, all that waiting had been worth it.

He assumed the slave lad was of noble family. Royal, perhaps. He'd heard how much these people prized their bloodlines. He'd guessed that Rufus would be a figurehead, a name who men would rally behind, who would unite armies of savages against Rome.

He'd gone to Constantius Scipio at once. Told him of her plan. Been ordered to go with her, to assist her in any way.

"See where she flies. Find out where her nest is. Then

we'll know where to strike." Those had been his orders, and he'd followed them to the very last word.

The fact that when Rufus had come away he'd been accompanied by a pair of Saxons – Flavia's blue eyes and Silvio's blond hair meant they could be nothing else – had added to his conviction that he'd uncovered a plot of immense significance.

He'd written as much to Constantius Scipio: set it all down in writing and made her carry the tablet to the spymaster herself. How pleased he'd been with that! How clever he'd thought it, to use her courage against her!

They'd got Rufus out. But – aside from their encounter with the bear – that had been the only part which had been truly dangerous. Once they'd reached Londinium, their path had been smoothed for them every step of the way. He'd delivered her to her tribe. The Wolf People: rumoured to be the most fierce, the most warlike, the most dangerous to Rome.

He had discovered their stronghold! That, at least, was useful information. He should have felt triumphant.

But – for him – things had fallen apart.

He'd known who Cassia's tribe were.

She had not.

How was that possible?

No, no, no! It was incredible. He could not have made such a huge mistake. Not him. It could not be, *it could not be* that all these months he'd thought she was something she wasn't, that he'd given her credit for a streak of animal cunning that did not, in fact, exist.

And yet there seemed no other explanation. He'd spun an elaborate web of supposition and ensnared only himself. What an idiot! He'd seen conspiracy where there was none. Janus wept! What would Constantius Scipio say when he told him?

What a disaster! So much money spent. So many soldiers paid to look the other way in Londinium and at the wall. So many bribes passed from hand to hand.

And all for what?

Cassia had never been a spy! There had been no plan to rescue a barbarian princeling! Restoring Rufus to his people had been a happy accident.

An accident that he himself had brought about.

He had never felt so idiotic. So ignorant. So stupid. Not since—

No. He would not think of that.

Yet if Cassia had been born a slave, as she said...

He could not doubt it! There in that wretched hill fort there was no benefit to her telling anything other than the truth. And her people had not known of her existence. They had embraced her as a long-lost daughter of the tribe, but one they had never laid eyes on until he had delivered her into their arms.

Slaves were made servile by the will of the gods. Inferior creatures, born only to serve. Did not the Greek philosophers agree on that? Aristotle, Plato? All the great thinkers of both Greece and Rome. His own father had drummed that knowledge into him.

As for the Britons, the Saxons, the warring barbarian tribes – they were savages with neither the wit nor wisdom to bow before the might and majesty of Rome. Uncivilized brutes, no better than beasts.

And yet he had seen nobility of heart and mind these past weeks not only in Cassia, but in Flavia too. Flavia – so stoical. Enduring every pain, every discomfort with silent dignity. Women! Who were only set on earth to be used by men.

So how was it that Cassia's courage matched that of any Roman soldier?

Her nerve was unparalleled. He'd seen her facing down a bear. Unarmed. Unafraid. A gladiator would have quailed. Yet she'd stood there and commanded it to leave Rufus alone!

And then afterwards – *gods!* – she'd kissed him back. He'd felt the ground under his feet being pulled away. Reality had skewed sideways. He was in danger of losing himself to her.

Venus be cursed! – the girl had wormed her way into his heart. He had caught her like a disease. Affection had grown like a tumour.

But a disease could be cured with the right remedy. A tumour could be cut out.

And it would be.

He was his father's son, was he not? If he could not master this one flaw, he was scarcely fit to be called a Roman.

III

He walked the length of that night entirely alone but soon after sunrise, Marcus quite literally fell into company.

Coming down a steep slope, eyes blurred with exhaustion, he missed his footing and tumbled, head over heels, rolling down an expanse of scree and landing at the foot of the hill.

It took some moments for his head to stop spinning. When he opened his eyes, there was a man standing over him, outlined against the sky: a muscled torso, a mass of hair and beard, the stink of horse.

Marcus was in enemy territory. He had no protection here. For a moment he thought his end had come and in his distressed state he would almost have welcomed it. But then the stranger spoke.

"Marcus Aurelius Aquila." The tone was faintly mocking. "What brings you into the wild lands?"

The speaker was known to him. A horse trader. An informer. Marcus had often pressed coins into his hand in the quiet corners of dark taverns in exchange for gobbets of information. He went by the name of Tertius south of the wall but no doubt used a different one north of it. When Marcus got to his feet, he simply extended a hand in greeting and said, "Well met."

"Indeed." A small group of shaggy ponies was clumped a little way off, the lead mare hobbled so she couldn't run away. Marcus fixed his gaze on the animals while the trader eyed him with more than a little suspicion. "You are alone?"

"I am."

He sniffed. "Then you are a very brave man. Or a very foolish one."

Marcus didn't reply. *Foolish,* he thought. *Foolish.* The word banged from one side of his head to the other like the clanger of a bell.

"Where are you headed all alone?"

Marcus thought of Cassia. Part of him longed to turn back. To retrace his steps. To explain. To unburden himself to her. Didn't the Christians do such things? Confess. Repent. Beg forgiveness.

But – though his father had changed the family's religion with each Emperor – at heart Marcus was no Christian. And he couldn't bear the thought of how her face would change if he told her the truth. He couldn't see her again. His only task now was to smooth over the catastrophic mess he'd made of things. "South, " he said. It sounded flat and dull. Deathly.

"Ride with me, then," Tertius said. "I could use some help. My boy was kicked in the head by that colt there two days back. I had to send him home to his mother. This many horses are hard to manage alone."

It was easy to believe the gods had directed their paths to cross. Easy to fall in with Tertius, to accept the mount he was offered and to ride south, towards Roman territory. Easy to keep an eye on the horses. To ride and not to talk. To ride and not to think.

Tertius wanted the animals to arrive at market in good condition. He did not push them hard, and when they came to patches of sweeter grass, he allowed them to graze awhile. He asked no questions, and Marcus gave no information. They moved, they watched the herd, they travelled in a silence that was broken only by the cries of eagles, the grunts and nickers of the horses, the wind through the heather, the babble of a stream.

At the end of the day they made camp. They shared a little of the dried meat that Tertius carried in a pouch at his waist.

When Marcus slept, he dreamed of Cassia.

It was three days before the wall loomed in the distance. It should have been a welcome sight. Civilization lay on the other side. Decent food. Good company. The Baths.

But so did Constantius Scipio. So did confession. Judgement. Punishment. It could not be avoided. He was a loyal son of Rome. He would do his duty.

The night after they arrived on the other side of the wall, he and Tertius went to the tavern. Knowing what lay ahead, Marcus drank too much, said too much and woke feeling as though his skull had been cleft in two.

Memories of the night before came in pieces, drifting into his head and making him groan with shame.

He remembered that he'd wept into his wine. "I had her all wrong! Right from the moment I saw her."

"Who, Roman?" It was all the prompting that Marcus had needed. Words poured out of his mouth as freely as the wine had been poured down his throat. Dear gods, had he told the man everything?

"Cassia! She was a slave. But I thought… I thought… Gods, what a fool I've turned out to be!"

After that he'd utterly abandoned himself to self-pity. Snivelled and whimpered like a child. How could he have behaved so pitifully? And what more had he said that he didn't now recall?

But what did it matter how much of the truth he'd spilled? His mistake would be known to everyone soon enough.

His reputation – such as it was – would crumble into ruins. He'd lose his job. Go home disgraced. The dread of reporting to Constantius Scipio was nothing compared to that of having to tell his father how badly he'd let him down.

But there was something else too. Something underneath that twisted like a knife in his guts. It was treachery against Rome. Yet there was no evading his fierce, hopeless longing to see Cassia's face again.

Venus wept! Was this how it felt to love?

IV

Marcus Aurelius Aquila was not the only Roman in this tale whose mind was mired in thoughts of Cassia. Titus Cornelius Festus could think of nothing else. And he was not without influence. A man with wealth at his disposal could never be ignored.

He'd seen the bitch Cassia right there in his room! Seen the fear in her face. He'd almost had her there in the palm of his hand! And she'd slipped through his fingers again.

He'd decided to remain in the city until she was found. Men had been bought who were ordered to turn over every stick, every stone until she was discovered. She wouldn't escape a third time.

His purse was large, but even so, it took some time and a great many coins to discover where she'd been hiding these past months. It took even longer to discover who'd placed her there and why.

But by the time Marcus Aurelius Aquila finally arrived back in Londinium ready to confess his mistake to his superior, Constantius Scipio already knew of his error.

He was humiliated. Shamed. Exposed as a fool. An idiot who'd grasped the wrong end of the stick and failed to let go. He was reduced to less than nothing.

Standing before Constantius Scipio – his head down, his eyes on the floor – Marcus felt as though he was ten years old.

Constantius Scipio never once raised his voice. It would have been easier if he had. The long litany of Marcus's errors seemed to take Scipio most of the morning to recite. The sun was high overhead when he at last concluded, "All this and more. You've helped a number of valuable slaves escape. Every master in southern Britannia has felt the effect of it. All across the country slaves are growing unruly and restless. You know how they talk. Gossip spreads like disease. As for Cornelius Festus – his estate is in chaos. This one girl has inflamed them all. She's given them hope." Scipio paused, and said heavily, "She can't be left to run free."

The sentence hung in the air. It was a few moments before Marcus realized he was expected to give an answer. He raised his head. Met Constantius Scipio's eyes. Read the challenge in them.

"You want me to bring her back?"

For the first time that morning his superior smiled. "Oh, I wouldn't trust you to retrieve a lost shoe, Marcus." He let the contempt in his voice sink in before he added, "But who else can I send? I'll not risk other men's lives for your mistakes. No one but you knows where to find the runaways."

"I can't bring them all back on my own!"

"No. Well, Festus doesn't much care what fate befalls the others. Kill them. Bring back their heads. Or leave them be – it's as you see fit. But he will have *her* back, and he will have her back alive. Or it will be your neck that feels the sword."

Marcus protested, "I can't go in and drag her out. She's among her own people. She's protected."

"There will be a way. I suggest you find it. You have an imagination, don't you? This time try putting it to better use."

V

The only place to go was the tavern. The only thing to do was to drink himself senseless. He found a squalid dive where his face wasn't known and ordered a jug of wine. But he was still only halfway towards oblivion when his sister slipped into his mind.

He'd not thought of Phoebe for years. But a vision of her suddenly filled his head.

Her, kneeling.

His father.

Her face.

Eyes tight shut. Trying not to cry out. Biting her lip so hard blood was running down her chin.

Instinct had propelled him across the room. He'd run at his father, yelling and screaming, fists flailing.

Primus, taken by surprise, had been knocked off balance. He'd landed heavily, cracking his head on the floor.

Marcus had seized his sister by the hand, pulled her up. Urged her to come with him. To run. To hide.

But she had not.

She'd merely looked at him. Looked with eyes that were suddenly those of a stranger; eyes whose expression he couldn't begin to understand. They were no longer those of his older sister. No longer those of a girl at all. Instead they brimmed with age-old weariness and sorrow.

She'd stared at him. One, two, three heartbeats.

And then she'd shaken her head. Turned away. Turned back towards his father. Knelt down on all fours. Lifted her dress.

Marcus drank deep. He was angry. Sweating. Feeling the same rage and confusion that he'd felt at ten years old.

He'd tried to save her. She'd refused.

Bitch. Two-faced, treacherous, self-serving whore!

Shock had carried him through the beating his father ordered. He'd barely registered the first bite of the whip. Rage and resentment had shielded him from pain.

He'd not wasted a single thought on her from that day to this.

Until now.

Why? Why was he thinking of her? What had happened to him?

Something had changed.

He drank. And drank. But the peace of oblivion eluded

him. Memories of Phoebe came thick and fast and when he finally left the tavern for his bed, they snapped at his heels as he staggered through the streets.

Phoebe. And her mother. Hera. The woman who'd raised them both after his own mother had died.

Sold.

She'd sung to him. Soothed him out of nightmares. He and Phoebe had clung to her in storms when thunder and lightning raged overhead.

Only the gods knew where she was now.

That night, alone in his room, he dreamed he was back in Rome.

His father's house. The corridor. Vast. Cavernous. As he walked along its length, solid ground became liquid beneath his feet. It heaved, sticky and fluid. Sucking with each step.

The noises. Echoing. Wails. Whimpers.

The door gigantic. Yawning open with a monstrous creak. Going in.

Seeing his father across a vast distance. And the girl kneeling on the bed, raising her head. Her anguished face. Looking at him.

A girl with Phoebe's blonde hair.

But Cassia's eyes.

He cried out. Snapped awake. Sat up, swung around, feet on the floor, standing, ready to run. Ready to intervene.

But the room was dark. Cold. It took a few moments for him to realize he wasn't at home.

But those eyes. They'd burned into him the way they had when Cassia told him why she'd run from her master. But no! No, no, no! This hadn't happened to Cassia.

She'd fled.

Why hadn't Phoebe?

The answer came, glib and pat, the way it always had. He heard his father's voice, whispering into his ear so softly. So patiently. *Because she was a slut. A whore. She'd wanted it. Planned it. Plotted to take her mother's place.* She'd teased and tempted Primus until he'd yielded. Women were like that.

He remembered his own response. A faint protest.

"She was crying."

"Women do," his father had replied. "It's the way they are. It means nothing. They do it for their own benefit. They're manipulative creatures. Don't give them the chance to tug at your heartstrings. They'll only exploit you."

And then another voice was in his head.

Cassia's.

"No."

In the dark stillness before the dawn – half waking, half sleeping – he heard her clearly.

"She had nowhere to run."

The truth settled in his guts like a lead weight. If Phoebe had taken his hand, they wouldn't even have got out of the room, much less away from the villa. Her situation was hopeless from the moment their father had touched her. And she'd known it.

Why hadn't he?

Pain bent him in two. He crumpled back onto the narrow bed. For the first time he saw that it had been easier to blame his sister than think about why she'd shaken her head. Easier to believe his father than oppose him.

A sob rose in his throat. This was Cassia's fault. Gods! What had she done to him? He curled into a ball. Shut his eyes. But he did not sleep again.

VI

A personality that had taken years to construct could not be taken apart overnight. There was no sudden moment of revelation. No clouds parted. Jupiter hurled no bolts of lightning from the sky.

And yet, in the days that followed Marcus's return to Londinium, there was a change in his perception. Everything seemed askew. He felt an unease that grew and spread until everything he saw, everything he touched, everything he tasted dripped with it.

Word of his disgrace passed from mouth to mouth until the whole of Londinium knew of it. He'd been able to find only the shabbiest lodgings in the seediest part of town. The men he'd once drunk with didn't wish to be tainted by association. Until he returned Cassia to her master he was dishonoured. Bad luck was infectious, he knew that. In their position he'd have done the same. He didn't blame his former friends. But it meant he was alone, standing on the outside looking in. Scarcely knowing how it had happened, he began to see the place through Cassia's eyes.

Soon after he came back to the city there was a games. Gladiators. Beasts. The spectacle would distract him from his troubles, he thought. But sitting there among his fellow citizens, an unpleasant sensation seeded itself in his guts. As the day wore on, it grew until tendrils of doubt were winding around his heart and mind. Once he'd have revelled in the slaughter, but he now began to wonder at its mindless brutality.

He found he couldn't walk past the slave market. Whereas before he'd seen only goods and chattels, now he saw people. Broken. Desperate. A few days after he'd dreamed of Phoebe, he saw a wealthy merchant squeezing the breasts of a young girl who stood on the auction stand. He'd had to fold his arms, turn on his heel, walk swiftly in the other direction to avoid intervening. For an insane moment he'd itched to slap the man's hands away. It had flashed through his mind that he should buy her himself simply so that he could turn her free. Madness. He couldn't save her! He couldn't save any of them. Slavery was the grease that oiled the wheels of the Empire. There was nothing to be done about it!

But he'd avoided the market and the area around it after that.

Yet there was no way of not seeing or noticing the slaves

that ran through the streets doing their masters' bidding. They'd been all but invisible to him a few short months ago. Now eyes seemed to burn with accusation from every face.

And it was not simply the slaves he viewed through shattered glass. It was his own countrymen. Where once he'd seen superiority now he saw arrogance. Pride. Corruption. When he looked at the Forum, he saw a monstrous edifice built on stolen land. He pictured the broken bodies of the slaves forced to construct it. These temples, these palaces, these public buildings: they were golden facades built on the vast, mass grave of native Britons.

He saw an Empire withered and rotten to the heart.

A Roman should not think these things! He feared he was losing his mind. His former confidence, his old assurance, his brazen swagger – the harder he tried to catch onto it, the more it evaded his grasp.

One day a sudden recollection dropped into his head.

He had been young then: how old? Five perhaps. Or six. He had been crawling through the garden in pursuit of Phoebe when he'd come face to face with a snake. It was a milky-eyed thing: blind, he'd thought. Bound to starve.

He'd taken a stone in his hand meaning to put it out of its misery. But he didn't know how to kill a snake, so he'd watched it instead. For no apparent reason it had started throwing itself about in the most hideous contortions. And then, before his eyes, its skin had split.

He'd never run so fast in his life!

He remembered the panic that had seized him. How he'd fled screaming for Phoebe. How she'd calmed him. How they'd crept back and found the creature basking in the sun. It had sloughed off its old skin and emerged, shining and new, a creature reborn, its eyes black and clear.

He was the snake now, he thought. He felt as though scales had peeled from his eyes. He was seeing the world afresh. His vision was sharp. It should have been intoxicating.

But when he thought of Cassia, and what he was duty-bound to do, he would have given anything to be back in his old, familiar skin.

Constantius Scipio left Marcus to consider his plans for Cassia's retrieval without interference. It was no easy task, and so he was given plenty of time to fathom out a scheme that would not fail. Days turned into weeks.

Night after night he saw her in his dreams. There on the bridge, her dress dripping wet. Standing, while he cut her hair. Red curls falling to the floor of his room. Cassia in her village, in native dress, dripping with gold.

And then one night he was there on the road with her. The oxen lame. The sound of an animal padding after them in the dark gloom. The bear attacking.

He was riding after her, through the nightmare of the woods.

Seeing her standing there, facing it down.

Kissing her.

Breaking free.

Watching her unwind her brother from the shroud. But the boy's face wasn't that of Rufus.

It was his own.

The dream did not fade with the sunrise. There was a message there that he could not comprehend. He sat and worried at it the length of that day. And slowly, slowly, he saw that meeting Cassia had been a tremor that started an earthquake. A hairline fracture had cracked the earth under his feet. Light was leaking into a dark crypt and things that had lain dead and buried for years had been exposed to the sun, little by little.

He began to perceive that he himself had behaved like Rufus. After Phoebe had been attacked by his father, after he'd been beaten – he'd been so afraid. Lost. Lonely. And then – when his father had come to him with open arms – he'd been grateful for every crumb of kindness thrown by the man who'd ordered his beating. He'd made an idol of him. Turned him into a god. Created a perfect statue of marble and gold and sat at its feet worshipping.

From that day to this he'd been in thrall. His father's fool. His loyal and willing slave.

The moment of realization was so shattering that Marcus was amazed the whole of Londinium did not hear the sound. The statue he'd constructed in his mind, the idol of his father, was falling. Smashing into pieces. Crumbling into dust.

Cassia had broken the chains that bound her.

Was it possible that he could do the same?

VII

It was another month before he returned to the Forum to give a full and detailed account of how he proposed to redeem himself and, when he finally did, Marcus Aurelius Aquila did not disappoint his superior.

His father had told him a tale once. That of a horse: a magnificent beast, black as night, with a perfect circle on its forehead that shone white as the moon.

Such a horse had never been seen before. It was a creature a god would be proud to ride. Man after man tried to tame it. Man after man died in the attempt. It was so wild that the creature was worthless. In time no man dared even get near it. And so it was decided that the animal would be slaughtered for meat.

On the day of its execution a young lad – twelve or thirteen years old, no more than that – watched men surround the horse, their spears poised. It reared and stamped, but was so magnificent that none of them dared throw their weapons. The boy studied its movements, observed its rolling eyes, its laboured breath. But he and he alone wondered what made the animal behave so. As it whirled and spun, he realized it was wild with fear, and that what scared it was its very own shadow.

Bursting between the men, he seized the horse's bridle and pulled its head towards the sun.

And all at once that rearing, plunging beast became calm. It stood, sweating, its flanks heaving. But it did not paw the ground or roll its eyes. It did not kick or bite the young man who held it. Slowly its nostrils ceased flaring. It lowered its head. It allowed him to stroke its neck. And then it stood still while he vaulted onto its back. He alone was able to ride it because he alone had found out its secret fear.

The words his father had spoken had been ringing loud and clear in his mind all week.

"Men are like animals, my son: each one has a terror all of his own, and with each man it is different. But find his secret fear, and you will put a bridle on the man. You will ride him, though he knows it not."

Find the secret fear.

Well, he knew Cassia's.

He had seen it in her eyes that night. Seen it again in his dream. Her fear of violation. Of being taken against her will.

He would make use of that, he told Constantius Scipio. "She also has a strong sense of justice. She wouldn't want someone else to be suffering in her place."

"Go on."

"I'll tell her that her master has bought a new girl. I'll propose we rescue her. I'm sure Cassia will come away happily if that's the plan."

"She'd be brave enough to come back this side of the wall?"

"I'm certain of it. And I'll have men waiting. The moment she's crossed over she will be captured. Imprisoned."

"And the others? You plan to leave them there?"

"No."

"He is less concerned about them."

"I know that. But I'd have them back for my own honour, sir. I can't rest easy until the wrong I've done is put right."

"What do you propose?"

"To use her as bait to tempt them out."

"You think they'll come looking for her?"

"They owe her their freedom. They won't give her up lightly."

"You'd risk a war with her people?"

"There is risk of one in any case, isn't there? But we have the advantage now: we know where their stronghold is. If they threaten to rise against us, why then, I can lead our men to their village myself."

"You'd do this?"

"Willingly. I've sunk very low, sir. I'd do anything to climb out of the hole I've dug for myself."

Constantius Scipio surveyed him thoughtfully. Marcus's eyes burned with zeal, with ambition and with suppressed fury against the girl who'd been the cause of his humiliation.

When Marcus left the Forum, there was a spring in his step and he had not a single misgiving.

He'd convinced him. His superior had believed every word. Thank the gods! Constantius Scipio had seen nothing of what truly lay in his heart.

Marcus Aurelius Aquila left for the north the following morning with the protective blessing of Rome draped about his shoulders like a cloak.

He'd sworn on his father's honour that the task would be done: before too long, Cassia would be delivered to her master.

It was a vow he would feel no remorse about breaking.

VIII

When he left Londinium, Marcus meant only to get back
to Cassia. He would tell her everything there was to know
about him, he'd decided: the plain truth, ugly though
it was. He must confess that he'd thought her a spy and
conspired against her. That, since then, he'd changed his
mind. Changed sides. Lied to his superior. Given a false
description of where her village lay. Vowed to bring her
back to her master with no intention of actually doing so.

What happened after that would be for her to decide.

Having turned his face to the north, he couldn't ride
fast enough. He could do with Perscus's winged sandals, he
thought. Or Pegasus, instead of a shaggy native pony. He
muttered half-crazed requests for divine intervention under
his breath yet for mile after mile he remained stubbornly
land-bound.

The gods did not help him. Indeed, difficulties beset

him every step of the way. But then, he was not doing the bidding of Rome's deities any more, was he? It was not surprising they cast obstacles in his path.

His horse was lame at the end of the first day. The replacement he bought turned out to be a broken-winded thing that scarcely lasted the length of the next before dropping dead two miles short of his night's planned destination. He'd had to leave it by the side of the road for wolves to tear at and go on towards the town on foot.

After that the weather turned. Riding on his third horse, it became unseasonably cold, even for Britannia. Rain poured in gushing torrents, which turned to hail and then sleet as he journeyed north.

Following his disgrace, his pay had been stopped by Constantius Scipio. But his father's name carried such weight that there were plenty of moneylenders prepared to deal with him. His bulging pouch of coins would take him across the Empire and back if he wished it. A shame that it could not buy him better weather!

A horse was faster than an ox-cart, but with the elements and with Fortune so against him it took him twice as long as he'd intended to reach the wall.

And on the very night he did, the first snows of winter fell.

Had it been a light dusting, such as might have been expected at that time of year, he would have gone on. But it was a heavy fall and overnight a biting wind whipped the drifts into strange contortions so that the land was unrecognizable from the day before. It continued to fall all that day and then froze hard the following night.

To travel alone into the unfamiliar wilderness with the snow so thick on the ground would have been madness.

Marcus sent a message to Constantius Scipio that he was unavoidably delayed. That he couldn't go further until there was a thaw. It might come next week. Or – which looked more likely – it might take some months.

And then he sat and waited in a small room in a seedy tavern in a desolate frontier town for the bad weather to pass.

The winter had come unusually early and it departed unusually late. It was six long months before Marcus was able to travel north of the wall. By the time he did, an entirely new plan had taken shape in his head.

IX

Cassia was crouching by the pool when he found her, a rough mountain pony tethered near the rowan. Her back was to him, but there could be no mistaking the colour of her hair.

She didn't turn as he approached and he wondered at her lack of caution. He might be a bandit, a warrior from an enemy tribe, a Roman scout … surely she should be more wary? Was she so lost in thought that she had not heard his horse? What was she thinking that held her so rapt?

He dismounted. Walked forward. She was gazing into the depths when his reflection appeared on the surface. In the water their eyes met.

Only then did she stand. Turn. Her face betrayed no surprise whatsoever.

And then he realized she had expected him.

He was a stranger on her land: perhaps word had been carried ahead? He must have been seen and not known it. And she'd come out from the hill fort expressly to meet him; chosen a place where they would not be overheard.

He'd gone from her in the summer. It was now the following spring. All these months he'd imagined seeing her again. He'd desperately hoped there would be joy in her eyes. But there was only doubt. Suspicion. Anger.

"So, the Eagle has flown north once more." Her voice was cold. "What brings you here, Roman?"

He felt as though she'd slapped him. All the words he'd prepared melted into the air. He took a step back. Folded his arms in self-defence. "Is that my only greeting?"

"You went away without a word. I thought you dead. What did you expect?"

"I'm sorry," he said. "I've regretted it every day since."

"Why did you?"

The time had come. He'd played this scene over in his head every day this last winter. The confession should have rolled off his tongue. But it didn't.

"I made a mistake. About you."

"Go on."

"When I first saw you… I didn't think you were a slave."

He'd thought she might react to that, but she simply asked, "And what did you take me for?"

It was in the lap of the gods now. Let them decide this as they willed. "I thought you were a warrior sent from the north. A spy, plotting against the Empire."

Fury should have followed that revelation. Violence,

even. Instead she laughed, throwing her head back, so he could see the soft whiteness of her throat. He wanted to kiss her there.

She seemed almost relieved. How could that be?

"A spy!" she said. "Me?"

"Yes. Your dress, your manner ... it confused me."

"And yet you helped me. You. A loyal Roman." Her eyebrows were raised. She was challenging him, he thought. There was something going on here that he didn't quite understand. "Why?"

He hung his head. "I was never a trader. It was a mask I wore. My task was to gather information. To pass it back to Rome. I suggested to my superior that I watched you. I was ordered to see what you did. Where you went."

"And helping Rufus escape? Was that a part of your plan too?"

"Yes. I was supposed to discover where your people had their stronghold."

"The bird flies free..." she said. "I heard you. There at the wall. For weeks after you'd gone I wondered what you meant."

"Well, now you know."

"I do. And I'm glad to hear the truth from your lips." She leaned closer to him. "But actually, I already knew it."

He was startled. "How?"

"You think rumours travel in only one direction? There is a horse trader. I believe he's an acquaintance of yours? He passed this way before the snows came down. He told me of the evening you'd spent drinking together. Said you'd wept into your wine the whole night over me."

He flushed red. He remembered so little of what he'd said. Gods! Had he declared his love for her to the entire tavern?

She was amused by his embarrassment and that, he supposed, was preferable to her rage. Yet now her voice had a harder edge. "I understand why you left. But why have you come back? Do you intend to betray us?"

"No! I could not."

"Why then?"

"I will tell you everything. It's not pretty. I've had to lie my way here. Your master … he's determined to have you back. I would never do it, but I swore on my father's honour to return you."

"And why wouldn't you? There's a big price on my head."

"I know. Since I met you my heart and mind have been at war with each other."

"And is the battle over?"

"It is. I'm no longer a Roman. If I go back to Londinium, I'll die as a traitor."

"And so what now? Do you propose to settle here among savages?"

"In time. If your people will have me. But first there's something I want to do."

She seemed intrigued. He used almost the same words she'd thrown at him when Titus Cornelius had found her in Londinium. "I need a Briton."

"You've come a long way to find one."

"I need one in particular. You."

"What for?"

"There's someone I'd like to help. I have a sister…"

"A Roman?" Her lip curled in distaste. "Why would she need my help?"

"Phoebe is a slave."

Cassia's eyes narrowed with suspicion. "Oh? How so?"

"Because her mother was. Mine died when I was born. Phoebe is a little older than me, but we were raised together. I'd like to see her walk free."

Cassia shrugged. "So do it."

"My father won't allow it."

"Buy her then. You have money, don't you?"

"He'd set the price too high."

"And so what do you propose?"

"To bring her out secretly. The way we did with Rufus."

Cassia was frowning. She stared along the valley for a while and then asked, "Where is she?"

"Rome."

"Rome?!" She was startled. Incredulous. "You ask me to go with you to Rome?"

"Only if you agree to it."

She stared at him, her eyes scouring his face. "I ask again. Why do you need *my* help?"

She had not turned him down. Not yet. His future

seemed balanced on a knife-edge. When he spoke, he chose his words carefully. "You have such courage. More than I've seen in any woman. Or any man." He paused for a moment, and then said, "Besides that you have a talent for quiet, clandestine action." He knew she'd often been afraid on their journey north. When the bear attacked, they all had. But whereas the others had been diminished by their fear, she'd seemed to thrive on it. Indeed, she'd never appeared more alive than at their times of greatest danger. Cautiously, he ventured, "I think you have a taste for it too?"

She didn't respond but he could see he'd hit upon the truth. There was a line between her brows that deepened only when she was thinking hard. He hoped she was already imagining leaving her homeland, making another journey by his side.

"You need my help..." Cassia murmured. She looked up. "So this is what brings you so far north?"

"I didn't return for the delights of your cooking."

A smile flitted across her features.

He grinned back at her, but her next question wiped the expression from his face.

"Tell me more about this sister of yours."

"It's a long tale," he said flatly. "I need to start with my father. He was – *is* – an important man in Rome. Very influential. He is – some would say – the power behind the Emperor's throne."

"So?"

"Well then ... Phoebe is my half-sister. We share the same father. But when I was ten – and she twelve – he took her for his mistress." Despite himself he found he was shaking with long-suppressed emotion. He couldn't control the tremble in his voice. "She was – she *is* – his daughter, Cassia! My sister. He made her his whore."

Ice-cold, she asked, "And you did nothing?"

"Oh, I did. I attacked him. And was punished for it. He took great pains to teach me the error of my ways. I can still hear his words. 'Slaves are not human beings! They're worth less than an ox or ass! They're chattels, to dispose of as their masters wish.'"

"And you believed him?"

"Cassia, any other thoughts I had were beaten out of me. I nearly died of my foolishness. I don't ask for your pity. But, yes, I became the man I was expected to be. I was the obedient son."

"But now you want me – a slave, the scum of the sewer – to help rescue your sister?"

"Only if you do it willingly."

Her silence seemed to last an eternity. Eventually she said with an irritable sigh, "I owe you a great debt. Whatever your reasons, I wouldn't have come home to my people without your help."

"There's no debt. I don't need to be repaid! If you come, you come of your own free will."

There was another interminably long silence. Cassia

261

breathed in. Out. In again. She raised her head. Fixed her eyes on his. And – at last – nodded.

He could scarcely believe it. "Do you mean you will come?"

"Maybe."

Arms outstretched, he closed the distance between them. But her hand came up, warding him off. "If I do this, I don't do it for you," she said. "But for your sister. No woman alive should have to endure such torment."

"We're bound for Rome then?"

"Perhaps. There is someone I must talk to first. If he agrees to it, I will come."

There was something almost reverential in her tone. Whose consent did she need to seek? Who had such power over her? Gods! Did she have a lover? A pang of jealousy squeezed his guts. Bitterly, he demanded, "Silvio?"

At that she laughed aloud. "No! Not Silvio. He is indeed my very dear friend, but he married a wife this spring."

"Oh?" Marcus tried to keep the relief from his face. "A woman of the Wolf People?"

"No," said Cassia. "Of the Deer. Their land lies to the west of here. They were our ancient enemies, so I'm told."

"But are no longer?"

"No. We are at peace. There was a gathering of the clans this last midwinter. Silvio met her then: lost his heart in an instant. Their marriage strengthens the bonds between our peoples."

"So the rumours are true," Marcus said. "The tribes are uniting?" For a brief moment Scipio's face flashed before him. How eagerly his superior would pounce on that piece of information!

"Does that worry you, Roman?" Cassia was watching him narrowly.

Marcus shook the vision from his head. "I told you," he said, perhaps a little too firmly, "I have turned my back on Rome." She looked doubtful and he could hardly blame her. What would it take to make her trust him? Time alone, he supposed. And action. His deeds would speak more convincingly of what lay in his heart than his tongue ever could. He changed tack. "Whose permission do you need to leave? Your chief's?"

She shook her head. "My brother's."

"Rufus?"

"Yes. He is… Well. You'll see how he is."

Marcus watched her walk to her horse. She had changed since he'd last seen her, walking with a confident stride – a swagger, almost. There was a knife strapped to her upper arm, he noticed. She vaulted onto the back of her pony with fluid grace and when they moved off, Cassia leading the way, she seemed almost to be part of the beast. She'd learned to ride well over the winter, then. He wondered briefly what else the Wolf People might have taught her.

Presumably she knew how to use that knife too?

X

The roundhouse was newly built, its thatch of lighter hue than others in the settlement. Its walls were smooth and as yet unmarked by growths of moss and lichen. He would have taken it for a modest native dwelling had it not been for the curious array of objects around the door. There were branches pushed into the ground either side, and from the twigs dangled what looked like totems and offerings. A bunch of leaves. Dried flowers. Feathers. Coloured stones. The small carving of a wolf. A tuft of grey fur, tied with grass. The fang of a large animal – wolf or bear? – threaded onto a strip of leather. At the base of one branch stood a jug of mead. At the other, a bowl of what looked like fresh blood.

Marcus was aware of a strange power even before Cassia held aside the hide hanging over the door and invited him inside.

A pungent smell of burning herbs struck him.

There was a fire but it was little more than a heap of glowing embers and there was no other light. Dimly he saw Cassia gesturing for him to sit. He did so. She took her place beside him and there they waited in silence for something. Or someone.

It was not until the figure moved that Marcus knew there was another person in the hut. Not until that person spoke that he realized he was sitting opposite Rufus.

If Cassia had changed these last months, her brother had been transformed almost beyond recognition.

The boy put back his hood and leaned forward. His face was lit by the embers' glow. He looked at Marcus but when he spoke, his words were for his sister.

"You waited by the pool?"

"Yes," she said. "And he came, just as you said he would."

"Eyes meeting on the water. I saw it in my sleep."

Marcus felt his jaw drop open. Was that why she'd been there? Because the boy had dreamed him?

Rufus extended a hand. Pointed a finger. "You want to take her with you."

It was a statement, not a question.

Marcus was unnerved. "Yes," he mumbled. "I want to rescue my sister. Cassia won't go without your agreement."

"You have it. Cassia will go."

Rufus leaned back against the wall. His face was once more in the shadows.

Was that it? thought Marcus. *Could it be so easy? So straightforward?*

No. It could not.

Rufus spoke again. "You must take Flavia."

"Flavia?" Marcus echoed. "To Rome?"

"No. To Germania."

"Germania!" Marcus could not keep the panic from his voice. It was in the far north, wasn't it? Beyond Gallia. Miles out of their way. A wild land beyond the limits of the Empire. A country of forests and wild beasts, and even wilder warriors. His father had terrified him with tales of the barbarians' savagery when he was small.

But then, his father had put many things in his head, hadn't he? False things: things that he no longer wished to have there.

More calmly he asked, "Why must we take Flavia?"

"Her ancestors call her. She must be returned to her people."

Marcus had no idea how to reply. It was Cassia who said, "If that's your wish, we'll take her, brother."

"Not mine," he said. "The spirits'."

Cassia leaned into Marcus. "She will be glad to make the journey. She's spoken of home so often. When death comes, she wants her bones laid with those of her people."

There seemed no escaping it. "Very well."

Marcus thought they would leave the hut then. Tell Flavia what had been decided. Make preparations for what lay ahead, but Cassia didn't move.

Rufus had taken a handful of something that he scattered over the embers.

It caught. Flared. The stench was overpowering. The smoke made Marcus's eyes stream. As he breathed in, his head felt lighter. His limbs heavy. Beside him, Cassia reached for his hand. Her palm was cold. Clammy. He wanted to speak. But found he couldn't.

Held in the grip of a peculiar inertia, Marcus looked across at Rufus. As he watched, the boy's head snapped back.

Rufus's eyes rolled so that only the whites were showing. His mouth opened. His voice, when it came, seemed not his own. "Eagle and wolf. Wolf and eagle. Stand together. Wall. Crest of red. Hills ablaze. Fire. Blood."

The boy's hands reached across the fire. His fingers stirred the smoke. It whirled. Seemed to become almost solid. For the most fleeting of moments Marcus thought he glimpsed something in it. Cassia. Flames at her back. Hair a scarlet halo around her face.

Then it was gone.

The smoke thinned. The fire died.

And Rufus was himself again. A boy. Nothing more. A boy who was dazed. Blinking. Getting to his feet and pulling aside the hide across the doorway to let the light flood in. Demanding food.

"I'm hungry."

"I will fetch you something," said Cassia.

"No," he said. "He can. Go on, Roman. Tell Flavia you're taking her home. Then bring me food. I need to talk to my sister."

Greatly disconcerted, Marcus did what he was told. He found Flavia and told her to prepare for a long journey. The old woman wept, taking his hands in hers and pressing her forehead to his knuckles, thanking him over and over again in her foreign tongue. He would have found her gratitude touching if his mind had not been so full of Rufus.

As he'd left the hut, Marcus had caught a movement out of the corner of his eye. It looked as though Rufus had pressed something small into Cassia's hands. And then brother and sister's heads were together, and they were whispering. Of what, he could not hear. But Cassia had glanced in his direction, and he guessed he was the subject of their conversation.

"What happened to your brother?" Marcus asked later.

"He's a seer. A shaman."

"Was he always this way?"

"No," she sighed. "He was always something of a dreamer. But things changed for him when I ran away. And since we rescued him... All those days he was a corpse, unable to move, unable to see? And then the bear... Rufus looked into the heart of death. The boundary between this and the spirit world has dissolved for him. He knows things. Sees things."

"Like my arrival?"

"Yes. And…" Her words dried up. She would not meet his eyes. What had Rufus seen that made her skin flush scarlet? There was a brief silence and then she said, "He tells me our fates are intertwined. That I must learn to trust you."

Marcus smiled. "For that, I'm grateful." He would have pursued the matter but Cassia seemed reluctant to discuss it. So he asked instead, "Does Rufus spend all his time at the hut?"

"No. Sometimes he is just a boy." She smiled sadly. Her eyes were bright, as though she was on the verge of tears. "Once in a while he is still my baby brother. He plays. He wrestles. He tells stories. But at other times? He moves far beyond me to somewhere I can't see. When the spirits whisper to him, he must sit in the dark and wait for the visions they send."

"And does he always see true?"

"It's hard to say. Visions come through smoke. The shapes, their meaning – they're not always clear."

It was too disturbing a subject. Marcus turned his attention to more practical matters. "So we are to take Flavia to her people. It will add to the length of our journey."

"We must do as he says." Cassia looked at him enquiringly. "Does that disturb you?"

"No, not at all." He sounded confident, but his guts churned. He wondered how the barbarians of Germania might react to having a Roman walking on their soil.

XI

The Fisher People dwelled on the coast, two days east of where Cassia's tribe had their home.

It seemed they were content to carry the travellers across the sea but it was a full week before they judged wind and weather right to make the crossing.

It was a week in which Marcus did nothing much more than let his beard grow. He knew how his father would see the place. Stinking nets, stinking hovels: a stinking barbarian village inhabited by stinking bog-dwellers. But he was flexing the muscles of his newfound freedom and was delighted to find how much he enjoyed the company of savages.

He passed the time engaging in contests with whoever challenged him. Boys. Girls. Old men. Women. Cassia.

Who could throw a stick furthest? Who could make a flat stone bounce off the surface of the water the most times?

Who could flick a knife into a target with the most accuracy?

Every time he faced Cassia in competition, she beat him. And in between, when they sat together on the shore and looked to sea, day by day she prised the truth in pieces from him.

He told her everything about himself until at last his soul lay at her feet naked and exposed. But hers? He had no idea how she felt now she saw him for what he was. He was on trial, he supposed. He must prove himself.

When the wind changed direction and the sea calmed, they finally set sail. The weather could not have been better, the Fisher Folk said. The sea goddess herself was easing their way.

When Marcus had first come to Britannia, the crossing had been a relatively short one at the place where the channel was at its narrowest. The coast of Gallia had disappeared from view at almost the same moment that the cliffs of Britannia poked their heads above the horizon. To go from the wilderness north of the wall to Germania was a longer and more hazardous journey.

The vessel was well constructed, but seemed such a small thing to be afloat on the vast sea. The mountains vanished and there was nothing but water. Marcus felt like an ant riding a leaf across an endless lake.

He lost all track of time. One day melted into another as he sat with Cassia and Flavia hunched in the stern, keeping out of the way of the ship's crew.

As they crashed from wave to wave, the years seemed to peel away from Flavia. She talked, telling them of her people, her childhood, her village. Of how she'd been taken by slavers and sold. She was more reticent about describing what had followed afterwards, whether out of consideration for his own feelings, or simply because she had no words with which to describe it, he didn't know.

She told stories too. Saxon myths, legends. Men and monsters. Warriors. Heroes. The tales poured out and he was gripped by them. He'd always been told that the barbarians of Germania had no culture, no art, no imagination. That Rome had offered them the benefits of civilization and they were too ignorant and too foolish to accept it. Yet now he was glimpsing a world that was as vibrant, as pulsing with life and energy as his own.

Occasionally Flavia would shift into the Saxon tongue and Cassia would reply. It seemed she'd not only learned to ride and throw a knife that winter. Holed up in the huts when the snow lay thick on the ground, Flavia had taught her enough of her own language for the two women to converse in words he couldn't understand. Sometimes they laughed, and he wondered if they were discussing him but Cassia's eyes gave nothing away.

The cold, grey expanse of water heaved and surged. The sail slapped and cracked in the wind. Marcus observed Cassia's every mood with the same intensity that the ship's captain studied sky and sea.

Extraordinary, he thought, that returning Cassia to her people had so transformed her. She'd not known the place existed until he'd taken her there. But somehow it was in her veins, in every muscle, every sinew of her body. As Flavia's homeland was in hers.

As for himself? He thought of the dry heat of Italia. The dappled shade of olive groves. Lemon trees in blossom. Azure seas. Home.

But thoughts of it were tainted now by the corruption at its roots.

Where did he belong? What land was his?

He'd made himself an outcast. In the darkness of the nights at sea he prayed he would be strong enough to endure it.

XII

One morning they woke to see that at last land was in sight.

Flavia was on her feet so swiftly that she set the boat rocking. She looked almost as though she would jump ship and swim the few miles distance to the shore. She fidgeted and squirmed like an impatient child the length of that morning. And when the boat's hull scraped against shingle, the old woman scrambled unaided over the side. On the beach she fell to her knees, gathering up handfuls of silt and grit, pressing them into her cheeks. And then she howled: a guttural, involuntary cry of long-suppressed suffering and its final release.

It twisted like a knife in Marcus's guts. Tears flowed down her face. But that smile of hers? He'd never seen anything like it. Only a statue could not have been moved.

He understood nothing of what was said to the coastal tribe they had landed among. The captain of the ship that had carried them across the sea was clearly well known. People came running from their huts to greet him. When he pulled Flavia forward as if to introduce her to them, there was an eruption of sound as her story became known. It was all noise and chatter and wailing cries. Marcus – who could understand not a single word – felt gravely disadvantaged. Despite the beard he'd grown, despite the native garments Cassia's chief had given him – he stood out so clearly as a Roman. Eyes darted sideways at him. All faces bore a look of deep and profound suspicion.

It was odd to be at the mercy of foreign people. To know they could hurt him. Kill him. Enslave him. He could not prevent it. Nothing, he thought, could be more unnerving than to have no control over his own fate.

Cassia seemed to guess some of what he was feeling. While Flavia continued to chatter in her peculiarly leaden-sounding tongue, Cassia said, "This is hard for you, I think? To be surrounded by strangers? And all speaking a language you don't understand."

"I can't deny it."

"Rest easy. Flavia is telling them how much she owes to you. You're perfectly safe."

There was a mocking edge to her voice. He replied sharply, "I'm on foreign soil through my own choice. I know perfectly well that Flavia never had that luxury."

Cassia didn't answer. But she did smile.

★ ★ ★

He couldn't fault them for their hospitality. These people gave freely of the best they had, plying the new arrivals with food and drink not just on that day but for several days afterwards. Though he itched to be moving on, it seemed they were not permitted to leave the village until the code of honour the savage enemies of Rome abided by had been satisfied.

When they were finally allowed to leave, they were given horses and a guide to take them to the next village, where they had to undergo the same ritual of cheerful welcome and noisy astonishment that Flavia had escaped from bondage.

It was days and days of travelling and stopping, talking and eating and drinking before they finally arrived in the place that Flavia had once called home.

And then…?

He had seen imperial processions in Rome. Horses, elephants, chariots driven through the streets. Displays of imperial grandeur. Of power and might. He'd seen chariot races and gladiatorial battles.

What happened when they entered Flavia's small village was not disciplined. There were no columns of soldiers marching in perfect unison. No salutes. No bread or circuses.

But by all the gods of heaven and earth, there was joy. So much he could taste it. He breathed it in as word spread from hut to hut that a lost daughter of the tribe had returned, as people came, incredulous, to touch Flavia, to embrace her.

There was feasting that night. The mead ran like a river and with each mouthful the declarations of love and gratitude grew louder and more passionate. The chief swore eternal kinship with Cassia and all her people. And Marcus – a Roman who had turned against his own kind – was hailed as the noblest and bravest of men. The mead had taken effect by then. Marcus felt a sense of comradeship with every soul in the hall. The women's tears flowed as freely as the drink. Tales were told. Heroic. Sentimental. Songs were sung.

And when the tribe's musicians were done, they turned to him.

"They want a song from you," Cassia told him. "A song from Rome."

Reluctant though he was, there was no escaping it. He stood. Cleared his throat. But then found his mind had emptied. He could think of nothing at all. No tune, no words, nothing. He reached into the recesses of his mind and plucked out only one: the song Hera, Phoebe's mother, had sung to them both when they were very small. He'd not heard it since she'd been sold.

The crowd were watching him. Cassia's face was full of encouragement. She was looking kind. Soft. Wonderful. He could make a home in those eyes. If she would be his country, he wouldn't need another. He would tell her that.

Just as soon as he'd got this song out of the way.

He began. A soft, lilting tune. It brought back a time of innocence. Of sweet, straightforward friendship. A time when his only love and loyalty were for his sister, not his father. Not his country. Not his Emperor.

He sang.

And was surprised to find that, at the song's close, his cheeks were wet with tears.

XIII

Mead made fools of all men, he thought when he woke the next morning. It was late and his head pounded, but he was determined, nonetheless, that he and Cassia would be out of this place and on their way as soon as horses could be made ready.

But when he ventured out of the roundhouse and into the bright sunshine, a war seemed to have broken out. There were two warriors wrestling, cheered on by a circle of onlookers. Not far from them two more men were going at each other with great sticks. In the distance a group of women on horseback were galloping at full pelt across the valley as if in flight from some deadly attacker, and yet no one was in pursuit as far as he could see.

It took him a few moments to realize that this was no enemy attack. Briefly he then wondered if all the sentiment and good humour of the night before had turned into aggression. Had they started fighting among themselves?

No ... there seemed no petulance in it. There was more an air of honest competition. Of excitement. Gods! Were these part of the celebrations of Flavia's homecoming? Were the tribe indulging in their own form of the Games?

By the time he finally caught sight of Cassia, he'd reached the far end of the village. There were a few people standing near the hut walls on the outskirts but she was alone with a sword in her hand. A few feet away from her, a warrior – twice as large and twice as wide as Cassia – threw down his own weapon and gave her a low bow.

Cassia turned at that moment, a triumphant smile on her face, and saw him.

"Marcus! Are you awake at last? Come. I'll fight you next."

His mind was working slowly. The tip of Cassia's blade was dripping scarlet – with blood, he thought – but then he saw it was too thick, too dark for that. Dye then. And her sword sheathed in cloth to blunt it, as was the weapon the warrior she'd apparently beaten now thrust into his hands.

To fight a woman was alien to him. Unnatural. But bets were already being made, coins were changing hands. He could hardly withdraw without looking like a coward. The intention seemed to be to mark, not wound each other. Ah well. He would go easy on her.

Raising his sword, he swung half-heartedly. Cassia dodged. His swaddled blade cut nothing but air. She laughed aloud and the sound provoked him.

He'd prove himself! The moment their blades met, his sheer power would overwhelm her.

But Cassia made no attempt to strike him. Her own sword was in her hand untried, unused. He came at her again. She danced out of the way. She was so light on her feet! There was laughter from the crowd and it annoyed him still further.

Marcus didn't think she had a plan. He assumed she was merely reacting to whatever move he tried against her. He admired her agility – albeit reluctantly – but she couldn't keep this up. Sooner or later she'd be exhausted. He'd beat her then: it was inevitable.

His wits were too addled for him to realize that each time he swung at her, each time she evaded his blow, she moved a little further to the left. Once, twice, three times more. It was so small a move he hadn't noticed that she was steering him. Moving him into position. Slowly, slowly, one hand's breadth at a time, she was turning him towards the east.

She dodged again, evading the swinging sword and then moving to the left. He was ready to strike, but at that precise moment the sun broke over the roof of the roundhouse. Dazzling bright light hit him full in the face.

And now, only now, did she use her own weapon, slicing it down across his chest. Had it not been blunted she might have killed him. Instead she left a streak of red dye across ribs and belly.

There was a great roar – a cheer of approval – and the contest was at an end. While Cassia accepted the congratulations heaped on her, Marcus stood with his mouth hanging open.

He was astounded. It seemed Cassia had not simply learned a foreign tongue in the dark winter months. She had learned to handle a sword too. How much more could she do that he didn't yet know about?

Strange! Fate was turning her into the very thing he'd once imagined her to be. A thing he'd feared and despised. In the months of his absence Cassia had become a warrior queen.

And he was delighted by it.

The night before they left Flavia's village, there was more feasting. The laughter was as long and loud as it had been on the night they first arrived.

But Marcus was subdued and preoccupied. Phoebe filled his head. He'd had all winter to dream of her rescue. But now the reality was nearer, he was plagued by self-doubt.

There was something odd too, between Flavia and Cassia. He'd seen them whispering earlier that day, heads close together. Cassia had pressed something small into the old woman's hands and he had the impression that whatever Rufus had given his sister had now been passed on. Whatever it was had made both women look in his direction.

He glanced over to where Cassia was now sitting beside the chief, talking with him quietly. A dog lay at their feet, snoring. The flies that had been circling its head, that it had been snapping at with only occasional success, had come to land and were now crawling over its hide.

The chief nodded his head towards Marcus and said something in his own tongue.

Cassia looked up, looked away and replied in words he couldn't understand. The two conversed a while longer. And then Cassia poked the dog with her toe. It roused itself. Stood shaking, sending the flies buzzing through the smoke-filled air. It snapped at them again, catching one and knocking another into the fire. The chief grasped Cassia's arm in his vast hand.

Later, Marcus asked Cassia what had been said.

"He asked if I liked you."

"And what did you reply?"

"That I did. I do. Then he asked if I trusted you." She smiled.

"And?"

"I said not entirely. You are a Roman, after all."

"Ha! What else did he say?"

"He said Romans are barbarians. He asked me why you couldn't stay in your homes. Why wasn't your own country big enough for you? He asked me what made you hack and kill and force Mother Earth herself to submit to your will."

"And what did you say?"

"I said I had no idea. But that it was the same in Britannia as in Germania."

"Anything else?"

"He asked if Britannia was vanquished. I told him she simply slept."

"Like the dog?"

"Yes. And if roused … I said she might shake the Romans off, as easily as flies."

"What reply did he make?"

Her eyes were blazing, but her voice was cold. Thoughtful. Calculating. The skin along the length of his arms prickled into bumps as she said, "He told me that if my country were to wake, she would only have to call. There are plenty of warriors who would come to her aid."

XIV

They were well provisioned. Two ponies. Packs. A guide to take them across the country.

They said a tender farewell to Flavia, promising that – even though it would add weeks to their journey – they would return this way with Phoebe if all went according to plan. If it did not ... well ... it was best not to speak of what might happen if they failed. Best not to even think of it lest they tempt the Fates to intervene.

They rode for some days, then bartered passage on a small vessel that took them along a river where vineyards stretched across the hills. From there they rode on the cart of a trader who was travelling to the town where he sold his wares.

There was no wall, but lines of ditches and defences stretched in both directions. Forts were dotted along it like beads on a necklace, keeping the Romans in and the savages out. Yet their cargo of wine was not only legitimate, but very welcome. The Empire's thirst was infinite and the cart was only cursorily inspected, then let through the gate into the town beyond, and Cassia and Marcus along with it.

Once they were on the Empire's territory, they parted company with the trader. When he was out of sight, Marcus changed his clothes, shaved his beard, and became a Roman again so they could pass through Gallia without attracting undue attention.

He'd brought a change of clothes for Cassia too.

"Am I to be your slave again?" she asked.

"No." He pulled a garment from his pack. "This time you're my wife."

"Indeed?"

"Yes. We're newlyweds."

Cassia raised an eyebrow and said, "A love match, I hope? I don't want to have been traded like a sack of flour."

"A love match? Why not? No one will question it if we choose to keep ourselves to ourselves."

"What are you suggesting?"

"Simply that there'll be no need to be sociable with strangers. We can avoid awkward questions."

"They'll still be asked," Cassia said. "We should have a story prepared. Why are we travelling? We must have some reason."

"I suppose so. In search of work?"

"Perhaps we plan to try our chances in Rome?"

They began to walk south, embellishing their tale as they went along, inventing names for themselves, and a past history.

"Where did we meet?" asked Cassia.

"At market. Our eyes met across the fish stall."

"Oh, please! Think of the stench!"

"Where then?"

"Somewhere with more romance than a crowded market place! By a mountain stream perhaps. Or a clear lake."

"Perhaps I rescued you from drowning?" Marcus suggested.

"I'd be more likely to have rescued you. Especially if you'd been drinking too much."

"Eurgh! Mead! Beer! Such filthy stuff!"

With Flavia and her people behind them, and with Rome such a very long way ahead, Marcus was overtaken by a glorious lightness of heart. Suddenly he felt like a child released early from his lessons. They were alone. Cassia was at his side.

He smiled at her as they walked. He laughed. Teased her. And she gave as good as she got. The innkeeper who rented them a room that night had no difficulty at all in believing them to be newly married.

There was but a single bathhouse in the town they'd stopped in. It seemed that women were allowed there only for the

288

hour after dawn. The rest of the time it was given over to the men's use.

After they'd eaten, Marcus declared that he was tired of reeking like a savage and would go and bathe.

She laid a hand on his chest. The tips of her fingers were on his skin, her palm warm through the cloth of his tunic. "Marcus…" she said softly. "The oil. Not juniper. If you please."

"You don't like it?"

"No."

"Very well."

He thought of her while he bathed. There seemed some kind of promise in that gesture. That request.

She was in bed by the time he got back. He entered the room nervous as a virgin bride.

A lamp burned on the table beside her. He'd been prepared to wrap himself in his cloak and sleep on the floor if necessary, but she looked at him. Smiled. Pulled aside the blanket.

And Marcus discovered that everything he'd said about Cassia when he'd sat with Tertius and wept into his wine, and everything he'd thought about her in the warmth of the mead-soaked barbarian hall was true.

With Cassia, he'd found his home.

XV

As they journeyed south, the landscape changed. The dark forests of Germania gave way to something sparser. Drier. The heat grew more intense day by day. To Cassia, it was strange and unfamiliar but to Marcus, the smell of olive and vine brought unwelcome memories.

One morning, when they lay late in bed, Cassia said, "Tell me the plan. When we reach Rome, will I still be your wife?"

"No. A slave again, I'm afraid."

"And you? Who will you be?"

She'd hit on the thing he'd almost worn his brain out puzzling over during the winter.

"I've thought long and hard about that. I know that if – *when* – Phoebe's brought out, we'll need somewhere to lie low for a few days until the fuss has died down. But Rome's such a public place – life is lived on the streets.

Everyone knows everyone else's business. We need to rent a quiet villa. And we need to prevent the neighbours from coming calling."

"How do you propose to do that?"

"You showed me last year how little people look at those who are grieving. I thought I'd be a young husband. A man who's just lost his wife — lost her in childbirth, perhaps? And the baby too."

"Yes," said Cassia grimly. "That will be enough to keep the curious away."

And so, in an olive grove not far from the southern coast of Gallia, Cassia became a boy again. Her hair had grown almost to her shoulders over the winter. As he cut it for the second time, Marcus experienced a sorrow for its loss that he'd not felt before. So many miles they'd travelled, side by side, sharing a room, sharing a bed. He wound tresses of her hair around his fingers. He loved to see it flaming red in the sunshine, dark chestnut in the rain. To feel it against his skin in the dark of the night. He pulled each strand taut before he took his knife to it. And then he dyed it with a concoction he'd acquired from a Gallic pharmacist. It seemed like an offence against nature. But there was no other way. A woman as striking as Cassia could not wander about in Rome alone: she would not be able to walk five paces before some thug tried to drag her into a hidden alleyway.

★ ★ ★

After another day's walking, they reached the coast. Here Marcus donned the mantle of grief that would carry them into Rome and, he hoped, safely away from it. He would not shave again. Sorrow would explain both his beard and his unkempt state, his inability to converse pleasantly with other travellers.

In leaden tones he enquired at the docks about vessels that would carry them to Ostia. As luck would have it, there was a merchant vessel departing with the high tide. It was just then being loaded with the last of its cargo. Stepping aboard, they were confined to a tiny corner of the deck along with half a dozen other travellers but the price was low enough to justify the discomfort.

The wind was against them. A long and tedious voyage followed, at the end of which Marcus Aurelius Aquila arrived in Italia, the land of his forebears, feeling so different to the young man who'd left two years before he was certain that his own father wouldn't have recognized him.

XVI

They took a house in a suburban district at the far edge of the city between the aqueduct and the eastern gate. Using the money he'd borrowed in Londinium on the strength of his father's name, Marcus paid a month's rent in advance. He did not even attempt to barter and the landlord – delighted to have a tenant so free with his coins – escorted them through the streets to both show them the way and open the place up. He was talkative and inclined to gossip but Marcus was unresponsive. When the man paused for breath, Cassia found an opportunity to mutter that her master was a grieving widower.

"He's not himself. His wife died only five days ago. Their infant son along with her." Word of Marcus's sorry condition travelled faster than they could walk. By the time they neared the street in which the villa lay, neighbours were calling their children in from their street games and adults were turning their heads aside.

The landlord stayed only long enough to unlock the gate and show them the principal rooms.

"I can arrange for slaves, should you need them," he said.

"No … no. My lad here will serve."

"A cook, perhaps?"

"No! I don't want strangers!"

"Very well. I'll leave you in peace but if you change your mind, send your boy to me. I can arrange for anything, anything at all. I'll give you the very best prices. I'm honest, you see? Unlike some I could mention."

A small cry escaped Marcus's throat and his face contorted as if he was about to start weeping.

Alarmed, the landlord hastily departed.

When the door was safely barred behind him, Marcus threw Cassia a brief smile.

"And so … we have a house." He sat down on a stool. "To business. We've arrived in Rome. All we need to do now is work out how and when we will leave."

"And who with," said Cassia. "Let's hope Phoebe doesn't react the way my brother did. We can't take her away by force."

"True. First I need to find her. I'll need to get her entirely alone. It will be hard: my father keeps her close to him."

"Can't we get word to her through the other slaves?"

"No. I don't want any of them knowing I am here. I wouldn't trust them to keep it quiet. Don't look that way, Cassia! I don't mean they're dishonest in themselves. You don't know my father. The very walls have eyes and ears in his house. He's a powerful man. There are too many people who'd try to buy his favour by betraying her. By betraying us. I must get into the house myself, unnoticed."

"Not easy!"

"No ... but again I've learned from you. The best place to hide is in full view. My father is fond of laying on lavish entertainments. He likes to display his wealth: his mighty power and influence. That will be the way to get in."

"And if he recognizes you?"

"He won't. I can pass as a masked entertainer. Or a musician, perhaps; a supplier of victuals. There are a thousand and one ways to hide. He's sure to be throwing some kind of grand festivity during the next few weeks. I need to find out what. Listening to the talk in the streets will tell me that, and yet..." He felt suddenly worried. "I need to move freely about the city. Can I do that in this disguise? Wouldn't a grieving widower sit in the dark and weep?"

"No," said Cassia. "Grief itches. It gives no peace. You're a man deranged with sorrow: you're more likely to walk the streets from sunrise to sunset than keep still."

He looked at her, pity in his eyes. "You've felt sorrow like this?"

"Yes. For my mother. But I've seen it in other people too. If you haunt Rome like a restless spirit, no one will question it."

XVII

After a week of walking in the city, lingering in taverns, wallowing in the public baths, Marcus gleaned the information he needed. His father did indeed have a lavish feast laid on the next week. Moreover it was to be for prominent traders from all over the Empire.

"He'll know very few of them well. It will be an easy crowd to lose myself in."

It did not take much more eavesdropping for Marcus to discover the name of a prominent merchant from Palmyra who had been invited: a man who was in Rome seeking new business opportunities for himself and his family. A man whose hair was long and plaited, who wore a beard as Marcus himself now did.

"I'll pass as one of his party," he told Cassia.

"But he'll know you for a stranger, won't he?"

"We'll watch from the corner until he goes in. I can

appear a few moments later – say that I was delayed. If I wear the same style of dress, trim my beard like his, plait my hair… Yes, I believe I can talk my way past the doorkeepers. And you'll come with me. A man like that always has a cup-bearer at his side."

A week later Marcus entered the public baths as a grieving widower. He emerged as a Palmyrene merchant: a wealthy man, in silken robes and finely tooled sandals, dripping with jewellery, his skin oiled, his hair plaited and beaded in the fashion he'd asked the barber to copy from the original.

Cassia likewise was transformed from slave of all work to cup-bearer, whose only task now was to be at her master's elbow.

They waited outside in the shadows.

Seeing the place he'd been born and raised in had an unnerving effect on Marcus. High walls concealed a perfect square of grounds from the plebeians' curious eyes. It was his father's private kingdom, the villa the crowning glory of splendid, ornamental gardens.

Marcus imagined walking through the gates. The approach to the house. The pool running the length of it, fountains spilling from the walls either side. Two avenues of cypress and palm trees. Steps leading to the entrance.

It was all designed to intimidate as much as to impress. To scream wealth and power and influence.

And inside the house itself: every pillar, every slab,

every tile of every mosaic was painfully familiar to him. He could see it all in his mind's eye. He could find his way blindfold. Marcus was satisfied that he and Cassia had planned this scheme in meticulous detail.

But there was one unknown factor, one thing that they could not predict or arrange.

Phoebe. He hadn't spoken to her for ten years. He knew nothing about her now. Would she come away? Or was she too broken to even consider it?

He stood beside his cup-bearer, silently observing the arriving guests, itching to get started but able to do nothing. He couldn't even talk to Cassia without attracting attention.

When the party from Palmyra arrived, resplendent in their finery, he felt a surge of gratitude.

As soon as the last of them had been admitted, Marcus hurried across the street, Cassia at his heels. He gave every appearance of having been momentarily delayed. He cursed his slave, complaining of a broken sandal strap, blaming the boy for not noticing it before. And then he was calling out a name – a fictitious one that sounded gloriously foreign to Roman ears. He appeared to be looking for his companions, rushing to catch up with them.

It worked. With scarcely a glance at either him or Cassia, the gatekeepers stood aside to let them enter.

Now keeping a very careful distance from the Palmyrans, he followed them through the grounds towards the villa. Up the marble steps. Between the columns to where guests were crowding into the vast atrium.

At its heart his father lay on a couch, graciously taking compliments from those who sought his favour.

Keeping his back to his parent, Marcus mingled with the other guests.

He'd hoped Phoebe would be one of the slaves who waited at the feast but he didn't see her there.

The original plan had been for him to point his sister out to Cassia. For Cassia to find an opportunity of getting her alone. Cassia, and only Cassia, could be trusted to pass word to his sister telling her where and when they would wait. And now the whole scheme had fallen at the first obstacle!

Well then, he'd have to follow the second scenario they'd imagined and go looking for her himself. It wasn't like he didn't know the layout of the place.

And if he was found?

It was a riskier strategy. But a merchant, a stranger in the city, one not familiar with the customs of Rome? If anyone were to discover him lost and wandering through the villa's private rooms, it could be explained away.

Briefly Cassia's eyes rested on him. She had work of her own to do that night. She'd slip away shortly on the pretext of refilling his cup. After that she'd leave the villa and its grounds.

She was readying herself to do so when the worst of all possible things occurred: Marcus was recognized.

The Fool. Felix. A hunchback his father had purchased years before Marcus was even born. An oddity, a freak. Bought to amuse guests with his deformity. A man who'd been jeered at. Tormented. Scorned every day of his life. Who'd never been anything other than kind to Marcus.

Felix was dressed in a brightly coloured tunic, bells dangling from his belt that tinkled as he moved so no one could miss the spectacle of him shuffling between them.

Marcus caught sight of him at the edge of his vision and turned aside. The one part of him he couldn't disguise was his eyes and they'd give too much away.

So the little man only saw Marcus from the back, but something in the outline of his master's son was too familiar to go unremarked.

Slave though he was, the familiar name escaped him: "Marcus?"

Most people will turn when they hear their own name being said aloud, whether the speaker intends to catch their attention or not. Amid a hubbub of conversation the ear catches it like a fish on a hook. But Marcus was practised enough to not blink or twitch or turn. He made no sign at all that the name meant anything to him. Any onlooker would have assumed the hunchback was simply muttering to himself.

It was Cassia who was startled. Cassia who dropped the cup she was holding. It hit the floor, spilling of red wine over her master's robes.

He reacted immediately. At once a stream of foreign words erupted from his mouth. He hardly knew whether they were those of a real language or whether it was something he'd made up on the spur of the moment. The tone of his invective was convincing enough, either way.

His hand was up. He had to strike her. But there was a moment's delay. A moment's stillness. Their eyes connected and he hesitated.

He must do it! Not to do so would be fatal. Her own expression urged him: come on. Do it. Do it now. Do it, or we're both lost.

And so he hit her. Hit her as a master would hit a clumsy slave. A smack across the face with the flat of his hand. A smack so hard that her teeth clamped on her tongue and she fell backwards onto the floor. And when she was down? A kick to the belly.

He was careful. It was for show, the sole of his foot connecting more with the floor than with her flesh, making a loud slapping sound, jarring his nerves from foot to knee.

She'd known it was coming. They both knew the blow had to fall.

But it took all of his willpower for Marcus not to drop to his knees and beg her forgiveness.

Felix had turned away. He was muttering to himself, "Not him. Not him. Old fool. What's wrong with your eyes? Just another bloody foreigner."

The danger had passed. For now. Cassia got to her feet. Marcus raised his hand as if he'd strike her again. So she cringed and cowered as any slave would. Picking up his cup, she went creeping off like a beaten dog as if to look for more wine.

And then she slipped from the villa, and disappeared into the night.

XVIII

The streets of Rome were thick with manure. Each night carts were driven in to clear them and, earlier that day, Marcus and Cassia had been to find one of the shit collectors to make a modest proposal.

They had not spoken to the first man they'd passed, nor the second. The first seemed too honest to be bribed, the second too watchful. The third, however, proved ideal.

Sitting in the tavern, loudly setting the world to rights, from across the street they judged him to be an indolent man with a grudge against the world. Moreover, when they casually strolled past, they could see his cart was ill-kept. Rotten planking was clearly visible in one corner and that would serve their purpose well.

They had split up then. Marcus had walked the block and then come from the opposite direction. He sat alone, the grieving widower, appearing uninterested in what was happening at the next table. It was Cassia who approached the shit collector, buying him a drink, sitting beside him and saying quietly, "I wish to hire your cart for tonight, man."

He'd turned and looked at her with suspicion. "Why?"

"For a joke."

"What's so funny?"

"Nothing. Not for the likes of me. But my master thinks himself a great wit." She took a long draught from her own drink and then spoke the full name of Marcus's father. "Primus Aurelius Aquila. Have you heard of him?"

The shit collector spat on the ground. "Arsehole, from what I hear."

"My master – who must remain nameless – would agree. Aquila is his rival in business. And in politics."

"What does a man like that want with my cart?"

"Not the cart. The contents."

"Oh?"

"Yesterday, Aquila abused my master. Right there in front of the Emperor! Said excrement was pouring from my master's mouth."

"He said the bastard talks shit?"

"Yes."

"Don't they all?"

"Between you and me? Yes. But now my master wants to pay him back in kind. He wants a load to be dumped on Aquila's front doorstep."

"Haven't they got better things to do?"

"Apparently not. He'll pay you well for this."

"Go on then. What am I to do?"

"You bring your cart. Leave it in the side street – the one nearest to the river. You need have nothing more to do with it. But you're to tell nobody. I'll empty its load when the time's right. And I'll bring the cart back to you in the morning."

"I want the money now."

"You'll have the money when the cart is delivered – with a full load, mind. Not before."

And now Cassia would be waiting in the street for the cart to come.

Inside the atrium of his family home and praying that he wouldn't encounter Felix again, Marcus began weaving through the crowds. He staggered just a little, giving the impression that he was drunk, but trying hard to appear sober. That he was keen to get through the atrium and into the gardens on the other side so he could breathe fresh air and steady himself.

But once he was in the shadows, he took a different route. Out of sight of guests and slaves he took off the sandals that slapped so hard and noisily on the marble floors and then darted sideways. Ascended the stairs. Along the corridor. Through one room. Then another. Towards his father's bedchamber.

He'd drunk nothing at all that evening, and yet the floor seemed unsteady under his feet. Shadows loomed, the walls closed in. It had the strange, disproportionate feel of his dreams.

The noise of the party repelled him. Men shouting. Girls screaming. Music. His father's guests, increasingly intoxicated, increasingly lecherous.

He paused for a moment. From the end of the corridor he could just see over the wall and down into the street. The muck cart had arrived. The shadowy form of Cassia was on it, working frantically, shovelling shit from one side to the other. Ramming the spade's iron blade between the rotten boards, making a breathing hole.

He must find his sister. And swiftly.

He hadn't entered his father's room since the incident with Phoebe. After that, it had been off limits. He felt a terrible sense of apprehension when, heart thudding, he pushed the door open and walked inside.

And oh gods! There was a girl in there. Not kneeling, but sitting on the bed, her arms around her chest, her head bowed. She did not look up. Merely curled in on herself as if by not looking she could wish herself away from here.

He knew at once it was not Phoebe. She had yellow hair and this girl's was black. She had obviously been put here to pleasure his father when the guests had left. Or perhaps she would be brought out earlier than that, for their entertainment.

He could do nothing for her. He had to force himself to go back out, to shut the door. The image of that helpless girl seared itself to the backs of his eyes. He had to forget it. He couldn't help them all! Come on, Marcus. Find Phoebe. Where is she? Suppose his father had tired of her? Suppose she'd been sold? Suppose this whole venture was too late?

Panic propelled his feet, but he didn't lose any of his caution. He looked into room after room and didn't find her.

The slave quarters, then?

Back through the myriad chambers, ducking into the shadows each time he thought he heard a slave's footsteps. Back down the steps. Through the atrium. Out into the gardens. Around the side of the villa. To the slave dormitories by the rear wall.

They were empty. Deserted. Every slave was occupied attending to the party guests.

Every slave but one.

Phoebe was there, alone in a corner. Curled under a blanket on the floor, a tallow lamp smoking by her side. Threads of her yellow hair caught the light. Glimmers of gold in the darkness.

She lay still. Asleep, he presumed. He approached slowly. Cautiously. He didn't want her to cry out in surprise.

He crouched down; spoke her name.

She was awake, but looked at him with no recognition. He was a stranger to her and yet she showed no fear. Only resignation. Dead eyes stared into his.

"It's me. Marcus."

A little life seemed to stir in her then. Her brow furrowed. "Marcus?" she repeated.

"Yes."

She looked dazed, as though not sure if he was real or part of a dream.

"I've come for you," he said.

A look of infinite weariness passed across her face. "He wants me? Now?"

"No! I do."

She recoiled. "You?"

Gods! She thought he was going to do to her what his father had. "No!" he exclaimed. "Not that. Never that."

"What...?"

"Run away. I know a place. Somewhere safe. He'll not find you."

She shook her head. "There is nowhere." She was looking at him as if he was simply spinning one of the fanciful stories he'd told as a boy.

"I have been there. I have seen it with my own eyes. The place exists and I can take you there."

"Where?"

"The far north of Britannia. Beyond the Empire's border. It will take us a long time to get there. But when we reach it ... you'll be free, Phoebe."

"Free?" Her mind seemed to wrestle with the concept.

"Free. I swear it. Will you come? Please…"

An awful silence. Drawn out. Thinner and thinner, until it finally snapped with her softly whispered "Yes."

"Quickly then."

He was expecting her to leap to her feet. But she moved like an old woman, sitting up slowly and with such difficulty she grunted with the effort. When she pulled off the blanket, he saw that she was grotesquely bloated around the middle.

Pregnant. Ready to drop. Hades! He'd never considered that possibility.

As Phoebe struggled to get up, he was startled to see a small face staring at him through the gloom. One so like his own he wondered if he was imagining things.

And then he realized it was a child. No more than one or two years old, he guessed. She must have been asleep at Phoebe's back. When her mother stood, she whimpered.

"Ssssh!" Phoebe put a finger to her lips.

The girl raised her arms, asking to be picked up, but with her huge belly Phoebe couldn't manage it.

"This is Marcus," Phoebe whispered. "He'll carry you, Julia."

A child too? That complicated matters.

But there was no time to debate. They needed to be on their way. He lifted the girl, and with Phoebe waddling awkwardly beside him they left the slave quarters.

Close behind them, in the far corner of the grounds

310

there was a door from the garden to the street. A great heavy thing of oak and iron, bolted from the inside so that brigands and thieves couldn't pass through. It had a lock too, the key kept hidden among his father's possessions, but Marcus knew from his childhood it was a simple thing, easy to trigger with a bent nail.

He set the child down on the path. His hands were shaking as he unfastened the gate. The bolts squeaked in protest, but the party was so noisy it wouldn't be heard from the house. *Keep calm*, he urged himself. *Breathe*. He took the bent nail and tried to force the lock. As a boy he'd only ever tried it in daylight, with Phoebe standing guard. Then, it had seemed easy. Now, in the dark, he couldn't see what he was doing. He dropped the nail. Had to scrabble around for it on the ground. Found it. Tried again. Sweat was beading on his forehead, running into his eyes.

And then he felt a click as the lock yielded.

They were through the door. And there – a few paces away – was Cassia and the cart. Without a word, Marcus lifted the child onto the back of it. Helped Phoebe climb in. Cassia made no comment to him either about the child or Phoebe's swollen belly. She simply told them, "Lie down. There. Face to the floor. See the hole? Breathe through that. Keep still."

The moment Phoebe and the child were lying down she threw a length of cloth over them and began to cover it with shit so they'd not be seen.

Marcus didn't move until she barked at him. "Get back through. Bolt the gate."

He did as she ordered him. Bolting. Locking. Leaving the gate and slipping back through the gardens and into the party.

That was that, he thought. It was out of his hands now.

But when he reached the house, it seemed the party from Palmyra were readying themselves to go home. He fell in with them as they left and they – already so far gone on drink and debauchery that they barely recognized each other – paid him no heed. They wound their way along the straight avenue of cypresses, staggered through the gates into the street and down the hill.

Ahead of them, Cassia had the cart underway. The oxen were moving, but each time she came to a pile of dung on the street she made them pause so she could scrape it up with the shovel and add it to her load.

Marcus and the Palmyrene merchants were almost level with it when there was a commotion from behind. A cry. A woman's call. Then a man's. Slaves were shouting, one to another.

And then another voice cut through them all. His father's, hot with anger.

"Phoebe! Phoebe!"

Yells. Commands. Feet, running through the gardens and into the street. Slaves, with torches held high, scurrying in different directions.

Though fear slid along his spine, Marcus paused, surveying the scene with the mild curiosity of a bystander, no more.

Cassia too looked back down along the road. Before long she was approached by one of the slaves who'd been sent in pursuit of the fugitive. "Did anyone pass this way?"

Cassia shrugged, as if utterly indifferent. "This is Rome, man," she said.

"So?"

"People passing all the time."

"A runaway slave? A woman. Pregnant. Child with her."

"Maybe…" she said slowly. "What's it worth?"

There was a moment of scrutiny while he assessed whether she had information or was simply trying her luck. He decided she was a chancer. Turned away. Looked at the drunken merchants and realized they weren't even worth asking.

Cassia shrugged. The cart went on its way, unexamined and undisturbed.

The men from Palmyra also walked on, and Marcus went with them. At the end of the street they went one way, and Cassia with her cart and hidden cargo went the other.

It was a warm night. As it trundled out of sight, Cassia walking beside, shovelling piles of muck as she went, Marcus was suddenly seized with fear that the heat of the night and the stench might suffocate Phoebe and her daughter.

Yet he could do nothing but stroll through the streets, a drunken reveller on his way home to bed. He parted company with the merchants at the bottom of the hill and returned swiftly and quietly to the villa, where he waited for the cart's arrival.

It seemed an age before the sound of iron-clad wheels on stone heralded Cassia's approach.

Nothing was said that could be overheard by a watchful neighbour. No torches were lit, no lamps carried. The cart was brought to a halt, and though the oxen huffed and blew, there was no other sound.

In silence Cassia and Marcus scraped aside the muck. When they pulled back the cloth, there was a dreadful moment in which Marcus feared they had indeed killed his sister. Phoebe lay horribly still. But then there was a soft cough. A pained, indrawn breath. She was weakened, dizzied, gasping for fresh air, but alive, thank the gods!

It was dark as pitch. Marcus bent down to pull Phoebe up, then lifted Julia from the floor. The child was limp, as if the stench had made her faint. Slinging her over his shoulder like a sack of grain, he hoped that was all it was. That she'd revive given time and fresh air. Cassia had Phoebe's arm and was helping her down from the cart. As soon as her feet hit the ground, Marcus steered his sister into the villa.

It was Cassia's job to drive on then, to pass through

the city gates and empty the load onto a heap at the edge of the farmland that skirted the city walls. From there, to drive it back to the man she had borrowed it from. It was a task that Marcus knew would take her all that remained of the night.

XIX

A silence descended when the door of the villa was bolted behind them.

Terrible awkwardness coupled with crushing fear. The seriousness of what he'd done hit Marcus like a hammer to the head.

Until now the reckless excitement of planning the scheme with Cassia had fuelled him. The fire had burned so bright!

But now it had died, leaving cold ash – and the wreckage of the woman who had once been his dear sister.

Pregnant.

Mother to a small child.

It drummed inside his head.

Pregnant.

Mother to a small child.

Julia.

His niece.

And … also … his younger sister.

His father. Getting children on his daughter.

There weren't enough curse words in the world to cover that.

Phoebe had been a stranger to him these last ten years and now that dark gulf seemed to yawn between them. He had not the faintest idea of how to cross it.

"Sorry," he wanted to say.

But sorry for what?

It was more than what his father had done. More than his own failings. It was the way men were. It was the Empire. The gods. It was all so very wrong. "Sorry" didn't begin to cover it.

So he said nothing. And neither did she.

Instead he busied himself with making her comfortable. Brought her water to wash with. Fresh clothes. Tore his cloak in half and fashioned a makeshift tunic for Julia. Burned the slave garments they'd both been wearing. Brought them food. When they'd eaten a mouthful or two, he pointed to the bed where the dazed, dead-eyed pair could sleep for what was left of the night. At her mother's bidding, Julia curled into a ball on the mattress. Only then did Phoebe at last break the silence.

"That was no muck-shoveller," she said. "Who's helping you?"

Tears pricked the back of Marcus's eyes. Phoebe had

always known what to say; what question to ask to draw a story from him. With unswerving instinct she'd hit upon the one thing they could speak of freely. It was easy to talk of Cassia and the land of the Wolf People. Far, far easier to describe what lay ahead of them than discuss what lay behind. He sat beside his sister on the bed while Julia slept. Told her most of Cassia's tale. And a little of his own.

"I am so ashamed," he said. "These last ten years … what I have done … what I've thought…"

"Hush. We both did what we were compelled to do. There was no choice for either of us until now."

A few words and she had absolved him. He was more grateful than he could express. He said only, "We have a long journey ahead. I'll leave you to rest."

But before he could stand, Phoebe grabbed his arm. She was trembling suddenly and a grim, deadly earnestness contorted her face. "If we don't get there … if we get caught—" she pointed at her sleeping daughter— "will you kill her?"

Marcus didn't answer.

Phoebe persisted. "I took my mother's place. She'll not take mine. She'd be better dead. I'd have strangled her when she was born if I'd had the courage. But I couldn't do it."

Marcus exhaled, a long hiss of air between his teeth.

"You carry a knife," she said. "A knife is quick. Kill her first. Then me. We can't go back." Phoebe's eyes burned into him. "Swear you'll do it. Promise."

How could he refuse? Though his heart felt like a stone in his chest, Marcus took his sister's hands in his and swore that if the time came, if they were caught and could not escape, then yes, he would kill them both.

While Phoebe and her daughter slept, Marcus sat and waited for Cassia's return.

Shortly before sunrise, stinking and sweating, she was back. He had never been more delighted to see her. As he approached, arms wide, she gestured to her shit-covered clothes. "Don't! Look at me! I need to get clean. I must be turning Roman. I've never been more ready to bathe!"

He ignored her. He needed to feel her warmth. Breathe in her scent along with the stink of manure. Reassure himself that this was real.

He held her until her muffled protests finally reached his brain.

"Let me go. You'll break my ribs."

And then he fetched her water and a cloth. While she washed, they talked about what they were going to do next.

They'd paid a month's rent in advance but had intended to stay for no longer than it took to find Phoebe, get her safely out of Rome and themselves back on the road to Britannia.

But it was plain to both of them that Phoebe's pregnancy was in its final stages.

"Her belly makes her so conspicuous!" he said.

"There'll be notices painted on walls all over Rome. He's bound to offer a reward. Every pregnant woman will be under suspicion."

"You think we should wait until the baby comes? Women usually scream when they give birth, Marcus. How will we explain that to the neighbours?"

"I don't know. But after the baby comes it would be easier to disguise her."

"And her daughter?"

"She'd fit into a pannier. A basket, almost."

"But will she stay still? She's very young. And what about the baby? No one can ask a newborn to keep quiet."

"But it could be drugged."

"Drugged?" Cassia looked aghast.

"Only until we're clear of Rome, no longer than that."

"With what?"

"Opium. A drop on the tongue. Enough to keep it asleep while we get away."

"And endanger its life?"

"No more than being caught would," he said. "She has made me swear to kill them both if that happens."

Cassia was quiet for a while. "Yes," she said at last. "There are worse things than death. For a woman, certainly." Another silence fell between them, but then she asked, "Suppose we took them out of here now, while the baby is still safe – and quiet – in her belly. Could we disguise her as a man?"

"No man was ever pregnant!"

"Oh, but there are fat Romans. My old master's stomach was nearly as large as hers."

"I don't know. It would need a certain swagger to be convincing. Phoebe hasn't your courage, Cassia. I don't think we can ask it of her."

They debated back and forth, but ended up feeling as though they were running in circles. By the time Phoebe and her child woke, no solution had presented itself.

XX

It was vital that nothing in the rented villa appeared to have changed that morning. Anything out of the ordinary would be noticed and they could not risk curious looks or gossip. Bone-tired though he was, Marcus went out into the city as he had every day since they'd arrived.

He was on edge, he supposed. His every sense was heightened. As he walked through the neighbourhood, he became aware of sounds that he'd paid no heed to before.

Women's chatter. Women's laughter. Following him down the street. From a balcony above there was a giggle, swiftly stifled. He looked up and there were two of them, staring at him. One matronly and plump. The other, unmistakeably her daughter. Young. Attractive. Of marriageable age.

She smiled. Flushed. Turned away.

Modest enough, but obviously interested in him.

He went on his way wondering if it had been a mistake

to adopt this disguise. In Rome, he knew a widow was a thing to be shunned.

But a widower? A young man, with money? His mask of grief would not keep people away for ever. It seemed he was already becoming a thing of interest. Maybe, even, an object of desire.

In the villa, Cassia was preparing food when she felt a small hand tug at the hem of her tunic. The little girl, Julia, had approached in silence and now looked up at her with fear-widened eyes.

"What's wrong?"

Julia didn't speak but pointed to the room in which she'd slept with her mother. When Cassia turned, she saw Phoebe sheened with sweat, squatting on her haunches in a pool of water.

The decision had been made for them. It seemed the baby was already on its way.

Marcus had said Phoebe's courage did not match her own. *He was wrong*, Cassia thought, as she watched the woman in her labours. Though the pains made every muscle tense, every sinew stiffen, every vein stand proud of her skin, she made not a sound. She had balled the hem of her tunic in her mouth and bit down on it with each contraction. Only her breathing told Cassia how much pain she was in.

Her daughter stood in the doorway whimpering with terror.

"She's not ill," Cassia told her. "Don't be scared. The baby's coming. You'll help me, won't you?"

She stoked up the fire. Put water on to heat. Fetched linen cloths. Tore them in strips. Set Julia folding and refolding them simply to take the child's mind off what was happening to her mother. And then all Cassia could do was wait.

It didn't take as long as she'd expected.

When Rufus was born, it seemed to last an eternity. But maybe that was because she had been young and frightened and unable to do anything but watch.

This birth was mercifully short. One moment Phoebe heaved and strained and the next an infant was expelled in a gush of warm liquid, plopping like a warm fish into Cassia's waiting hands. Without a word, she did what she'd seen women in the slave quarters do to a newborn infant. She wiped its impossibly ancient-looking face with a dampened cloth, checking mouth and nose were clear, so it could take its first breath. Dimly registering that it was a boy, she placed him on his mother's chest.

Moments later, clutching her son to her, Phoebe gave another heave and the afterbirth was passed.

Taking her knife, Cassia cut and knotted the baby's cord.

At that point he opened his mouth, drew in a deep breath, and began to cry.

It was not loud, but there is no sound on earth like that of a newborn baby. Here, in a quiet neighbourhood, coming from a rented villa where only a grieving widower and his slave were meant to reside, the sound could spell disaster.

For half a heartbeat Cassia and Phoebe looked at each other in horror. But then Cassia let out a yell followed by a curse. She kicked over the vessel of water, sending it clattering across the room. Julia curled into a ball, hiding her face against her knees, but Cassia could not help it. For all their sakes she had to mask the noise of the baby's cries. She carried on swearing and cursing herself so any of the neighbours that heard would think she was a slave who'd had an accident with some domestic task or other.

Her efforts at drowning out the baby's cries were assisted by a cat, which – no doubt attracted by the smell of blood – had leaped onto the wall. Cassia shouted as though she'd lost her temper. "Mangy fleabag! Get away! Get out of here, you old bugger. Oh Hades! Have you shat in his bed? Oh, what will Master say? He'll have me flayed alive."

She continued yelling angry nonsense until the baby was suckling. It seemed a long time before all was quiet once more.

When Marcus returned, he was stopped in the street by a neighbour, an elderly gentleman outraged at having his afternoon nap disturbed.

"Your lad was making a terrible racket in there. He needs a good beating."

Marcus had been up all night and with the shadows beneath his eyes looked like a man on the edge of insanity. The neighbour clearly thought him incapable of administering the required discipline.

"Want me to come in and whip him for you?"

"No … really, that won't be necessary."

"Don't you go letting him get away with it, mind. You show him a scrap of mercy and he'll be robbing you blind by the end of the week. Lads like him need keeping in their place and the rod's the only way to do it."

When Marcus finally got through the door, he and Cassia had to go through the pretence of a beating for the neighbour's benefit. He took a stick to a bundle of cloth and she yelped convincingly in response.

Phoebe's daughter watched.

"Poor child," said Cassia when they were done. "She must think she's entered a madhouse."

"It's no worse than what she left behind, trust me. In time she'll thank us for this."

"If we can get her out. It's a long way home."

Marcus took Cassia's hand. Squeezed it. Both knew they needed to leave Rome and the Empire as fast as was humanly possible.

They had started to draw attention to themselves. And with a newborn baby in the house, matters could only get worse.

XXI

The birth had been easy. The recovery was not.

Phoebe bled. Much more than Cassia's mother had done. Much more than she'd seen any woman bleed after giving birth. As soon as one bucket of cloths was washed and dried, another was soaked through.

It was fortunate that the villa's small garden contained overgrown beds of plants that were both culinary and medicinal. Cassia boiled brews of raspberry leaves and spooned them into Phoebe's mouth while Julia stood by her mother's side, eyes wide with fright.

In the days that followed, cooking and washing and worrying was all Cassia seemed to do. The leaf tea helped to stem the alarming flow of blood, but she was well aware that it left them with another problem. Raspberry was so associated with women's troubles. How could they explain to the landlord that his male tenant had stripped every plant in the garden down to a bare stem?

No fever followed the birth and for that Cassia thanked the Mother Goddess. Yet Phoebe was severely weakened and there was no cure for that but time and rest. The very two things that were not possible.

Marcus too was worn out with worrying. They could not risk the baby crying and so, reluctantly, both Phoebe and Cassia had consented to his purchase of opium. The infant slept soundly. Too soundly. When awake, it was not feeding as it should. If they did not get away soon, he feared that Phoebe's rescue would condemn her baby to death by starvation.

In the city streets, each building he walked past seemed daubed with notices describing his sister and her child and offering a reward. A reward that increased with each passing day. Every tavern heaved with men speculating on where the runaway was and how she might be captured. As time went on the talk got louder and more threatening.

How were they to make the journey back to Britannia? Not on foot. In her weakened state Phoebe could not even walk across the villa's atrium. Ride then? But his sister had never sat astride a horse and – even if her balance was good – she would be in danger of fainting with the effort. A cart then. Perhaps they could pull off the same trick they had played with Rufus? But no. Phoebe could not pose as a corpse with a newborn infant that needed frequent feeding.

But all this was ridiculous in any case! There was no point solving the matter of how they were to travel until he'd solved the problem of how they were to get out of the villa unobserved. He was increasingly aware that the neighbourhood women watched his every move. They would not even get the length of the street. He needed some almighty distraction so all eyes would be turned the other way while Phoebe and her children left. But what? He beat his brain to pieces but his ingenuity failed him. He was out of ideas. Well then. She could be moved out at night, he supposed, but even that was a risk. They had been lucky before, but would they be again? He was beginning to feel Fortune had deserted him.

Fortune. The goddess, Fortune.

He stopped so suddenly that a man walking behind thumped into his back, knocking Marcus off the pavement and into the street. He barely noticed. His mind was suddenly ablaze.

He'd been so busy thinking of his own problems he'd given no thought to the city's rites and rituals. It was almost midsummer. His heart started to beat faster. There was a festival fast approaching that could be of use to them.

"In two days' time," he told Cassia that evening, "offerings will be made to Fortune. The whole of Rome leaves the city. Vast crowds cross the Tiber to the Vatican fields. And then they try out the new harvest's wine. Thousands of people, all on the move, Cassia. And not one of them sober…"

XXII

They had only two days to prepare. But that was all the time they needed.

Marcus purchased a carpentum – a covered carriage suitable for the transportation of a Roman who was wealthy but not outrageously rich. He carefully selected one that was not so opulent it would attract attention, yet not so run-down that it could not make the journey. He paid for it but refused to have it delivered to the villa. Instead he arranged to have his slave collect the vehicle on the day of the festival.

And then he went in search of sound horses that could pull it. Again, he paid and told their owner the same story – that his slave would come for them two days hence.

Next, there were minor details that would nevertheless be the key to success: suitable clothing. Jewellery. A wig.

And then it was a matter of waiting for the time to

pass, hoping and praying that nothing would happen that might cause them to run sooner than they planned.

Fortuna's festival dawned. A day of noise. Of celebration. From the moment of sunrise there was a hubbub and tangible excitement even in the villa's usually quiet neighbourhood. People, dressed in their finest clothes, poured from their houses and into the street. Soon the roads were choked with a multitude that flowed like water down Rome's hills, across the Tiber and out to the Vatican fields.

Only when they were certain that the houses around them were empty of people, only when the neighbourhood was quiet, did Cassia leave the villa.

She collected both horses and carriage without incident but knew it was not permitted to drive a vehicle through the city in the hours of daylight. The streets were too crowded in any case for her to get through.

When darkness came, she set off, and for the first part of her journey she was still going against the human tide. But little by little it turned as drunken Romans began staggering back from the Vatican fields, over the Tiber's bridge and home to their beds. Full to bursting with fresh-made wine, many of them retched and emptied their bellies onto the ground. The stink in the warm night air was vile.

But Cassia knew from long experience the off-putting effect of certain stenches on the curious. The rotting corpse of a dead animal had saved Rufus from being looked at too closely. Perhaps she could make use of what Fortune had provided?

Stopping briefly she pulled off her cloak and pressed it into one of the many pools of vomit that dotted the streets. She threw the cloak into the back of the carriage and then drove the horses on. With that smell rising surely no one would look too closely when there were passengers inside?

She reached the corner of the road where the villa lay. It was quiet. Most of the revellers had not yet returned home. And those that had were lying, insensible, in their beds.

Marcus had been looking out for her. The moment she reined the horses in she heard the creak of the door. Then he was there, coming along the street, a sack in either hand that he threw to Cassia. While she stowed them beneath the seat, he went back to the house. He came out with Phoebe, one arm around her waist supporting her, the other cradling the baby. After lifting them both into the carriage, he returned for Julia.

As soon as he and the little girl were safely inside, Cassia urged the horses forward. Phoebe's face was covered by a hooded cloak. She slumped into one corner, Marcus in the other. To a casual observer they would look like drinking companions who had fallen into a stupor. Julia and her baby brother were lying between them concealed under Cassia's stinking, vomit-soaked cloak.

They were heading towards the city gate when a man hailed her and asked her to stop.

"Where are you going?"

She jerked her thumb at her passengers. "Taking them home."

"Give us a lift, lad. Go on. You're heading my way. And their wits are so addled they'll never even notice."

She couldn't refuse without causing a scene. Cassia nodded and shifted along the seat to make room. He climbed up beside her.

Her heart thudded hard against her ribs. She had to force herself to remain calm. Having him on the cart might help matters, she thought. They would look even less like fugitives. If only the baby did not wake, if only the child did not stir. If only he didn't ask any awkward questions. All would be well. It had to be.

Her unexpected passenger smelled strongly of wine. His head would no doubt ache in the morning, but for now he was at the stage of loving the whole of mankind. Rome was the best, the greatest, the most powerful city in the world, and its inhabitants were more like gods than men. He spent a long time praising the people he'd been drinking with that evening. It was a long litany of names and histories that meant nothing to Cassia. She gave no answer because none seemed required. As they plodded on through the streets, he finally turned his attention to her.

"You're a good lad," he told Cassia. "The best. Quiet. Respectful. I like that. Lucky to have you, they are," he said, jerking his thumb towards the carriage's other occupants. "Are they kind to you? Do they treat you right?"

Cassia assured him the occupants of the carriage were good and generous masters. "That's good," he said. "You've got to treat your slaves right. Got to be kind. Fair. They need discipline, mind. Got to know their place. They're not happy unless they know the rules. But once you've got those laid down, you can rub along together very nicely."

Her companion rambled on, talking of slave management, and then his sons and his family. Each revelation was punctuated by a series of loud belches. By the time they reached the city gate – and were stopped by the guard – there was little Cassia didn't know about him.

"Where are you heading?" demanded the man on duty.

Cassia's passenger answered for her. "Home."

"Lucius!" A second guard greeted the man sitting next to Cassia by name. "What are you doing up there? This isn't your carpentum."

"I'm hitching a lift with my friends here."

The guard glanced briefly inside and clearly took the occupants to be his fellow drinking companions.

"Been making a night of it, eh?"

"The whole city's been doing that. Fortune be blessed!"

"Except for us poor sods on duty."

"I'm sure you'll make up for it."

The guard laughed. Bidding them goodnight, slapping the rump of the nearest horse, he waved Cassia on through.

And that was it. Before too long, the city of Rome was behind them.

Her passenger was truly a man sent by Fortune, Cassia thought. And a man who was completely unaware of his own part in this drama. He began to doze intermittently, waking himself up with the loudness of his own snores. When they reached his home, he ordered her to stop. Telling her once more that she was a good lad, the best, he climbed down and staggered off. Cassia addressed silent thanks to his departing back.

She clicked her tongue and the horses obligingly carried on along the coast road that led towards Gallia.

The cover of drunkenness could not last beyond the end of that day. By the evening – on a quiet stretch of road when no one was in sight – they changed their story along with their appearance.

A wig for Phoebe. A fine linen dress. A cloak. A veil. Jewellery – of paste and brass, admittedly, but enough to convince a casual observer that she was a wealthy woman. A richly embroidered tunic for Julia – who now looked like a young boy. A shawl for the baby.

As for Marcus? A shave. A haircut. Cassia took her knife to it and Marcus saw on her face the same regret he'd felt when cutting hers. A change of clothes and he was transformed from grieving widower to Phoebe's husband.

If anyone was hoping to win the bounty on her head,

they'd be searching for a fugitive: a desperate runaway. Not a family of affluent Roman nobles.

They went onward, skirting the coast of Italia, crossing the mountains into Gallia.

Each night, when they were compelled to stop and rest, Marcus and Phoebe took the best rooms in the inn. Cassia stayed in the yard with the horses.

There is little more to be said about that journey. It was long, tiring and tedious. With Phoebe's health being so poor, they travelled agonizingly slowly. The baby – no longer drugged into silence – made full use of its lungs. Its cries shredded their nerves.

They moved under the shadow of a constant dread. Like actors on a stage they felt as though every eye was on them, that every move was watched and that every word was scrutinized. The terror of putting a foot wrong – the prospect of what would follow if they were found out – was a burden that was almost unbearable. It filled their sleep with nightmares, it turned food to ash in their mouths.

But, in truth, they had no need to fear quite so much. As they journeyed through Gallia, their passing was hardly noticed.

The inhabitants had more important things on their minds.

Stories of unrest among the barbarian hordes on the eastern fringes of the Empire had begun to spread like a fire through straw. Absorbed by their own concerns, at first Marcus and Cassia paid them little heed. But soon they saw for themselves that the rumours of trouble were true.

One morning they were forced to leave the road to make way for a legion of soldiers. Men in bright armour. Helmets crested with red. Marching. It was said that they were being sent to suppress the savage tribes. That troops all over the Empire were on the move.

After twenty days they reached the frontier. The border town was far busier than it had been when Cassia and Marcus had come into it from Germania. Word of the rising was being passed from mouth to mouth. There was talk of reinforcements being sent to fortify the Empire's defences.

Several wine-traders were in town who, having sold their goods to the army, were heading back to the vineyards. Amid all the commotion it was easy enough to buy passage with one of them. The guards were more concerned about preventing hostile strangers coming into the Empire than letting fugitive slaves out. The cart they were concealed in was not searched.

Once in Germania they had no guide to steer them, but it seemed that word of a Briton woman and her Roman companion had spread among the tribes. The pair who had travelled to the heart of the Empire to free a slave had become creatures of legend. As had the slave woman who had inspired them to make the journey.

In the first village they reached, they were greeted as heroes, welcomed as friends and honoured guests. Phoebe – who had lived her life in the shadows and in shame – found herself looked upon with respect. Admiration, even. It was a novel experience, but not an unpleasant one.

They were fed and feasted and sent on their way with oaths and promises of friendship. It was the same in the next village. And the next. Until, some fifty or more days after leaving Rome, they were back with Flavia's people.

It was exhilarating to be so lauded. Extraordinary. But besides their own personal triumph their actions seemed to have greater significance. These two people had dared to strike at the very heart of the Empire and they had succeeded. It had set people thinking: what might others do if they put their minds to it? Whispers of rebellion turned into shouts. The tribes were itching to rise.

Marcus had once thought that the Roman forts were strung along the walls and ditches like beads on a necklace. Now he wondered if those fortifications were not more like a rope around the Empire's neck. A noose, that was within a heartbeat of being tightened.

PART III:

EAGLE AND WOLF

I

Did I say there were only two players in this tale?

I lied.

There is, of course, a third. The villain who began it. Without him there would be no story to tell.

Titus Cornelius Festus.

What was he doing all this time?

He was a man who prided himself on his patience. In matters of business he would sit, like a spider in its web, waiting for the right moment to suck the blood from his rivals.

But the girl had tried him beyond the limits of his sanity.

He'd been informed by Constantius Scipio that Marcus Aurelius Aquila had sworn to return her. He'd made no objection. He could hardly go after the girl himself. Marcus had caused the problem: it seemed only right and fair that he should be the one to solve it. But, by all the gods of Mount Olympus, when that young man brought her back, he'd pay the price for his mistake! Titus would have his head on a platter by sundown.

He had waited in Londinium for news of Cassia's return all that winter – irritable, ill-tempered and seeking relief in the delights that various brothels had to offer.

Seeking relief, but finding none. The illness that afflicted him had worsened and spread and the healers seemed to have run out of remedies that might cure him. There were days he felt himself rotting from the inside.

Sickness made him superstitious. When spring came, he consulted a soothsayer, who advised him to travel to the wall himself.

He was a wealthy man. It would not do to ride. Slowly, and in splendour, he was carried from town to town. If he'd been younger, if he'd been well, he'd have sampled every whore in every brothel along the way before moving on.

But he could not. And the knowledge of that didn't improve his temper.

All that way! The further north they'd gone, the worse he'd got. By the end he experienced such extremes of discomfort he'd hardly known what to do with himself. It wasn't the illness alone that plagued him. He'd been eaten alive by insects. Drained by bedbugs, sucked dry by fleas.

He had hoped she'd be captive by the time he arrived.

In his dreams he was stiff as a battering ram with the anticipation. His waking state was disappointing. But if he could not actually take her, if his condition prevented it – well, he would think of something. She would suffer. She would be punished.

When his carriage was finally driven into the frontier town where Marcus had been holed up during the snows of winter, there was nothing.

No sign of him.

No word.

Not even a whisper.

Nothing.

Had she killed the man who'd gone after her, Titus wondered. These pagans were well known for their savagery. Had Marcus Aurelius Aquila been beheaded? Mutilated? His privates cut off and put in his mouth? He'd heard rumours that savage women did such things. But if that was the case, they'd have heard of it, surely? Savages loved to boast of their brutalities. It was part of the game.

Had he been attacked by wild animals then? There were wolves and bears in those wild hills and he'd travelled alone. It was possible. How else could a man vanish so completely from the face of the earth?

The arrival of Titus Cornelius Festus and the questions he was asking began to spark rumours among the natives and the slaves in the town.

This girl who'd escaped from the south. She'd fled all

the way from the other side of Londinium! Gone back to steal away her brother from right under her master's nose. She'd taken two others to freedom too. And now she'd surely bewitched the Roman who'd been sent to capture her. Slaughtered him, maybe – put his head on a spike. The red-headed girl was a warrior queen. A second Boudica!

It was not long before Titus Cornelius Festus saw the same glimmer of hope in the eyes of the slaves who walked the streets of that sodden northern town. It was all nonsense! How these fools gossiped. And yet – *that bitch be cursed!* – those stories had the power to inspire the downtrodden. To make them restless. Discontented.

Something must be done.

Daily he harassed army generals, centurions, common soldiers.

"She is my property! Mine! Go after her."

They should annihilate the entire savage tribe that harboured her, he told them. They could not – would not – be beaten by a slave! It was not just him the woman was laughing at – she was spitting in the face of the Emperor.

A slave, roused to rebellion? It would not do. She would encourage others. They were all facing a loaded ballista. Couldn't they see that? It would only take one hand on the lever to send the load hurtling against the walls of the Empire. Before they knew it, the whole edifice would start to crumble. If slaves rose up against their masters, civilization would collapse – and then where would they all be?

Day after day, Titus Cornelius Festus harangued whoever would listen to him. They paid him little heed. They could not go into enemy territory without provoking a war. Cassia was not the army's problem.

But Titus was a man of money. He could pay whatever was necessary. He had almost persuaded himself to hire a party of mercenaries when he decided instead to consult another soothsayer.

And – praise the gods! – the old crone said that if he would only sit tight and wait, one day soon Cassia would come to him.

II

They left the shores of Germania in fair weather, the wind strong at their backs, the skies clear.

Marcus stood looking out across the waves, thinking about their melancholy parting from Flavia. He knew Cassia doubted they would see the old woman again and this last farewell had pained her.

It was no surprise that Cassia would feel sorrow. What was unexpected was how greatly Phoebe had been affected by it. She had known the old woman only a few short days. Yet they had spent most of that time conversing in whispers. He supposed that Flavia could understand better than either he or Cassia all that Phoebe had suffered. Whatever had passed between them, his sister's load seemed lighter. She was more content. He had begun to catch glimpses of the girl she'd been and hoped, in time, that some of her wounds would heal.

She was not the only one who had changed in the space of a few short days. Julia had not spoken a word – not in the villa, not in all the time they had been travelling. Yet there in Flavia's village Marcus had woken one morning to see her playing with the other children. She had laughed. And with that one sudden sound it was as though a dam had burst. After that she could not stop chattering.

The stinging of his wrists interrupted Marcus's line of thought. He rubbed them to ease the soreness and then stood staring at the pattern of whirls and dots that were freshly pierced into his skin. The night they'd been made ran through his mind.

As they had sat around the fire that first evening in the Saxon village, Cassia had told him, "You are truly one of us now."

"I know it."

Cassia had looked at Flavia. Some secret signal seemed to pass between them. The old woman had slipped away and returned carrying something which she handed to Cassia.

A small pot of pigment. A bone needle.

"Rufus gave them to me before we went," Cassia said. "I left them in Flavia's safekeeping. My brother told me that if we were successful, I was to mark you as our own. You will be one of the Wolf People. If you are willing?"

"There could be no greater honour."

Later that night, when there'd been talk that the risings

in the east would ignite flames of rebellion in the west, Marcus listened with no feeling of disloyalty to Rome. If the Empire was to crumble? Why then, it was long overdue.

He smiled into the sea. Cassia's gods had shaped him into something he could never have imagined. He hadn't escaped from the Cyclops under the belly of a sheep. He hadn't chopped the head from the gorgon Medusa. But in his mind and heart he'd slaughtered the monster who'd held him in thrall. In freeing Phoebe, he had also freed himself. He was his own man now. He could be the hero of his own life. And with all this talk of uprising... Who knew what Fortune had in store for them next?

They were within sight of Britannia when their luck at last began to run out.

There was a change in the wind. Bitter cold. As if it had been hatched in fields of ice. No longer at their backs, but in their faces. It was enough to furrow the brow of the man who steered the ship. He tasted danger in the air. The vessel had to tack back and forth in zigzags across the water, sailing twice the distance to make half the headway.

The waves that until now had been nudging them homewards were a barrier that slapped the ship's bows and cascaded salt spray over the deck.

Little by little, however, they continued towards the coast.

Next dawn, clouds were gathering on the horizon. White. Small still, but growing a little larger with each heartbeat. By mid-morning they were the size of trees. By noon they had billowed to gigantic proportions. With every passing moment they darkened. From oyster. To slate. To pitch.

They had hoped to make land in the village of the Fisher People before nightfall. Marcus and Cassia strained their eyes scanning the horizon for it. Just as it came into view there was a crack of thunder. A bolt of lightning tore the clouds apart. They spilled their load, and sky and sea erupted into a violent storm.

To have come so far, to be so close to the homeland that Marcus had spoken of and now to be in such danger was more than Phoebe could bear. Hunched in the stern of the boat, she wept, clutching her baby to her chest. He in turn began to howl as though his lungs would burst. Julia whimpered and there was nothing Cassia or Marcus could do to soothe any of them.

They edged closer to the shore. With great difficulty the master of the tiny vessel steered them through the jagged rocks and into the bay. In the lee of the cliffs his task became a little easier. Closer. Closer.

And the Fisher People had seen them. Through wind and rain their shouts came from the shore. Yells of encouragement. Prayers.

The ship was driven forward on the crest of one wave. Sucked back out on another. The sea was playing with them. A cat with a mouse.

The hull scraped against rock, sending a shudder along the length of the timbers. It was then knocked sideways, dipping so low in the water that Marcus feared it would overturn. The crew fought to right it.

They were closer. Closer.

They could see the Fisher People's faces now: anxious. Desperate. On the beach, ready to do what they could to help.

When at last the hull hit the shingle, the crew dropped the sail and jumped from the ship to haul it onto land. The villagers waded out to help. Strong hands reached in to take the crying children: the baby. Julia. Phoebe. They were safe. Safe!

But Cassia and Marcus were not. They hadn't reached their journey's end. Fate and Fortune had not finished with them. Indeed, their game had barely begun.

Cassia had one leg over the side when, without warning, the wind balled itself into a mighty fist and thumped the vessel so hard it reared like a horse from the sand. At that selfsame moment Neptune sent a great wave crashing onto the beach, scattering people, hurling them to the ground, washing through the ship, then lifting it, tugging it back out to sea.

Crew and villagers were too busy saving themselves from the sucking waves to do anything about the ship.

Marcus and Cassia were carried away on a vessel that neither of them knew how to steer. He crouched in the stern, appalled, so horrified that he could neither think nor act. Cassia was on her feet, struggling to raise the sail. But it whipped and snapped and the rope slid through her hands, burning the flesh. And then there was a loud crack. A scream of timber as the mast split along its length and came crashing down.

They were helpless. Tossed like a leaf on a mountain stream. Adrift. Marcus prayed. To Neptune. To Jupiter. To the Christian god. To the spirits who spoke to Rufus. To any divine power who would listen.

Whether Cassia's gods mocked her, or the gods of Rome were laughing in his face, Marcus didn't know. The ship didn't founder on the rocks, and that was, he supposed, some mercy. But through wind and rain he could see that they were being pushed further away from the shore. And then – oh gods, no! – cliff by cliff, bay by bay – they were being driven south along the coast.

It was not in sight. Not yet. But he knew that with each clap of thunder, with each bolt of lightning, with each howling gust of wind, they were being taken nearer to the wall.

How long they were tossed on monstrous waves, Marcus didn't know. The length of that night and the whole of the following day, certainly. Then another. Whether there was a third or a fourth, he couldn't tell. Time meant nothing. They had entered Hades and could see neither sun, nor moon, nor stars. Marcus stopped fearing that they'd be washed from the deck, or that the vessel would go down. He was numb to the core. As was Cassia. All they could do was cling to each other.

And then one morning they woke to find they had run aground. Overnight they had been swept into the mouth of a river and carried upstream. The ship had beached itself on mud flats as the tide ebbed.

They were alive.

But they were on the wrong side of the river. The wrong side of the wall.

Occupied territory.

Marcus and Cassia prised themselves apart. As the horror of their new situation revealed itself to them, they exchanged a look.

"We got through the wall before," Cassia said. "We can do it again."

"Of course we can," agreed Marcus.

They lied to each other with reassuring smiles. But both knew that the last time they made the crossing the soldiers had been bribed to look the other way.

Fortune's wheel had spun. The goddess had turned her back on them.

It was impossible to believe that they would truly escape this time.

III

Every soul in every town the entire length of the wall knew that a red-haired Briton and a Roman were being sought. The dye that had concealed Cassia's colouring had worn off as they'd travelled through Germania. It was a flaming beacon of scarlet to anyone who saw it. Every soul knew there was a price on their heads. And so it didn't take long for word to reach Titus Cornelius Festus that the soothsayer had been right. Marcus Aurelius Aquila had walked into town. And Cassia was with him.

They had trudged the length of that day and it had rained without ceasing. They were chilled. Frozen half to death. Sodden, dizzied by hunger. When they reached the outer edges of the small frontier town, they stopped in a tavern with a roaring fire. They had no money, but the innkeeper seemingly took pity on them. They had not even begun to eat the stew his wife put before them when Titus Cornelius Festus arrived.

Cold, dazed, immensely weary, Marcus and Cassia only realized they were surrounded when the innkeeper suddenly left the room. They turned. Stood.

Ten men, built like gladiators. Not Red Crests. Not slaves. Hired thugs, whose only loyalty was to the purse they would earn for Cassia's capture. Ten men against Marcus. And Cassia. And they with only their two knives to defend themselves.

They heard Titus approach before they saw him. A wheezing, as though each breath might be his last. A rank stench of sickness.

When the circle of men parted and Titus Cornelius Festus squeezed between them, Marcus could see that Cassia's former master was close to dying from the disease that his own vices had brought down upon his head. And yet a creature teetering on the brink of death is at its most dangerous.

"Marcus Aurelius Aquila, I believe!" said Titus. "You have delivered her at last! I'd begun to think you were dead. What took you so long, man?"

The sight of her former master dizzied Cassia. Revulsion washed over her so strongly she was almost knocked off her feet by it. She found herself clinging to Marcus for support.

Her gesture wasn't lost on Titus Cornelius.

His eyes narrowed. He was angry. Incensed. But there was no shadow of suspicion about Marcus's treachery to Rome. Not yet.

"Is that how it is?" Titus Cornelius looked from Marcus to Cassia. "Gods, have you had her? Have you been making free with my property?"

From the corner of his eye Marcus could see that Cassia's right hand was creeping up her left arm, fingers slowly inching towards her knife. She was not beaten yet. But if any of them saw what she was doing, it would all be over. He needed to keep their eyes on him and him alone.

"Cassia is not yours," he told Titus.

"You've had her!" The man exploded with fury. "You were supposed to bring her back a virgin. You've soiled my goods!"

"What of it? What she did, she did of her own free will."

"Free will? What rubbish is this? You think she's yours now? You will pay a mighty price if you think to buy her."

"Cassia belongs to no one."

"You swore to return her!"

"I did." Marcus nodded solemnly. "On my father's honour."

"Well then."

A pause. A grin. "He has none."

"What?"

"The oath is worthless."

Marcus held up his arms, showing the newly made marks at his wrists.

Whether their significance was understood by Cassia's

former master was hard to tell. He made no reply. Because at that moment she spun on her heel. With one flick of her wrist her blade darted across the room, and into the throat of Titus Cornelius Festus.

IV

The look of surprise on his face would have been comical if there had not been so much blood in him. It spurted from the wound in his neck, hitting the whitewashed wall, turning the world red.

Marcus had his knife ready. They could not hope to win, but gods, he would slay as many of Titus's henchmen as he could!

But hired thugs do not do the job they are paid for when the man with the money has died. Hired thugs are more inclined to rip the purse from his dead waist, to tug the rings from his hands, strip his body of valuables and disappear into the night before the watch know anything untoward has occurred. The paid henchmen of Titus Cornelius Festus did not lay a finger on Cassia or Marcus.

Yet a citizen of Rome cannot be killed in a public tavern without consequences. Cassia and Marcus were barely out of the door when the innkeeper looked in and saw the blood dripping down the wall, the knife protruding from a Roman throat. He gave a shout. Just one. But it was taken up, passed from mouth to mouth. Then came the clanging of the alarm bell. In the distance, there was the noise of the garrison being roused to action.

And if the soldiers had awoken, so had the people of the town. Drawn out of their houses by the commotion, they poured into the streets.

Cassia and Marcus ran, but each path they took was blocked. There was a price on their heads, and no one yet knew that the man who would have paid it was dead.

There was no getting out of the town. Lane by lane, path by path, they were being backed towards the wall. It loomed behind them. The only way through was the gates – a vast pair, as tall as two men – but they were shut and barred. The crowd surged forwards, and there was nothing Cassia and Marcus could do and nowhere for them to go but up the stone steps that led to the top of the wall.

They stumbled, slipped, clambered, leaped and soon both were standing outlined against the sky.

Below them, native Britons. Slaves.

And behind the townspeople, the Red Crests. Soldiers, baying for the rebels' blood.

Orders were given. Weapons were drawn. Blades glinting in torchlight. But they could not advance.

The crowd would not part to let the soldiers through.

There was a whispering.

"It's her!"

"She's come!"

"The Roman's with her."

"Did you see his wrists? He's changed sides!"

"He's one of us!"

"What are they doing?"

"Why are they here?"

"What are they up to?"

And then Marcus realized that he and Cassia hadn't been chased through the town by an angry mob. They'd been followed. The crowd below was hushed. Expectant. Waiting for something.

Cassia was quicker to grasp the situation than he'd been. Her voice rang out. "Britons! Slaves! Cut your bonds. Seize your chance. You are your own masters now."

Silence. Then whispering. The whispering became a murmuring. And then some in the crowd started pointing to the hills beyond. The soldiers were looking there too.

Marcus and Cassia turned.

A flame had appeared on the crest of the nearest hill.

A small figure, on horseback, holding a torch high above his head.

He was a long way away, but even at that distance Cassia knew it was her brother.

Below her the murmuring changed to shouting. Rufus

was moving his torch. Slowly, slowly he swung it in an arc to the left. Another flame flared.

He raised it again. Moved it to his other side. And at his right a third torch was lit.

The crowd stood transfixed. Three torches held motionless on the hill. A moment of silence. And then Rufus threw back his head and howled like a wolf.

The cry was taken up, a dozen, two dozen, three dozen men, baying for blood as the torch-bearers either side of Cassia's brother swung their flaming sticks through the air, and ignited two more.

Torch by torch, lights flared, until a line of flames across the hill cut the night in two.

And then the chanting started. Warriors. Calling Cassia's name.

The people of her tribe had heeded her brother's visions. Their moment had come.

Native Wolf. Roman Eagle. Together on the wall, exactly as Rufus had foretold. Cassia, with the flames behind her as Marcus had glimpsed in the smoke. Her red hair, cut short, standing in spikes, framing her head like a halo. Or a crown. Torches held aloft, the Wolf People's warriors began to advance towards the wall.

"An attack!" called a voice in the crowd.

"Rebellion!" cried another.

"War!"

There was a moment of silence.

The soldiers began to push their way forward. But the crowd still would not let them pass. Men and women packed together, standing their ground. Protecting Cassia. Protecting Marcus. Holding back the Red Crests' advance.

Yet there were other soldiers on the wall. Two, three, more – coming from either side. They would reach Cassia and Marcus long before the warriors of her tribe could save them.

The two of them stared down into the darkness on the other side.

They regarded each other. Smiled.

"We might die."

"We might live."

"We do it together."

Hand in hand, they jumped.

V

And so the story ends. With a birth or a death. Sometimes both.

Sometimes neither.

I am a singer of songs, a weaver of words, a spinner of stories.

A dreamer of visions. A shaman.

When I was a boy, I saw the truth long before it happened. Cassia, on the wall, rousing Britannia from her sleep.

My sister was the spark that lit the fire. Slaves rose against their masters. Britons joined with Saxons to contest the might of Rome. Some took weapons and fought in the front line of battle. Others worked secretly in the shadows. It was a rebellion that burned for a year and was then extinguished.

Or so the Romans said.

In truth, it was never properly doused. The embers smouldered. From time to time they flared and were dampened, only to flare again. On and on it went. It has taken most of the years of my life, but Rome has fallen. The Empire is dead.

Some said that Cassia was the beginning of the end. She, and the Roman Eagle she had bewitched. I would agree.

But how did they do it? What was their fate? Did they survive that jump from the wall?

What of Phoebe? Did she find her way to Cassia's people? Her children – did they grow up free? Did they, in turn, fight Rome?

I am an old man now, and weary. My voice grows weak. The fire burns low. I do not choose to answer.

I will say only this.

They lived until they died. All of them. And all of them played their part.

But wars and warriors, blood and brutality: these are subjects that do not interest this particular wordsmith. There is neither beauty nor poetry in battle. To hear that tale, you must find a different teller.

Or you must dream it for yourself.

AUTHOR'S NOTE

It's hard to say precisely what triggers the idea for a book or story. With *Beyond the Wall* it was several different things over a long period of time.

It started when I first saw Hadrian's Wall. I was probably around seven or eight and we were on our way to Scotland when we stopped off to look at the ruins. There was something magnificent about that extraordinary feat of engineering. But there was also something haunting about looking over to the other side, knowing that this was where the Roman Empire had ended: that "civilization" had come this far, but no further. We must have been doing the Romans at school because I could picture the soldiers standing along the top of it very clearly. I could imagine them − so far from home − looking out across the bleak, barren lands beyond, fearing an attack.

I also grew up with the story of Boudica. Every time

we went to London, I saw her statue on the Embankment. The image of a woman in a chariot – a warrior queen leading her people in battle against the Romans – caught my imagination.

I was fascinated by the idea of the Roman Empire. I wouldn't have been able to put it into words then, but I also felt disturbed by it. I could see there was a splendour to the architecture, a magnificence in the art, but it seemed to me that there was also an arrogance: an absolute conviction in Roman superiority. Maybe the Empire was well and good if you were top of the pile, but suppose you weren't? Suppose you were one of the oppressed, the colonized, the enslaved? Life would have been very different.

Years later – whilst researching for *Buffalo Soldier* – I came across a lot of stories of slave escapes in America's Deep South. I was reading widely about slavery throughout history and came across a line that said that the difference between the situation for slaves in the USA and in the Roman Empire was that in Roman times slaves had nowhere to run to. I remembered that first sight of Hadrian's Wall and the land beyond and the idea began to grow in my head.

I started to read and wonder more about Roman Britannia. And then I came across the Great Conspiracy when, in AD 367, slaves rose against their masters. That year a Roman garrison on Hadrian's Wall rebelled and allowed "savages" to come pouring through from one side of the wall to the other. Native tribes united with Saxons from Germania and attacked in different parts of Britannia.

The rebellion was defeated but never entirely crushed. Trouble continued to flare along the Empire's borders until, in AD 409, the Romans finally withdrew from Britannia.

We don't know the "barbarians'" side of the story because they had an oral rather than a written tradition. Frustrating for historians, perhaps, but perfect for a novelist. In this book, I have played fast and loose with strict historical accuracy. *Beyond the Wall* is simply an imagined evocation of what might have happened and how it might have felt to have been part of something like the Great Conspiracy.

Enjoyed *Beyond the Wall*?
We'd love to hear your thoughts!

🐦 @tanya_landman
@WalkerBooksUK   @WalkerBooksYA

📷 @WalkerBooksYA

IN A
WICKED WORLD,
CAN AN HONEST
MAN SURVIVE?

Hell and High Water

TANYA LANDMAN

CARNEGIE MEDAL-WINNING AUTHOR

Hell and High Water

Shortlisted for the *Guardian* Children's Fiction Prize

It was a man. Drowned. Dead.

Lying on the sand, waves breaking over his back.

The body should be moved, but Caleb

couldn't manage it alone.

Yet who in this godforsaken place would help him?

When his father is arrested and transported to the Colonies,
Caleb is left alone. After a desperate journey in search of an
aunt he's never met he receives a strange, cold welcome.
Then a body washes up on the nearby beach and Caleb is
caught up in a terrifying net of lies and intrigue. Soon he and
his new family are in mortal danger.

———◦•◦———

"Beautifully written and wonderfully paced"
Guardian

"Gripping … Landman's research is impeccable."
The Times

"An amazing novel which left me lost for words – everyone
should read it. Can I give it eleven out of ten?"
Guardian Children's Book Website

WHAT
DOES IT
MEAN
TO BE
FREE?

WINNER · WINNER · WINNER
CILIP
CARNEGIE
MEDAL
2015
WINNER · WINNER · WINNER

Buffalo Soldier

TANYA LANDMAN

Buffalo Soldier

Winner of the CILIP Carnegie Medal

What kind of girl steals the clothes from a dead man's
back and runs off to join the army?
A desperate one that's who.

World been turned on its head by that big old war,
and the army seemed like the safest place to be,
until we was sent off to fight them Indians. And then?
Heck! When Death's so close you can smell his breath,
ain't nothing makes you feel more alive.

———•—•———

CAN SHE
ESCAPE HER
DESTINY?

the Goldsmith's Daughter

TANYA LANDMAN

CARNEGIE MEDAL-WINNING AUTHOR

The Goldsmith's Daughter

In the golden Aztec city of Tenochtitlan,
people live in fear of the gods.

A girl born under an ill-fated sky, Itacate is destined to a
lifetime of submission and domestic drudgery. But she has
a secret passion, one which she can tell no one for fear of
death. When she falls in love with a Spanish invader and
her secret is endangered, Itacate must fight for her life.

Can she defy the gods and escape her destiny?

———◆———

I WILL
LIVE
& I WILL
FIGHT
FOR I AM A
WARRIOR
APACHE
TANYA LANDMAN
CARNEGIE MEDAL-WINNING AUTHOR

Apache

Shortlisted for the CILIP Carnegie Medal

I was in my fourteenth summer when the Mexicans rode
against us. Twelve moons later, I took my revenge.
And though Ussen has drawn visions of a terrible future
in my mind, I will not be vanquished. I belong to this
land: to the wide sky above my head, to the sweet
grass beneath my feet. Here must I die.

But first I will live, and I will fight. For I am a warrior.

I am Apache.

————— • • • —————

"Magnificent ... a disturbing but exhilarating experience"
Independent

"Beautifully written and unforgettable"
Time Out

"This novel is a masterpiece... It deserves to become a
modern children's classic."
Books for Keeps